Zarat

Zarat
Notes of the Becoming
or
An Uncommon Disdain

By Zarat

Written by Philosopher Stephan Pacheco

The 2nd Book in the Manifest Utopia Series

NOTES:

I am a nation unto myself. These are the rights I posses:
I serve no other nation or ideals but my own.
I will not tolerate a threat to my sovereignty or to my Freedom.
I recognize no force other than my own.
I will not obey invaders to my nation that threaten my
right to pursue happiness.
In my Humanitarian effort I form an open Committee to accept and
aid others in obtaining True Freedom without Power.
I will not create nuclear weapons, and would not permit their
detonation in an ocean full of Existence.
I will not create war on another person's nation, unless the opposing
nation threatens my own sovereignty, or that of my Beloved's.
I will believe only my own Just Cause and recognize no other,
for I am an Emperor for life, and my decisions are
absolute within my boundaries.
I hereby recognize the Freedom of all other nations and will strive to
help them turn away from the Nationalism that is Pride.

WARNING

There are many false enlightenments.
The Dark Society takes many forms. It's blindness knows no bounds.
It is in the conformist. It is in the rebel. It is in the intelligent. It is in
the stupid. It is in the same patterns that play out again and again in
the societies of the ignorant. It is in our Reasons. If you believe, at
any point, when you read my works that my works insight violence or
promote fear, anger or the assumption of power over anyone...You are
part of a false enlightenment. My works show the path to peace
through the violent internal trails.
We have the ability to create peace and love and move beyond our
arrogance and self loathing. We have the power to be humble and
pure again. We have the power to have no power. We will be free.
We will disassemble ourselves and only truth will remain.
Stop the cowardice that makes you think that you deserve anything.
You do not deserve peace. You do not deserve fame or money. You
deserve nothing. Be humbly nothing. And what you have will not be
what you are, and what you can obtain will become limitless.

Dedicated to all those that always told me I was wrong because they were scared of things that might happen to me. There is nothing that could ever (and I mean ever) happen to me that could be bad or harmful. I fear no consequence. Know that and begin to know me and the truth of my free reality.

For Zarat (age 27), and for all the unfinished heroes that left behind their Great Works in order to be Free.

Crawling Caterpillar
Know me by pieces.
As a Friend unfolds to you.
A kind limb extends.

It's "American" if it exists at all in America. It's natural if it exists at all in Nature. It has the potential to exist if we can imagine it anywhere in our Imaginations. Don't let anyone that was here before you... try to tell you that reality isn't real, and that your mind isn't powerful--some will. Be Free. Consider your Force. And be anything you want to be. You are the Definer. You are Alive in this World.

<u>Acts of War</u>
(Before you is a Hero's Mind. You must make an effort to know a Friend, and to Break Free.)

ACT I

The Rise of Will

Page...13

ACT II

He Draws the Long Knife

Page...83

ACT III

The Holy American

Page...139

ACT IV

A Hero. His Suicide.

Page...219

<u>The True Introduction</u>
by Philosopher Stephan Pacheco

Beyond is the life of a young Man. His memoirs, his reasons, his views on what you might choose to become and the mind you might use when you get there. When browsing these pages, in order, or at random, think of him. Think of where he was. What he was doing. How old he was. The length of time since the last entry. How deep into the book is it? Has he won or lost for the day? What else has happened that isn't there? Listen to him. He is your friend. My friend. He is so simple that he will seem complex, but .he is so simple. so much so that he is, completely, Human. Struggling, like all of us, because of what we have chosen to do in our epic lives within the flash of that Silence that comes before a thought. Don't look for him to please you, just accept him. Just be with him. Be there for him, like he will always be there for you. This is a chance to know him better than anyone. It is a chance to know yourself. Like the most important friend, he will help you with that, and try to teach you how to overcome what you thought were its limitations.

To another great sacrifice, fighting a war in his head, so that we don't have to. I now yield the floor to the Philosopher.

INSTRUCTOR'S GUIDE: Why is Zarat thinking what he is thinking? What is he balancing, again and again? What is he dismantling? Why does he think? And why does it only matter to him? How does he build himself? What does he want to be? How will he save Humanity?

Zarat's Introduction:
The Truest of Introductions
How to See in Slow Motion

The ego is a construct of our insecurities and fears. Our ego is a series of psychological occurrences that cause our stress, sadness, anger, annoyance, loneliness, everything that we writhe while feeling. Beyond these basic surface emotions is a deeper mind. A mind that feels one primary emotion while feeling these other more shallow emotions. This emotion is Bliss.

The technology we have developed leads to the rise in evolution of this emotion. And deeper than that is the truth. Bliss as an entity. As we cure the psyche from all its greedy wanting we are able to see through the smog and enter beyond the shrouding veils and witness the soul itself. And as we realize that we cannot see it and that we are it, all fear falls away and we are very calm because we learn that though we can lose our minds and our lives, we cannot lose our souls. This technology presented in art that lies beyond is presented with love for all to advance.

ACT I

The Rise of Will

Our Great Hero, Zarat, has been trapped in himself for some time. Likely, thrust into a depression from the loss of his cause, and striking death of his Love. Had Zarat been around other people, they may have pulled him out of it. He is alone. Zarat seeped back into this current society, as people do, for warmth, for food, for a touch of technology. Unable to enslave himself to people that would use him cheaply, he struggles for the opportunities to survive, forcing him to steal what gluttons don't need. Here we find him...working his mind awake and forcing his spirit to burning life to fulfill the debt of a promise he made truly. The Hero will avenge the story untold. He would give his life to Freedom, compelling him to end the reasons that love power.

<u>A Warrior Speaks Softly</u>

"I have seen every face come the age I am. I have felt every inflection.
No look strikes me more deeply than the movement of the gaze that
knows it may never see me again, and it wants to remember me.
My love, you will not remember and you can never forget.
This is the promise of my correct statement."

Students: Everyone knows that there is no way anyone can hold power
in the true path.

What happened to the past six years? How long had *she* been gone? What stopped it? What stopped his momentum? What stopped the dramatic story of Zarat?

"*Girl*?" into the nothingness. "Are you within me now? Did you drown into death and fade into nothingness. Free from this place. Free from stagnancy, from that horror of having greatness stir constantly within you but knowing you cannot release it or you will fail again. Are you free from the waiting?" Zarat sat. He felt a burning in his belly. He tried to raise the burning up into his third eye. He tried to pull it. He tried to push it. He tried all visualizations of movement he could. He began to swirl it back down to his belly. The red heat moved up his front. He thought it would move up his spine, but it didn't. He wanted to see her. He needed to glimpse something familiar and good in the world that had broken his heart with blind cruelty and dumb selfishness. In blind abandonment. What happened to that small group of revolutionaries that he fought with in that first fun battle? They didn't have the truth in them. It was never what they were. There must have been only three that had any truth in them. One died. One wandered off. One sits trying to figure out what the fuck happened to his war. And what the fuck happened to the warrior he loves to be. Violently and offensively he reaches out for it, his mind cramped and cursing. How can He make that old mind again? What will He have to lose to have it again?

Fat

Zarat looked down at the credit card that he had found on a drunken night of laughing. He might as well use it. If the man had not cancelled it after a year it is his own fault, or it is Zarat's gift anyway. Either way, he had created a rational to overcome the programming that holds a dark society together. So he filled up the gas tank in his truck and headed to the store.
As he entered, a large woman bumped him and walked in front of him to grab a cart. "Excuse me," Zarat. The fat bitch said nothing. She was absorbed into herself. "Hey, fat cunt!"
The fat bitch turned around. "You knew I was talking to you because your fat, right? Or is it because you always act like a fucking cunt?" Zarat.
"What the fuck is wrong with you! Who the fuck do you thi," the fat bitch's words of rage were cut short as Zarat's fist quickly crashed into her face. She stumbled backwards in shock from the blow, but more in shock of the fact that someone would dare to resort to the necessary measures to stop her disgusting ego. Zarat laughed in himself and smiled at her shock to reality. He grabbed her by her shirt and slammed her against the wall.
"Listen you nasty bitch. You have a disgusting disease inside you. I call it the fat disease. I see it all the time. Those that have it are almost always grossly overweight, like you cunt. You believe that you have the right to have and have. To take and take. That is how you got so fat. You live off of others. You want everything that is yours, and your piece of everything that is someone else's. You cut people off, believing it is your right of way. Maybe it is the spite you have..."
"Get the fuck off me right now!" Fat Ego.
Zarat head butts the diseased thing. "Shut up."
People are starting to gather. He speeds up his teaching.
Zarat, "Maybe it is the spite you have for their consequences to your gluttony and selfishness. I mean the consequence of being ugly in this society. I don't know exactly, but there is definitely some self hatred in there you cruel bitch. I know that I am supposed to not judge you because you are a fat cow. I know I am supposed to except you no matter what, even though you are, or especially because you are, a fat cow. But I won't, because it symbolizes your personality. You are a greedy, horrible bitch. You need to see that and you need to change that. Be better than what you are comfortably being. This is not your world to consume." *She is the "fat cow", not because her body is fat,*

Zarat's shirt is grabbed by a security guard and he is flung off of the diseased. The large man tries to push him against the wall. Zarat smacks a flat hand up into the oppressors genitals. The man recoils. "You should learn to take a shot in your balls. You'll fight a lot better," Zarat. The guard lunges at him. Zarat pulls out a 300,000 volt stun gun and lays it into the man's belly. Zarat laughs at how easily this small dick was eliminated. Zarat walks out of the store. One bloody woman left behind with something to complain about for the whole of her sick life and one man in his own shit left to think about hatred and revenge his whole life in verbose flurries of "how he could have taken that angry kid if he hadn't been a pussy and used the fucking stun gun." Right. Zarat would go further, hurt the other more. Zarat programmed himself to win without limitations. Zarat will win. Zarat walked and wished that "they" would accept the failure of their situation and their lives as a whole, but he knew that they would cover themselves with more lies and delusions of how important they are. Oh well, he taught all he could. Zarat needs to go shopping. Zarat needs a new shirt.

<u>The Beast</u>

Within all people is the possibility to be all other people. Every person that you may criticize you can become. It is why training is effective. It is why the weak become the thinking process of whatever field they go into. It is rare to see the true Independent. That glorious person that is uninfluenced by the thought around him, but able to consider it. And rarer still is the god that has overcome the psychological influence that can force a person through pattern into such situations. While many people have used many people to fight wars by merely tricking soldiers to be able to justify and feel good about the slaughter, not expecting society to damn murder, the truly free have the choice to act, without the need for belief. If you have the greatest belief, if you have the most faith, it just means you are the manipulated. Only an idiot knows. It is a great weakness in democracy and all society, it is the same psychosis that won't allow it to be fixed. The assumption of power is the most sure sign of a low intelligence. It is why in a situation of group rape and group murder, like is common in every military, the group becomes more and more savage when it is honored to do so. Tag 'em and bag 'em. Watch the bodies hit the floor. The weak will always become what the group sanctions and praises and glorifies. And they will always think it is good and strong, no matter what the means to succeed in the group. But not the Independent. He is free from this societal warping, mini or large scale, from his wife or his country. He never needs praise. He can choose all paths. (So he likely walks in the middle where he can't hear the worshipers of themselves trying to recruit him to another fake story.) We do not need to trick ourselves, or use others. With or without you. This is why our Beast is Best. Free from the need to reason we destroy while you are trying to think of why you should, or more likely, for someone to tell you why you should. If someone is telling you a reason, they are gaining, and you will not. This is the trick of power, but you will always believe you will gain, until you don't, until you can't, and you will have no ability to. The Beast in the Independent, the Free man, lives while you are trying to figure out how to. Free from fear, even when the body feels it, he fights all those that seek power, at least for a time. He does so, because he sees it everywhere in the Darkness. But the weak are vast, and he knows he will not win. But his Beast is Free to sever whatever cause he dreams, or have no cause at all. If you are afraid or angry, you may be his prey. While you think of how to trick him so you may have power over him, he already knows what he is doing. He has already acted and you have already failed. He is what you think you are. The cage cannot rattle, because he can see that there never was one. The Beast is Free.

<u>Leave "Home" Immediately</u>

Your parents will try to pull you towards a path. Once… people, people that breed, believed these paths to believe that they were gaining in life. They used these paths to beat and meld their children into. To survive. But now, all these hard lines become laxed, as the system becomes the path. And with this system there are many ways to get in. Many paths to come around. Leave home early. And listen to the things of "value" in every life. Find the obviously reoccurring patterns of reasons and notice what they mean. Pretty little. But the flame is significant. Burning, without the need for the continuous lie of justifying an eventually perpetually depleting value. This is where we find purity in our spirits. This is where we are alone, and not alone.

If you want to be free from hating everything that is not like it used to be as you age, then you must escape the parenting nature of judgment. We must live in a New Society where we are not forced to be liars. Where we may speak honestly. Where we can make a case, to see if love guided the just cause, or to see if the pursuit of power or fear, defense provoked any action. A period of detoxifying emotions would be needed, but not a period of confinement and degradation. A period of calming. A gentle period. Without stress, not within stress, not the atmosphere that breeds what caused whatever it was that placed them into politics. … It is too easy to reason in the direction of trying to make our helping efforts not have negative effects…too easy to want and try to matter… here we seek Independence from people that make these thoughts that justify our punishment. To be Free we must make an earnest effort to not acknowledge anyone that believes they can claim ownership of us. No one physical should own you, and see this without hatred, and you will be Free.

Children, notice when the reality is built on doubt. We are more alive when we have been shaken off our stilt, because we remember why we moved to the beach when we fall on the sand. Can you realize that you are not going anywhere with all this instruction? But you'll become something that can go anywhere. It is easy to heed the physical world and stay alive, the rest can come with a "Yawp!".

<u>Mercy, "tough guy"</u>

Only those that have stolen, murdered, and borrowed pieces of other's lives to continue, only the ones that faced the moments of desperation, that turned and returned from the utter brink of life and lifelessness, have the heart to protect the weak that could never want to think it. These are the friends of mine that couldn't believe how close these ancient reflexes of survival are, just stealing and killing, are to them. It is knowing what nothing is, and how little is needed to fall into the war against ourselves, a war we don't feel sorry for, because we know it is anyone who damns us that repressed something every human is, a survivor, but in those that talk of Heaven and Hell a slow perversion and fascination grows like the erection in the shed. And all they need to be told with gentle authority that a persecuting coward can believe in, is that they never had to contemplate and mangle and turn and twist and attempt to not think about, an innocent fleshy erection. We that have seen, living and dying and sex, and calmness, and peace, that know that baseness of war, that sought it, and damned ourselves to end Damnation, we Common Criminals, we hold ourselves together as the Forgiving Citizenry. And if all could come to know a simple song that haves and takes and needs a little, then prison would be as irrelevant as we know it is. Eternal Damnation, the embodiment of the extended prison sentence, the lie that police should use force, turn the righteous into cold impersonal friendless retaliators, making a war that is not naturally there. Only those that believe in Heaven and Hell are bringing damnation to anyone. All religions with this idea, are false. All enforcers are misguided, like all criminals they try to stop, both sides, and every side needing to be broken of the same limited and false arrogance, both believing and fighting within the same concept, neither believing the other side could be "saved", and there in lies the trap, the lie, and the war, being able to be alive is the only prize, and to know peace and no threat in that time is our award, there is no damnation. It is a lingering lie left behind by the rich believing it was a necessity to protect their wealth from the "poor", or those that need to survive, but now, we can all survive. And the caves will open unto sky. But the criminal and the police officer must see how their choices are the same. The only difference being security, and a place to sit and judge, while the other, the "criminal", must remain in movement.

But, some of us, will stop the flow of illusion, because there are no more disguises we believe in. We, like them, see power and no power. They will not be the power, and no one will.   The memories we end stop the flow of every side. We are not on your side. We are on equality's side. And we will never exist, so you will never find us. And we will always exist, so you will never feel alone. We walk amongst everyone. If you feel hate or sadness, you have lost, reason towards love, utopia, dependant on nothing, while having more.

"I could wreck the world and make it as I dream it. I feel time bend
as I flex in it. My influence warps it."

I do not want to be anything. Only free to be nothing.

<u>Ticking War</u>

Our enemy uses us as a toy. Part of their game to warp and use. It is not possible to change them. It is not possible to stop the ethos of those that truly control. It is factual that to stop their strongest, their most controlling, some people have to be strong enough to do what they don't want to. Some of us will be lucky enough to enjoy our burden. If one has the strength to not have to walk a beaten path of constant pleasure, than one can be free. If there is no will to stop those that seek control, the destroyers, your teachers, then freedom* will always have an asterisk by it.

<u>This is True, It is Not to Please You</u>

Moving from place to place.
Feeling fear.
Too much danger.
Soon something could build up and
close in.
Real Danger. I take risks. Real risks.
I make---enemies.
My time and my life are in jeopardy.
You may feel this in your life,
at least once.
My many threats have made me
feel this far more times than average.
This is the feeling of fear that you
will feel when your life is near end,
a time of true mortal danger.
But to me it is only something my
body feels. I calm the illusions
fear makes in the brain.
I choose as logically as I can in
the situation and in the state of my knowledge.
I knew I would feel this, I saw the course I would choose very very
young,
and I taught myself how to silence this overwhelming feeling.
Most of the other abilities I've gained were of a side result to this
quest
towards Freedom.

There comes a time when I need something
new.
Safer. Calmer. Until the next risk.
The path of a Hero is hard.
I still don't like the feeling of fear, which
warns me like a beacon,
or what fear naturally triggers in the reflexes of
defense I have in my body and mind that
I must deliberately and constantly meditate into what bliss can be.

Epilogue:
My hands are stiffer. How long will I be able to write?
What toll will the keeper ask?

Beauty to the Dying.

<u>To Be or To Not Be</u>

I knew that *she* would give me anything. So I made myself be careful what I asked for.

You! Reader. You. I will speak of Her whenever I wish. This is my existence. My living. My mind. It is a life! It is not meant to please you. It will never be thus. And if you ask me to, I will not stand for it. Freedom. This is why we are living. Against your Pride. Your pleasure. Your want.

Touch gently my hand and you will see that it is not hot, but are you brave enough and wise enough to reach out? When you do you are no longer concerned with me being your Brother or your Attacker, when you are just willing to see what it is and not be afraid of it before hand, then you will be ready. Reach out and grip hard, the ride is strong, you must be strong to take it.

What can you be on the other end of our training. Will you be Free? Will I?

<u>Types of Words</u>

When walking the path of no power, when fighting and existing and becoming more and more purified by confronting yourself you will hear many words that appear to be against you.

"Stop. You're embarrassing yourself," from the two most insecure liars I've ever met, I state with love. Everything They say is a reflection unto themselves. Like the King seeing the Coward in the Mirror. They would be embarrassed because they think that their image is who they are. I was fine and always unaffected by what the image was. Everyone that criticizes you, every <u>one</u>, does so because judgment makes them feel better about the person they don't want to see in themselves. Judgment is always aggression masking fear. There is always weakness in the yelling, in the pointing of weapons.

Every person I have ever seen that claims to be against addiction and drug use has feared drugs because they are an addict. Addicted to something like bliss, or adultery, as I understand was the fate of Sid's parents. *She*, our Nameless Hero, spoke of him, not even knowing that *she* did. His own parents doubting the human path, even forcing drug tests, because they thought that drugs could take control of themselves, because they were weakened by fear, they masked with an untrue, unwilling to damn themselves love. He was never that weak. I'd assume. Or else *she* would have never spoke to him, and never fondly of him. True love, expects damnation, and rides straight for it.

What people try to control is the fear of themselves. This fear of the person that you are is the root of all oppression. Those that preach the loudest against a human condition are always the most prone towards it. This is why you should never follow a leader. The Darkness over compensates to avoid the Truth and the development of Genuineness. The path is alone, against yourself.

<u>What was I thinking?</u> The ego. It exists. Greed. The want for comfort, the want for power. It is a choice to not use these things. It is a constant choice to decide not to be the weakness. How can I make sure I do these things? Meditation. To stop my mind from thinking it. To break the pattern. How can I overcome the exact thing I am? Think it, and release it. Act with it, and gain nothing from it.

American Christians

"So, you're a Buddhist?" Concerned American Christian.
"Ya. I guess. If you need to call me something," Zarat.
"So, what's that about?" Concerned American Christian.
"Well...It's about overcoming our general urges. These things that make us do what we normally wouldn't want to. It's about not wanting, not having to have..." Zarat.
"What do you mean? Not wanting? How are we supposed to not want?" It laughs at Me, "We just sit, we just die?"
"No. But we don't fear death. Let me give an example. Let's say that there is water over there..." His eyes jumping to interrupt me...He starts to...He forces me to talk over him..."Look, even if there is someone who is keeping you from that water. Even if you had to kill him to get it..."
"What are you talking about? ·Even if you had to kill him???!!!" Christian.
"Listen, there is no right or wrong action?" Zarat.
"I don't think God would want that?" Christian. It, the Christian, now ready to kill me to prove that it is right. Without Reason. Instantly.
"Look, you asked me. Don't you see that you've become the anger that you have against me? You are irrationally persecuting me. There's no love or tolerance in you. You hunt for reasons to hate what isn't like you. And you aren't sure what you are. You're the same sicko that burnt witches and committed genocides on the Native Indians! The same person that has destroyed society after society with this Pride. You are every enemy you could ever have. I mean, Jesus Fuck! What the fuck is wrong with your diseased mind?" ZARAT.
"You're the one going to Hell, buddy." Christian. He laughs at me again. Why would he laugh at that?
"You are Hell," So Spake Zarat.

How can we save the world from this? How can we reach through the illusion and save this man that would sooner kill me than hear unto me? How could he not see that he was forcing me into the Final Solution? And how could he not see that that was the only thing I could do to stop his oppression of all other people he would meet for the rest of his life? I chose the path that could go the limit. Poor, poor, suffering Hitler. Little Adolf. He cared so much, that he went so mad, and suffered so great. And using power to do it, using power to stop power...it never works...and it's the only way I see to stop the leaders of the Zealots, because they won't let it go, and they cannot be helped. They are too stupid to see that we are all wrong, and they are remnants of Darkness handed down by generations of tradition, existing here and now with their handpicked thoughts of blind belief, ready to face me, in this moment of Freedom. Forgive me Compassion. Though, there is no need. I hate this path. I hate that I am the only one that has the strength to walk it. The only one I know that is left. When will I walk no more?

In an instant, with a breath, my mind is wiped clean and my karma is pure again. And I can see simply and kindly again. And I am Free from the judgment of mankind. Free from the thought of the pain I made to stop pain. Without pride, I strike with great power, and gain no power. Amen. Damnit.

<u>You're Discomfort</u>

You think that discomfort is my fault. You blame me for it. You admonish me. And I had better not do it again. And you enslave me because I am not pleasing you. An entire evil society. That thinks you are evil because they don't understand what you are saying, because it is not what they expected to hear. They expected you to advance them, pleasure them, they instinctually use people. You make governments grow, and they make governments grow. And they are afraid of you making them any different than the shaky image of what they want you to think they are. Your weakness, your fear, your lack of control disrupts your ability to form a good society. You are letting your slave mind feel the discomfort. You are on a path to oppression, like every society that has fallen, when they lose contact with Life, with the dirt beneath their feet. When they judge to death. When they hang, when they burn, when they capture, when they collect, when they create suffering to answer suffering, when they take eyes for eyes, when darkness thinks it's light and it rules the world, when all it holds is the Power to Kill. It doesn't matter what reasons they are using to oppress, it has always been done with a smile, and encouragement, and the injection of Pride. It matters that it has happened, and they formed institutions to propel its perpetuity.
Before the white man came, with the Portuguese and the Slaves and the ability of using, there was heaven here. There was Earth itself. There was food and there was abundance. It isn't "Man" that's responsible for the destruction as they would have you think, it is the type of Man that you are choosing to be. It is the type you are being forced to serve.
The OverMan is the cure to your sickness. It will be some time until we are thanked for it. The cure lies on the other side of your discomfort, be human and face this world calmly, without fear of death, touching the life that you find discomforting. Then you can understand how you are your discomfort.

Libertine.

<u>Don't Believe in Yourself</u>

Bitch, redneck, nig, asshole, breeder, Jew, faggot, queer, dike, whore, skank, All of Them. Every group that heard these words. Every one eventually made it a word of Pride. Those that were offended began to yell it out to each other and smile. They took on happy tones. Good for them right. Wrong. Once it happened Pride was chosen. A special interest group formed around the concept of selfish gain. Pride made up an image of what it was to be that look. The mob mentality spread the idea of the image to others that wanted to feel safer, as is the myth of belonging. Since the image spread there came to be a more uniform thought of what it should look like in the group, and those that belonged first began to persecute and disallow others that weren't like the image that they now believed they were. Tyranny comes all to simply from Pride. Everything, every pattern, repeats again and again. There have been few generations free of war. You can identify yourself with one of those words, if you feel Pride from them...you have lost...chosen the Dark Path. The way of suffering. Suffering is what you have brought by belonging to your narrow minded image of people you want to criticize to be more like an illusion you've imagined, all while trying to avoid an image. So you have lost. Now choose a new way. A new path in your thoughts. There is a path beyond Pride.

<u>The Nature of Our War</u>

The Dark Society is populated with supremacist power mongers that want nothing more but than to form a perfect world where they can live forever and no hardship ever befalls them. The supremacists are not delineated by the color of skin, by ethos, by creed...no matter what their reasons they seek supremacy for themselves. And if they are not able to have power and security in your society they will ridicule and eventually kill you. This is the nature of lusting for power. See it in the tears of the wanting victims. See it in the manipulations of every conversation. They do not want equality, they want superiority over nature, humans, animals, and for any god they want to believe in to serve them and reward them for anything they have done. And if their god will not reward them they will damn god as well. Beware all members of the Dark Society. They will not trust you until you are one of them and they can have what they want. They want anything you can produce. They will give you money for it, so that you become like them. So long as power and supremacy over all things is sought, Capitalism will definitely fail. Like all systems have failed for the same reasons of greed, pride and power. Everyone wants the same thing. For the Dark Society to end this and save itself and return to the Light it must fix the psychological dysfunction that it pursues and believes itself to be. Everyone must stop fighting to prove that they are right. No one is. The enemy of all in the light are those that believe in their cause the strongest, every cause. And those that group together for power, any power. Because individual want is so fierce and grouped wanting is so vicious the Dark Society has lost all logic and tolerance. There are no facts, only illusions, behind those illusions are the selfish, those struggling to hang on, those that lose everything they want because they forget to notice what they have.

<u>Let It Loose and See it Abide</u>

A great problem in the Dark Society is that people adjust themselves by feeling bad to those that are disgusted or feel bothered by something. We are adjusting to the mentally ill. The disturbed. The sick. The bothered. The betrayed. It creates a society of persecutors and slaves. Crying mothers and fighting children. The weak become stong and the strong become weak. We must realize that reactions are psychological responses not the will of gods and rulers. If we overcome this weakness to cater to the disapproving, which was installed in us by the ridiculing of our parents, we can overcome a world with perpetual tyranny. Hoorah!

There is a mindset that I can rise up into. The mind of the crusading hero. Not by becoming greedy and short sited. I am sure that I will not become the Dark form of a crusader because I vow that I will seek no power, and there is not power I delusionally think I serve, though I feel the calming power. This is a mindset I speak of that I can simply choose to become. Some people wrongly believe that they are these mindsets, this presented energy, this personal image, this identity. But it isn't true. There are levels to personal advancement as seen in society. There are those that imitate a personality type, which is most people, driven by Envy. There are those that selfishly and forcefully define that image that is imitated. Both cowards, shaping a world they don't want to face factually. Then, there are those that discovered that every personality is within us. If we experience enough, highs and lows and enough reasons we see that anyone can be justified. And we can be anyone within our intellectual capacity.

There is a way of thinking that allows me to place my mind into a sense of happy, with no fear, a mindset where everyone enjoys me, loves me, and posts no harm or criticism towards me. And this in turn allows people to let me be free from them. As they stand in awe of what they want to be. And they are happy and more relaxed and they laugh without shame or hesitation. And they bring Freedom instead of persecution to those around them.

I can access the power image, that which intimidates. That which controls and owns. That which survives. That which too many think is themselves when it is only a technique available to anyone.

I can feel every depth, every bit of passion anyone has for anything. But I have full control to be able to apply it anywhere, not just where I can gain from it. My calmness is my choice. My fearlessness has been developed in the discomfort I have faced.

Watch me as I enjoy my limitless potential in every randomly occurring movement of reality.

And I can be as eloquent as anyone I've ever known. I adapt in an instant. And ease people's hearts that want to persecute me.

Patience...Patience...Patience...Patience...

The Systems "They" Keep Secret
Walton's

Written to make you feel less afraid. Because, you are in a Free country. And your heart should reflect that. The poor and the rich feel like criminals. Everyone tries to portray themselves in a false sense of perfection, when humanity is right next to them. The intelligent know it. They know the power is not so strong as it would like us to think. It is a mirage. But the illusion has become real in your mind. Calm it. Smile. Don't stare and doubt. Upper Middle Class. Holy handed. Security is independent, and cops don't care that much because they can't do that much. And what they don't know is vast, it is why they believe so awesomely in untrue circumstantial evidence. Everytime I have been questioned by the cops that came to search me, routinely, because I pulled something from the inside, and I knew what had actually happened because I totally did it, the evidence they found didn't have anything to do with it. So I instantly knew that they would never catch me. And I knew not to point the possibility of evidence that I had already fully considered. I rule, Zarat spaked coolly. 6 times. And they always thought that I was suspicious. Because I didn't know what questions they were going to ask, but I still instantaneously came up with the answers to their questions. "Am I authorized to make a copy of this key." It is why I can speak so freely, even if I go on living after I kill my Philosophy, thus my current reason for being. I know there is no evidence left behind. And no link worth the time. Plus, there were always people that would love me, because of my true and perpetual kindness that easily gushes for Real Beauty, thus my seductions. But the Father would teach me how to slow my reactions, even if I knew the answer the second he asked. Because then their stupid minds would feel satisfied. These cursed men, damned to seek satisfaction. None will feel it when they die. Not a single one. There will be the doubt in it that will pull them into their hell.
I want them to think that. Feel the damnation they wrought with want. The Criminal and the Cop want the same thing. To feel like the other one won't do something to them. To not feel afraid. They will always be the same Dog. This is why in the end, the vanquishing of fear is a main theme. This is why there is a story.

Walton's only really monitors electronics and jewelry. And unless you look like what they think shit looks like, and yes you can pretty much tell, but if you don't look like it you can easily get away with it.

Don't look like a criminal, is the key. Be an individual. Don't buy into the thug style. You think you're being an individual by looking like a criminal, looking tough, but...oh why explain it kid...Anyway, when you need to, when the risk is important enough, because you are poor enough, or you like the rush and want to keep your edge for adventure, simply take something from one area, and move it to another area. If it is electronics, which, don't because they put alarm sensors inside the answering machines now, take it out of the wrapper. Under a shelf so there is no video evidence. From that moment forward, you have always had that spiny black-light in your pocket. It is yours. Believe it. You came in with it. Maybe you wanted to find another like it. Be Free by not feeling crushed by the penalties they threaten you with. And love the enemy that would trap you. For real, and he will be your friend. See yourself in him.
These are the jokes folks. But they are referencing very real things. And are very true. Like everything in these Great Works. Believe what you want. You'll only remember what you need at the time. You can only do that if you're not willing to believe anything. Who cares if the answers are in the contradictions. The height of Physics and the height of Philosophy are proving that. It is the next level of logical mentality.

Zarat will not tell you who speaks on within me. I will not confess them to feel free. I will keep their burdens. The burden is heavy now. But I believe it will one day be light.

….
….
some time had passed.
…
When the Father came, he had no fear. He came to test the metal of the system. It was a big path. But one that seemed easy for the Patient. He called out everybody. Told him he loved them. Sat down with them, and they all began to talk. Focused on the grandeur of the concept of the Free and the Compassionate Society. That which can care about the person sitting across from you--fighting you---hating your thought---but believing in the prosperity and equality of each other's life that lets them speak unto our beloved ears.
Shit is, is that he did it. The "revolt" was just punctuation. And I was just the Calligraphy of it. The Great Society the Paper. And the Father, easily the ink.

<u>To a racist. or To a cop.</u>

Zarat: "Nostradomas said that blacks will one day rule the earth. Do you know why they will rule the Earth? You see. The blacks are overcoming the lies. And not because they are better or worse human beings, not because they are blackies, but because they are in the right random circumstances to make themselves that. They were so ridiculed. So hated. For so long. They accepted that they would not take less than everything they could get. So many already have nothing. So many have had nothing and know that you still have yourself when you have nothing. So they can risk more. And with nothing, or the acceptance that if you lose everything and have nothing, like the illusioned walls of a prison, it is not that bad. It is copable. Why not go for everything? Why not risk everything? However, there is darkness in this strength. There is power sought. There is spite used. This Dark Society has not even been destroyed yet, and already the new one exists. Already, the dreams of lost prophets, like Martin Luther King Jr. have been warped and used. In the next society there will be many that will not walk hand in hand. Friend to Friend. When will the darkness die? And how many times must it be destroyed?"
"Oh ya. I bet you think women will rule the earth too."
"Possibly. There is enough fear and hatred and total lust for power within the realms of feminism. The right to be justified is a dark right. There is much spite. Much darkness. If it happens, some lost hero will overcome the lies that he is weak and foolish and can change nothing, just because he is a man. Someone or something always comes to destroy darkness.   But it is not like these things are important. These scenarios have happened before, and those scenarios inevitably followed paths of power and eventual destruction. Man, Woman, nigger, cracker, white, black, slant, meld, prick fucking bastard, it doesn't matter. Anything can be good. And anything can be bad. It depends what the wanter wants to have, but also what side you're on."

<u>For the Animals</u>

"How long have you been sitting here?" animal.
"Awhile. I have noticed how similar all people are to all people. It seems as if there are only certain ways, certain designs in which to interpret the world. Certain egoic structures. Just as there are only so many ways you can make a functional engine, or a grilled cheese sandwich, you can add ham or a tomato, but without the cheese it's just not a grilled cheese sandwich. Perhaps there are only nine personalities, maybe only three sub-types to each. Western man is very very slowly figuring out the patterns in which its environment works in, but its ignorance shines through in everything it does. It misses so much. The Dark Society only sees useful things of power. It misses the useful things of peace." The formation of every defining thought is driven by defenses and impulses that are programmed into our mushy blank infant puddy bodies. We can choose to not function with the instincts that don't function anymore. But we must return the mind to childhood, without defenses, before defenses. The earlier one needs to defend themselves, the sooner one is oppressed, and the harder the changes are to make. All psychological issues stem from the inhibiting of freedom. We must make ourselves free once more. No matter what the circumstance we must direct our minds towards the Single goal. Towards overcoming goals.

Notes...Flashes...Sensations...

<u>A Sovereign Nation</u>

I may not be king of the world, but I am king of myself. I determine everything I do or that I let happen to myself. I am king of my own nation. For we are all nations unto ourselves. We are all free to do as we please. Those of the Dark Society may try to present us with consequences, such as jail time, or public humiliation, or other techniques of fear, but we have the choice to do as we please regardless of these weak consequences of humanness. For every life, as for every nation, there is a point of consequence, points of failure, and a point of death, and between these points of occurrence we have the option to do what we think is right. I am a nation of a man in a nation of men, in a society of lies and fear. I will not surrender my nation to the darkness and cruelty of those that seek power or to the blind hypocritical pawns of their police force. I am king over one nation. I have power over one nation. I have no reason to fear consequences. There are countless consequences to living, and most of them are not from the Dark Society, although it wants you to think it is all powerful. I choose to live, so I choose consequence and it enters into me with every breath and brings me closer to pain and death. And I do not fear this pain or any pain. Pain comes. And pain goes. It always, eventually goes, even if the going is my own death. But it always goes. The Dark Society is useless in its pursuit of power over my nation. I am king forever. I cannot be overthrown. My lifetime. I have a hope that one day the Dark Nation stops its war upon My Nation. I hope the Dark Nation understands that nations can disagree and have different ideas and do different things that affect other nations and that these wars they fight never had to happen. There could have been ease and understanding for the many ways there are to interpret this foolish world. But still, there will always be peace in My Nation. I have that choice. My Nation is unconquerable.

Zarat makes me understand what "I" means. He teaches me what the living "I" can be. And that I have no limits to what "I" could have existed as, or what I continue to exist as.

I hear *her* whispers in my mind. *She* is present still. As I touch this world less, they, my *lovers*, grow louder to me. The dead touch me, their spirit is not away from me.

With the loss of the Right to Property, a place to exist, high rent, and the concept of debt, those that seek power secured it. Restriction is everywhere, and all designed to make you join the economic system. All so that someone can own you and profit from your life, far more than you will profit from it. Realize it when you see how your "boss" speaks to you, like you owe him something. We can't live by rivers and lakes so that we must have apartments. We can't stay more than 14 days in a trailer so that we must work and work to live, pay high rent, want more things, and people think we are safer and better off. Camping restrictions deny people the right to live free. To not have to be a part of this slave system. Everything. Piece by piece we have been brought to our knees so that a few may walk upon us. All that have control, all that have any authority, these are those individuals that assumed it, that took your freedom, because they asked you if you'd give it up, but it didn't seem like a question, that was the trick, it sounded like a statement. All, never to be trusted, all traitors to a Free Society. All steeped in arrogance and Darkness. All your masters, until you stop them.

The path to freedom begins when you pursue all that you fear. Face everything that makes you uncomfortable. Anything that makes you insecure or nervous, or terrified or angry or sick---pursue it. Seek it. And become calm. The soldiers of freedom must not be swayed for any purpose. We must not be able to sell out. If we fear nothing, if we know we are already complete, we cannot be bought off. We cannot be penalized. We know slaves are made that way.

Your Wife, My World, Your War

There is a fact in conflict that arises in every relationship. And in all but the rare rises up a reflex of snapping tones and threats towards the imagined risks that may or may not threaten a person's identity or ability to have. This is the secret tone of the Dark Society. Those living amongst compromise and a hypocritical dual reality that overcompensates when unrestrained, because it always feels restrained. Restrained by the underlying tone of the threat of penalty, the simple threat of someone yelling their betraying opinion at you. A person suffering as they contort, because they believe in a reason that they want to last forever, when only the concept lasted a second.

Side by side, look at *her*, watch *her* graceful touch fall upon every basic task. And watch *her* as *her* judgment falls the second *she* realizes *she* could have had it, the second *she* felt the guillotine in *her* mind offering that cold feeling of being able to sever and become angry and controlling, the idea of the reflex that believes it must issue a Punishment, a Penalty, so that *she* can remain happy…though it could occur, it did not control. Realizing in a moment that it was only a feeling, a selfish one, one *she* felt, one he felt, and that didn't matter, one that did not come in between the love that kept them permanent in a world that was hardly even here, here in the place that is constant, the place where my soul is present. There are ways to go, if we don't have to believe we are what we instantly and psychologically think. We must see that we are the violators of the peace. In every instant we choose for ourselves, our place, and our Sin. For Sin to cease, it must fall away. What you believe has to be done, does not have to be done.

The Real War starts as you draw the line against yourself. Agreeing to stop yourself from contorting into what you have always hated to see in other people. First you will notice that long thought process trying to place yourself, shape you, create a view for others to see you as… second you will stop wasting your time, as you realize more and more that you have already mattered as much as you can, that your worth is a living presence, everything else is jewelry. Then you will finally come to the harsh border where you address the instinctual results of being slighted. Then baser and baser, to where an axe swings at your head and you counter calmly, blocking the arm and holding back the blade, because clearly the situation is fine, after all, the axe is not *in* my head, and peace is due in an instant if it suddenly is. What is it that I fear?

<u>Ancestors</u>

My Grandfather, a man who lived a life before me and had been at least a quarter of everything I might be, once told me that he had an Inferiority Complex. Which bode to me that he noticed that I may face something like this. This man had thought his whole life. Reason for Reason. Carved by a hundred rigid self believed restraints and molds. So, later I came to realize that he meant that there was a problem and he sought a solution and someone told him a name for something. But what was the problem? What was he trying to solve??? What would hinder him in this particular society that he chose to inevitably participate in…and even love…That's right. The same as myself. I can notice. He could see the scheme, but not do the deed. What? My God. The restraint. In my mind. Holding me from Greatness….Is it all a theory we can never be? Are we as false as every Imagination? Can no Great Sway of Reason for Purpose and Will spring to Save the Mass?

Praise be to All who were raised by Animals. The Beast holds the Wisdom, You are the Burden. Praise be to all those who fear the tie of the chain! And become Brave and Strong and Smart and Wise to Resist It!!!

Bam! - Bam! The pOuNdInG rhythm of the Yawp!

Further in we notice another risen mound of occurrence…
This condition came to me noticed as weak by his son. A mere condition of mind. Often, to be great at one thing, another thing, another side, will simply be weaker. And it seems that while growing and aging a person can make an observation of their parents, judge them, form choices, based on the weaknesses they see, this is why the teenage babes grow so cruel, so criticizing, mocking, and noticing, you can't stop their Survival, but we can be calm with it and let it roll. Attempt to interject and be destroyed, our futility the same damnation our parents drove themselves to with the want to reaching love that comes from trying to hang on to what we never owned and don't need to, but still must protect. Therefore: We can be anything. But first, we will drain life from who we are born to, then we shall retaliate against everything our parents have rejected from their parents to believe in, or we fail and believe in what our parents believe, as we are meant to be Independent, but our initial response as we Turn away from our parents is to become the opposite, but this is if we live blindly, without hearing

what people are saying.   Listen. And listen and believe in the flow of the intention of the soul feeding you a word and eventually, by caring, we will become exactly what we see everyone else already being…but that's only if we succeed in Capitalism.   However, if we succeed in the newest and funnest revolution, the Revolution Against Ourselves as the Coming Tyrants by trying these new reasons out while we're Young and formable and willing to think what anyone can, and should, then we will be something entirely different. Open your hearts, and do not reach out. And be Present for all who may love of you.

<u>Emotions</u>

It is not that emotions are wrong. Emotions are fine. What we must realize is that these emotions have certain responses. They do things to us. And we can use the impulse to direct ourselves towards a wiser more advantageous outcome. A different emotion. A better one. One we don't even expect exists. Where we gain, but do not take.
People are controlled by responses to being slighted or rewarded. They experience anger or sadness. Because they didn't get, or did get what they wanted. Want. They are driven by want. When we are addicted to our Want then we become slaves to these destructive responses. We can direct these responses by becoming calm in situations that turn us into these people we don't like to be. We are calm by no longer needing to win and no longer minding when we lose.   The metaphor for the choice of releasing this greed is "Let it go…" It is what the choice feels like. You just start to notice when you are out of control when you are trying to keep control. And you let go. Stop letting it whip you around. Notice. Choose. Now, from all of this…What if you were calm, what if you could invoke anger logically, and in doing so learn how to remove uncontrollability and confusion from the rage. Then you could use it to kill (metaphorically, maybe) an oppressor, someone telling me they have authority by their dark tone, a cop, suddenly, in a situation of casual questioning. Maintain Our Freedom. When an oppressor talks to me, I am always thinking of the way to maintain my Holy Freedom. My Right by Vow. Given as a Promise by the existence of my Holy Spirit, the Body of god. By going deeper into meditation and letting go of the things that control us we slowly realize that our want is far far more effective with a curve in it.

<u>The Grip</u>

She held no grudge against you. Father. You know. The greatest and hardest gift to give another human being *(No. Living creature.)* is the willingness to kill them. When you see that the fuse has been lit and they will be dead soon...To end them so they do not have to waste in their decay. My loves, my animals, my comrades, the thankfulness and the awe of the power that stares back as you shatter your heavy heart and feel the gravity of the soul. True charity will stun you. How much do you love? Enough to be so brave, to silence every interaction you have ever known with a click. A bang. Or the tear of a knife or a saw, or a heavy revolutionary sword crashing down on the soft hair of a *Girl* that knows *she* cannot lose *her* innocence.

I have always seen reality. Honestly, truthfully, exposing the beauty that you know shamefully. Letting it slide past my rhythms and show you god on the inside. A rapture insures. Your heart feels stopped and it has never beat so fast. Don't think you have had it. You are probably wrong. Have no pride in the answers you find, cling to no teaching, there is more to know to form a real opinion. Dive deep.

Be careful. Where there is light, the absence of light, and if you are there you will attempt to adapt to it. Search for the light. Exist in the Light. Sometimes you won't want to adapt. Keep Equality as a heavy rock inside you. Have it. Let no one move it.

<u>Stop Looking for Satisfaction</u>

We are not going to change our identity to please you. We are not going to pretend that this is fine and that is good and we are not going to play a harp for you to dance to. If the truth happens, we have faced it. Your weakness gives you your pain. We've told you how to deal with it, how to be no one, but you keep picking illusions. And we will keep laughing as we shatter yours and you are left crying, feeling like you have nothing. When the truth is, you'll always have nothing. Ownership is a lie. It can exist in concept, but not as a concrete reality. Because you enter the world with what you had. Maybe you are a bit more conscious. But there is only one thing you have.
I'll mock you as you die, because we are not sad like you are. Though we know pain, like you. Though we will miss you, we also see a wide smiles across the bellies of all sentient beings.
The reason the revolution of the 1960's failed, is because the young were willing to think beyond power, but as their parents aged, they felt that endless tie to them. And when their dying parents asked them, "Do you believe like I believe?" They did not have the courage to say "No. And how selfish are you to ask?" But they believe in it, and the child told his father what he wanted to hear. And that changed him a bit. Eventually, we all face the same road. And the beliefs we grip to won't exist, as meaning is given to us in the falling of our caring, psychologically complex, relationship falls. And only the ones that know who they are, only the ones that swim naked in mountain lakes, living without lies, will know how pretty it is. Everyone else will suffer and not realize the thrill of it.   Unafraid we balk the gesture of death. While you reach at everything with your eyes. My eyes, though crying, still remain unafraid. Gazing at you, always knowing that what you began as is what you end as, and it has probably happened many times before.

<u>Upper Middle Class White and Other Colored Boys</u>

People have been sold a mind. Most people have. Taught a way to think by those that will supply what they are interested in. And they look at other groups that have been sold a different way to think, because they are in a different type of economy, and see NO VALUE. Doesn't matter if they are looking up or down, but this view is widely spread amongst the prosperous. If these types can't enjoy you at the level they want then why insert you into their reality? You are as soulless as a dog is to them. As soulless as a car, or a tree, or feces. Which means, they don't touch life. They feel empty. Like a two dimensional plane. When they reach into themselves and look for what I tell them to look for, they feel it, like a mist, but they pass through it, and can't hold it. Because they are looking for it. Still reaching with their imaginary arms, which are the soul's arms, now the soul just needs to turn the arms in, and touch itself.

You don't want the empty feeling. You think you want the social laughing in the face of people feeling, hell, you even think it's who you are, but you only think that because it was what you had to become to deal with this thing you thought was pain, this "hole in your soul" crap you made up so that you could feel justified, and thus, safe. So, obviously, you need to stop defending yourself. Be willing to be hit, by anything. This is the heart of the Hero. This is your new path. Accept what is spit at you, and try to understand why spit happened, and try not to let the conclusion of that mean anything to you. It's just a thought. It is not who you are.

My mind is a small business. Managed. Pumping thoughts back and forward between departments that work on the same thought in different ways, each adding its input the way it can, like the individuals that become addicted to these parts of the brain, that they think are personalities. I am the Walrus.

<u>Zarat's Image Training</u>

Zarat's early training was thus: With my mind so vivid, so strong, so amazing, I could see all things. Things of this world, things not of this world. I was not trapped by the limits of foolish philosophers that could only know what they see. Early, very early, in my life I felt the idiocy of fear. I saw what it made people. I did not want to be like these people. So fake. So pointless, escaping death, only to live, and nothing more. I would sit, always alone, and I would delve deeply into the pain that others had programmed into me. The fear of being hurt, and harder yet, the fear of those I loved being hurt. Imagined them raped. Bloody. Beaten. Lifeless. Dead. Myself as well. Some of the Dark Society speak with their false axioms of ignorance like, "You can't ever die in a dream. I always wake up before I do." Bullcrap. The weak just can't face it. As I faced more and more, as I let go and accepted more and more demise and suffering I could be dead for great periods of time in sleep. Various things would happen, but usually and mainly, was darkness. This darkness was the dream eventually stopping. Sometimes I would remain asleep. Sometimes I would fade back awake. In time, I knew that I could face anything, because I had. Though there is nothing like the actual deeds of ending or creating suffering in lives, the visuals were well tempered in me. This facing of all fears, anytime I felt them, was a great key to my advancement. Before I met the *Girl* and proceeded more heavily down the physical side of pain, until I realized that no pain, not of the mind or the body, meant anything at all. And any meaning I would give was a lie, a perception that only deluded me for a time, and often kept me from fully facing it. This is why the technique to silence the mind is so vital.

The deeds the mighty Zarat has done I do not go into great detail of. It is not important, but for that person that was purified by it. What is important is how I was able to do it and not be harmed by it. Not ultimately. This world never touches the soul of the person that knows the soul is all that it is.

<u>Hmm</u>
Though I feel that the suffering I have left on the hearts and mind's of those I've cared for is unfortunate, (those women and men that have felt the rush of my overcoming passion,) I also know that it is them who chose to suffer from it. The *Girl* proved it to me by existing untouched by me. My rage, because of my caring, caused many pain as I was

51

younger. It was powerful and I didn't know that it was just a feeling, caused by something in my psyche, entirely distant from the feeling. Time passes, and people affect people. Your life is wasted and affected by my life in this world by your own choice to let it be.   Be simple. Exist. And move.

The Gift of Change

A great burden for the Dark Society's old rules is the fact that people believe that they must cling to the identities that they initially develop. The dark consequence is that the warrior will not know the vulnerability of love. The lover will not know the balance of solidarity. The modern Capitalist will not know compassion and the Monk will not know prosperity. We must free ourselves to flux within our own changing realities.

<u>Shatter the Ego, See the Soul</u>

In relationships most people go the cowards way and seep into a point of accepting and dealing with the comfort levels of their companion to avoid the growing anger from not dealing with the problem. Vulnerability, speaking, baring, this is the path to a good relationship. If hearts that are able to love each other approach one another barriers drop and the weights of life conflicting with life that is around life becomes free. There is a Hero's Path. It lies on The Edge where you are not afraid to lose what you have, it is near death, where you have to accept your own passing, where we are no longer afraid to let things go, even as you feel its fear. It is where we risk ourselves for the small sake of living. With real love, honesty is natural, but you must be willing for the honesty to crush you, the receiver, do not be afraid of the shatterings, they are natural. Wallow together in your vulnerability. See the truth of how you weigh on people. And see the beauty in those that don't mind how you hang upon them, slightly bending their lives. And those that are saddened by the hero's because they feel slighted that they are not recognized, when what they don't realize is that there are others that are hard to bend. Do not cling to your control, and let us drift in the wind that is our brother.

The Thoughts Are The Events. The Moments of Philosophy From the Eyes of the Present Distorted by The Mind Cleansed in The Spirit and Repeated Without It Never Needing to Matter. Pride is an illusion. Pride is an avarice extension of ourselves that means nothing, and sickens who would try to love you.

Most people growing up try to direct themselves to please a crowd so that those of the crowd might pay him advantages. But, I grew up reading the works of those that fought to take this country from the British, only for the same mindset with different reasons assuming power in it anyway. They made it so the money has to come from the source, them. And I read about tyranny and the violations to a Man's right to choose to be Free, to constantly not have to worry about intervention from a "policing" body. A group of worriers and complainers, forcing us to leave our shades open so they can know what happens behind them so they can feel about it and tell us what they want to do with us so they can feel different about it. They grew like fungus within society. And so growing up I trained to be able to take out that room of people that would be swept with fear. I did not train on the technical aspects, the words, I did not care about the image. It was a hard thing to be. All I needed to know was how to load a gun, aim it, and pull the trigger, all which I found extremely easy to do. I trained to have the will to go on when everyone is convinced that they must hate you, hunt you, and have the urge to kill you, and overcome the programming to let someone else hurt you, someone you don't need to know, the police, any police, anyone that would categorize one person here, and one person there. Those that trick us out of our rights, those that take the pay, those that believe they are right, and they conclude on so little information. The police's only thought is how to take a randomly occurring object or circumstance and make it point towards you, and you only have to be associated with the "incident". I trained to fight anyone that would assume authority over me, and I trained to kill anyone that was trained to kill anyone else. This is the Defense of Freedom. Can you hold yourself bravely, violence the last and final solution?

And others rise up, looking at each city as another chance to grab that power that festered Envy in them. Most of them are not white, but poverty is Universal and envy is easy to take, triggered by a successful image. And Envy and Pride spread. And the world grew more dangerous, and I had to be able to fight against them too. To know what "why?" expected, to know how they wanted me to act. To be tough enough, and care about them. To be tough enough to care about them. That's what the population that will not be called "slave" wanted. Or they'd kill me. Just like all Pride would.

I exist in this society. I am present. And if your power, pride and envy did not exist, I would not exist. But don't worry, I am not afraid anymore...and I will maybe not need to feel like I should hurt you. Maybe I can leave you to shatter your own ego instead...but you have to not want to matter. Life is mattering, all men have just forgot.

And if Freedom of Speech didn't exist, then far more would have died than have already. Our Rights are Important!

<u>Sitting, Thinking, Interrupted by Uselessness</u>

The taste of purple. A fake taste. A taste that didn't exist until society made it up. Colors in my mouth. Rotting there. So easily I see my own destruction. Not of my teeth, but of my mind. Seeing the rot first. Habitually seeing my own destruction is my pain, a path of negative self-destruction, because I am not guarding my mind. Trapped and rotting. How will I stop it? I do not need to, but will continue to struggle to live.

And directing uselessness properly.

Zarat:
"We will not negotiate with tyrants."

Zarat:
"Fight any that take freedom."

Zarat:
"We will not assume power."
"But we will manage what is powerless."

Zarat:
"All people have every right to do anything, except take freedom away from others. The militant nation of restrictors takes our freedom and they feel safer and more justified with more guns between the rich and the poor. Desperation breeds crime, oppression spawns crime, inopportunity makes crime."

Zarat:
"Plan prosperity for your neighbor while he plans it for you."

<u>Grandpa</u>

Zarat sat amongst the timber and recalled a Logger he knew. He recalled the kindness and willingness to teach his understanding and his ease. His Grandpa was a man of constant beauty and silent secure courage that few understood or even saw. When his death came he went to it. They say that it was the Cancer that took him. And so, he became a statistic. Another that died to Cancer. It must be cured, so many say. But it does not have to be cured. It is true that death brings sadness for those that shall miss the human that died. That is unavoidable, regardless of what anyone believes about death. But no, cancer must not be cured. Though I think it will be, and we will suffer a little less. Cancer is only a taker of life.   A necessary thing, doing its job well, like all disease and bringers of death it merely struggles to exist and will die as well. Life is supposed to end. It must end. And it is fine that it does. When his force began to leave his body and death began to overtake his body, he excepted it with understanding and courage. His often chilled body filling with such heat. He took it without fear, and so, his journey into anything that may have followed for him was a journey into heaven. All is heaven if you do not fear it. All is heaven if you are open to understanding it. And hell is what you are to afraid to understand.

If, we are beyond good and evil, If, we realize that "good" is what the fearful label as those things that keep them alive and that "bad" is what does not keep them alive, If, it is seen as that simple, Then, the Mind can be witnessed as something that is perceiving, interpreting, and growing, meant only to stop and take all that power away. It cannot be taken personally, our imperfections. We are only noticing new ways to find what is the underlying cause of a simple action, actions that are either beneficial or non-beneficial. All we need to do to have peace is change the perception of what is bad, look at the same situation, and find what is good. There is goodness to every side. And understand that it is a slow and painfully honest process, that will make the world easier and easier with each recognition that faces a discomfort and becomes calm in its circumstance. And as time passes the power of these falsenesses will become less. And being Beyond Good and Evil will not just be something we can say or think. It will be what we are. This is the Great Path. The path away from persecution and a path to fearless Compassion. There is a path for every person to peace. Every person with a desire to be Free. Free from ourselves.

The book plays like an album, with hundreds of singles. Rocking it since 1998, For the People.

A Poem...

"My Friend"

There amongst the high timber
I hear your teaching breath.
The knowledge of the silence
from a man who understands.

I hear your teachings on the wind
as it roars through the trees.
And in the river
in the mud
behind the growling instant of natural impulse.

Do you see me in the timber,
there amongst the trees?
Do you know that I now think of you?
Do you feel my endless care?
I lay unanswered questions light upon the wind.
They are carried into nothing. Far into unknown.

He was an inventor,
that lacked the random gift
of a money making thought.
He made an inventor in my mind.
Though he could not have known its path.
Created by words. By a Spirit bled to Silence.
I am your invention. A product of your love.

<u>May We?</u>

Can you believe how great you are when everyone tells you you are not? Because they cannot see that they are.
Can you believe that you are nothing when the image of having is so over elevated?
Can you be a star without need for fame? Can you know what you are and have that not matter? There is a balance when we don't need to reach out anymore, and when the fists strike us we fall, but we realize we haven't moved from the soon to be corpse of our living human body.

<u>Beyond the Mind, We Can Affect the Mind</u>

Within the mind. Devoid of contact, although it is all around me, and flowing fully through me. I am part of it, but the ego tries to tell me I am separate. Why does the ego lie? Why does it want to survive. I must drive deeper. Drive deeper into "no-thought". I must have no thought. Many have journeyed there. Many have faced the many fears associated with no thought. Great masters have said that a key, or the key, to enlightenment is to have no thought. To be void, non-attached. I must push further. I must not be afraid of leaving my body and not making it back, even though there are things I love here in this life. These things will end in their own time anyhow, as will what I am trying to cling to, the person that is the glorious Zarat. I must face it. I must not be afraid of losing anything, including myself. Let me search for the ultimate silence. The *Girl*, the *holy one*, has been there. Or has *she*? Did *she* go far enough? Did *she* pursue the same path? Stop thinking it out...Stop.   Force the silence. The thoughts only arise more fiercely when forced. I hear music tracks that I heard ten years ago. I hear ancient voices from my past and see images that have never existed. Illusions of the mind. I must not force, although that is my tendency. I want to make things happen, but... I must allow the thoughts to be let go. I must face nothingness. I must see for myself what there is to gain or to be when I am void of identity. Do I still exist? What do I lose if I don't exist?   In truth, I lose nothing.   If I do not exist, all that I have known cannot exist in my reality because my existence is gone. I am gone. All of my interpretation and fear and questions and connections and love and hate, are gone. So, even if I lose everything...I lose nothing. But, why am I still thinking about it?   I must let go.

I   must   let   go.
Nothingness.

                                        Why aren't I leaving my body?

Why aren't I exploding into nothingness?

Why is nothing happening?

I feel untouchable.   Unafraid.
All fears are gone, because what I know I am right now is unharmable. I am the "what" the mind cannot understand, even though the mind tries to make these words for the path. I am Zarat. And I hang on, so that others may follow. I try to remember so that I can tell others the way. Without those that try to keep the mind I would not know that this is the path. No mind. But...is the mind still there, even when I don't deliberately use it? Yes. I can recall everything that I thought in the silence and before the silence. The mind is simply not as frantic. It is not trying to force a remembrance. I do not need to force this. I do not need to make enlightenment happen in any amount of time.
Ease sweeps over the body. Muscles that Zarat never realized are even tense...relax.

Nothingness.

     The mind. The body.   Always so tense. For no reason at all. I have nothing to be, nothing to become, I am already the peaceful spirit. What a silly joke. What a silly thing. We try so hard to find the peace, but we are already at peace, we simply have to realize it.

Nothingness.

                    Silence.   The fearless
void.
                          Beyond the concept of death.

This spirit, this peace, is what we realize we have always been, and
have always had access to realizing, in our lives as we are dying and
then become dead and so, distant from this form.

We are already dead.   We are
already free.

Only a physical form covered in mites, organic material, stuffed with
stinky guts and decaying utilitarian existence is trapped on this earth.
And really we can leave whenever we wish. By meditation. Or by
suicide. Or by trauma. Or by any means. But if we are not afraid of
this world, if we are non-harmed by being here, then we have no reason
to leave and no reason to stay. But we must always be somewhere. So
why not here.

Why not anywhere.
Beyond Silence. Nothing.

The soul eases and changes the mind.

<u>The Schizo Theory</u>

I know what you think. I see the pattern of your reflex. You. Reader. Reading. Sucker. You think the *Girl* had separate personalities. But *she* didn't, and if *she* did, they would have all been geniuses anyway. But it is a conclusion you come to because you don't understand. You don't understand that when *she* thought, the thought was gone, and a new one existed, a new formed theory, a tomorrow, a past *she* couldn't keep because it distracted from a tomorrow *she* was being allowed to imagine. Practically. For everyone, and *herself*, *she* always always gained the most, and *she* knew how precious that was. You miss that *she* could think an entire series of devastating thoughts about *herself* and come to the raised conclusion at the end that it was good because obviously they were "problems" or imperfections in the illusion of reality. *She* knew that the delusional, like *she* was, would find ways to theorize against anything, frighteningly slashing just like *her* instincts wanted *her* to...and *she* was no longer driven into thought. So thoughts could come from anywhere. Any of the minds *she* could have had if the situations of *her* life were different, and *she* used the mixed genetics of *her* lineages to help *her* use different aspects of interpretation. *She* was dynamite.

If anything by the misperceivers, the image users of understanding (lawyers, scientists, dog catchers) it can be called Self-Induced Non-Detrimental Schizophrenia, that rotationally leads to certain states of elevated consciousness. Jerks.

In a Field without Cause

Zarat had sat in the fields not speaking. He laughed in himself when he realized how strange it was for him, or anyone, to sit in a beautiful field by a stream for so many hours and not speak to the person that is next to them. *How sweet that one is that sits beside us in silence and we need not speak to?*   How strange to so many that there was no particular purpose to sit and think and be. But in the silence that surrounded him, he thought...Within the Dark Society there is much hatred, greed, and insecurity. This comes from the society's tendency to force people to hate and fear being human. If one hates being human they will fight to propel society, because society covers humanness. It attempts to create an image of humanness, rather than accepting the simplicity of being human. The person will fight to overcome their humanness. This repression of emotions, such as all sexual emotions (*and we all have <u>every</u> sexual emotion whether we try to deny it or not*), violent emotions, even repulsion of our filthy bodies and environments, breeds anger and ironically breeds violence and sexual cruelty. The Dark Society uses the dark technique of shame to perpetuate itself. This dark technique produces generation on top of ever growing generation that does not intend to be cruel or prejudice, or harmful to those other people trapped in the same generation, the past generation or the growing generation, but the Dark Society takes good people and warps them. The society covers the truth and equality of a human being and fills the human being with ego, with shame, with raging cruelty that reveals itself to the person as goodness struggling for its place. The fact that the most vicious people with great force and drive within them have tried to conquer the world with their "good" or "right" ideas that are completely contradictory of another philosophy that slaughtered the minds or bodies of countless innocents is proof that the root of us all is goodness. But the *want* for goodness creates an illusion that keeps us from seeing the darkness. The root of us all is the goodness that is found in the silence of our spirit. It is the defining essence that makes us all Equal. It is what makes compassion possible. This is how we hate our enemy. And upon earth this spirit is accompanied by the equality that we are all dirty, imperfect, ever-struggling human beings. We are human, we are not the gods we try to make ourselves. We must not be afraid of ourselves. If we are so afraid, we will drive ourselves into extinction, ashamed of our own "imperfect" design. The hardest trick and the most difficult thing for the destruction or conversion of the Dark Society to overcome is that the Dark Society believes that it is doing good. But again and again, the story has been told and the examples have risen and fallen that tell us that the pursuit of shame and repression, money, and superiority of opinion, has only brought pain and devastation to the world. The most difficult thing for today's spiritualist, or searcher of unbiased truth, is to not be absorbed by what the society tells you is good. Those truly on the path must deny all the teachings of so many loved ones to overcome the darkness. It is difficult to fight the opinions of those that you want to have matter. The technique of Honesty is the key. Through the dangerous veil of honesty, covered in the shroud of no fear (or courage) and using the technique of non-attachment, look deeply at the people that teach you, look deeply at the millions of opinions that are thrust upon you (those that approve of you and those that disapprove) and see if you can find peace from the person that is teaching you. Do not try to find money, or title, or a figure of authority or even respect, these are no grounds for accepting "knowledge". See if there is peace. Is there peace or is there only the same fear, anger, aggression, defense, battle for security, greed and selfishness that you are trying to avoid becoming or that you are trying to change yourself from being? In the Dark Society it is difficult to be honest. From the Dark Society we are taught that the opinion of others is the most important thing. It is, after all, why we have our jobs, keep our families, and the reason we struggle for anything in society anyway. Honesty is the key upon the path. To be honest we must face and present the emotions that the people of the society do not want us to use to make their lives uncomfortable with. The Dark Society believes that emotions, such as kind love and affection, are things that should be left away from the professional world of the society. To be loving and honest is not what the people of the society want to see or experience, but they want to believe that it is what they are. Emotions of other people make people uncomfortable. These uncomfortable people don't know how to deal with their own emotions, and they certainly don't want to have the burden of dealing with other's emotions. So, the loving meet with persecution. The affectionate meet with shame. But the courageous will bring love anyway. From Socrates, to Jesus, to Buddha, to Nietzsche, accepting persecution without taking it personally, with love. The brave have stopped the darkness, at least within themselves. If you are the brave that walks this path and you find that through honesty love is what you want and you present love as what you offer to others and you accept other's random opinions without rage or aggression, but only as opinions, then you will find that directly under the disguise that everyone tries to show for the sake of the society is the want to love and the desire to be loved. It is not the desire to be accepted and glorified, as they portray for the society, but the desire to be easefully loved, kindly loved, not for their opinions, but for that which is themselves. Religions were supposed to tell us that we are loved for our very self, but somehow they lost their way in the darkness too. It is not an omnipotent god that sits in judgment that loves us while feeling shame for what we do that is outside his law, but it is ourselves that is love and ourselves that make shame. And it is this love that is the honest root of us all that is the truth. And if you must have it, it is this love that is the final truth, the final "god". It is not away from us. It is, in fact, what we are. And everyone that has ever lived has felt it, no matter how much clutter, shame, and fear has covered this endless beauty. It has been felt through contact with children, or wives, or pets, or parents, or salvation, or being alone in the mountains. Or it was felt in the regret of an ambitious pointless life. Love is what we all want. What we feel from real love is our definition of peace and freedom. It even remains the definition from the Dark Society. So, that power of liberation that we seek in the forming of nations, or from the hands of God, is actually already here. We, you, have the opportunity to let it happen, to make heaven on earth, simply by being what you really want to be. Stay constantly focused on the path of actual peace and be always wary of what the darkness is doing inside of you. Over time, with vigilance, the darkness can and will fall away. The ego can fall away. The Dark Society can return to Light. And love and compassion can let you laugh at the friendship and goodness that is all around you.

<u>Reno</u>

I can feel. I can see the anger thrust upon me when I drive my car too close to another I did not see. I see that want to have a place as my blinker blinks and my "neighbor" won't let me over. I know that they are not this darkness that puts pride into every simple action. I can see. I know that their spirit is like mine, at peace, and calm, but their situation is that of angry desperation. And their rage is proof of their fear to be weak or not in control. I know. Anger will come to me as they all assault me at once, oblivious to the assault that is their being, concerned with the proof that they must matter. Where is my war? How could I kill them all? How will that stop any of this oppression that has become natural to those that loudly demand the word Freedom, and curse it? Mostly, I Zarat, though not that deep, can hold ego or let it fall revealing the wisdom that allows me to listen to another person. Hmmm. I am unafraid to lose control with or without the ego. My life is a ping on a footnote that is attached to everything, just like every other person's kindness or cruelty as displayed in every simple action.

I wish there was enough kindness in this ashy filthy city to grant me the opportunity to have compassion. I am trapped by money in a place of rot. Stench. Pride, in every rich woman's walk damned with the genes that made her think she was pretty, and every ghetto Black's voice proclaiming his majesty for the Praise of the Prideful, and pride is in every poor white boy that knows he should already be so much more. Angst and desperation and belief in ourselves, built this city like a stain seeping across decency as it absorbs and drowns any caring person to its sullied depths. It is hard not to *want* to leave a place like this. It is hard to care so much for people that care so much about their own goals. This is where the War, every part of it, began.

What sadness, masking desperation, masking insecurity, fueled by the greed of the image conscious, lost in Darkness. I pray for a war, fueled by my ego, which will always fuel the Darkness, so that I might burn cruelty to the ground. I listen to the voice of my ego, painting a reason for destruction, knowing my soul will never believe it. And knowing my soul has no reason to stop it.

(This was the time after the San Diego Freemasons came, and all good people left, knowing the trap of fighting, and those that stayed worshipped or were victims at a Dark Alter of image and false ritual, devoid of human spirit and pro-slavery. The unsettling sensation of Rape, Rapists were everywhere.)

Building the Mind to Do What He Wants

It is really hilarious that the society that begins in so much light, and then grows to become the Dark Society, creates the tools of its destruction by the mere elements it was created in in the first place. Comfort. Breeds Sloth. Sloth Breeds Apathy. Apathy Breeds Ignorance. Ignorance Yields Angst. Angst Yields Anger. Anger Yields Revolt. Revolt Yields Humility. And the Dark Society fades.
Or/And Success Breeds Power. Power Breeds Arrogance. Arrogance Creates Delusions of Grandeur. Delusions Breed Fear. Fear Yields Lies. Lies Yield Mistrust. Mistrust Yields Hatred or Apathy. Hatred or Apathy Yields Failure of the Structure of Society. All Societies are doomed from the natural human response that has occurred in the same pattern within all societies that have ever existed. There are different time periods that pass, but the escalation of environments that affect the society, from building, to arrogance, through to power, and abuse, to anger and apathy, to destruction. All societies rise and fall. All because man has not mastered himself. He seeks to master and warp everything else in the world to his desires for the success of himself and society, but he fails to fix himself. And so, spreads the seed of the Dark Society, of pride, of its functioning tools, into another ignorant generation. Society can exist without a government to force people to obey its rules. There are eons old societies on this earth right now that have succeeded in it under several kinds of governments because they taught their people to understand themselves. But what if you had no one that sought and exploited the power from the top of society? That country was created once, in a light time tainted with the avarice breath of darkness. The truly Great Society that almost existed for more than ten years, failed because those that sought power, security, and control *(the Great Possessions of the Dark Ones)* seeped quickly into the new opportunity. A power structure was created within a Constitution. But we were free from 1776-1787, if not for James Madison's preservation of our Rights we would have none at all, because minds that control seek power in a certain way and seek their preservation and continuation like any letch struggling to keep a job and keep their feet out of the mud.

Is my ego not the program made to destroy this? Am I the only one that has the ability to make a functional war against it. Aren't I designed to stop it, as it was designed to rise? No. But it is possible I could let myself believe that. Where is the Father to guide us? Why am I alone, to suffer in my own greedy mind? Why will I talk myself into creating another useless war? My way will not know peace. My way is surrounded by Hell because I choose to let it keep bothering me. Do I want to play out my destruction?

<u>False Ethos</u>

One of Capitalism's greatest flaws is one of it's current prime prides.
Specialization. The idea that money gives people the opportunity to
become a specialist in their field. It sure does. It also makes them
completely devoid of knowledge on any other subject, especially that of
the inherent value of all other souls, even the souls right in front of their
faces, the human ones. I see a Dark Society of prideful fools. Idiots.
All the time. Again and again. Yelling at me to do what pleases them,
them with only one thought, though not even conscious, the thought
of my value for them. Do I leave them safe and powerful? What a
problem. Ruled by the increasingly stupid and self centered.
The next biggest problem is that foods can be eaten from around the
world. We can have whatever we want whenever we want it, so long
as we have the money for it. There are plenty enough that get what
they want. Eating outside of our habitat is devouring the world too
quickly. The virus of humanness is deadly to everything. Beware the
Dark Society and the temptation to serve it to get what is easier. Have
money, but don't own life. They used to call it keeping your feet on the
ground. Humble your mind.

False Philosophies:
"Torture the Earth and It shall yield up it's secrets."
The wanters will destroy everything so they can have something for a
second.

"The eyes are the window to the soul."
The eyes are a window for the soul to see out of the black cave-like
darkness that the body holds. The soul can see when it is out of the
body. This is fact. You can leave your body and look down at it. Eyes
only allow us to see as human. The soul is seen in the energy that
surrounds a person, this can only be seen by masters.

"I think therefore I am."
The falsest and one of the most detrimental philosophies to ever be
thought. You exist without thought. Consciousness continues to be
present in the Alzheimer's patient that has a malfunctioned mind. It is
so damaging a philosophy because it pulled people's consciousness into
deep self-justifying selfishness. Darkness. Pride in anything a person
thinks. The loss of free will, because!, a person is trapped to believe in
everything that the mind thinks. A person cannot guard the mind from

being cruel, or angry, or defensive, or murderous. The person is the mind. And choice mostly falls away. And the weak reign the Earth. Much bad philosophy is the cornerstone of the Dark Western World. That which seeks to own you and everything else. Would you give up what you "own" to save the world, or to even save a single person, or even your flesh and blood...I doubt it. I've seen the veil of coldness fall triggered by belief systems that don't matter. Money means so much to you. The illusion of staying alive.

Plus:
On the plus side, the Specialists will die off quickly, once the society begins to crumble, destroyed by those that will not allow nature to be retarded into slavery again. Power is the largest illusion the darkman has lied about so far.

<u>Nothing Personal, Broad Aspects with Real Human Punchlines</u>-and routes to insecurity that reveal anger to defend and then violence to stop the defense…but we're working on these human things aren't we? Actions. Be strong. Be un self-conscious.

People wear their societies like robes.   Flaunting the ultimate cleanliness of success. Using every ounce of money to believe that they are something. Something better than the mud. Trying to hold it all up. When in fact the great burden is shouldered by certain people. Tasked to a job. A job people have proven can be done. While the rest of us should be calm, allowing our neighbors to do as they please. Take people out of desperation. Never make anyone feel like a Criminal. Let people not need to do things to meet a justification. Let people believe that the "something good" to believe in is themselves. Then the goal will be easy and reasonable to attain. And maybe the sin of Educators in the Dark Society would curb, and they would not think themselves so worthy of the dimes they pillage from us with Unions. They would not try to create an upper class to move themselves into as the "builders" of the society. When in fact they have only herded the flocks. But this is a great task. But a humble task. A task of a Shepherd. Not the task of anything amazing.

<u>Sub-Types</u>

There are two types of Existentialist. The violent. And the non-violent, or the Buddhist type. It used to be the Christian and the Atheist. But christian doesn't mean the same thing as it used to. Both sides of the existentialist mind are pure. Simply, one side chooses violence, like the good man Ted Bundy and the Marquis de Sade, or the non-violent, like Jesus and the Dalai Lama and other Buddhas. These are different paths in the same forest. Both paths created by the rational. Both paths sought for through the mind. Both paths overcome the fear in the mind and ascend to what the person dreams to be. Both are free. As is shown by the continuous preaching of both Ted Bundy and the Marquis de Sade as they were both imprisoned. As continued the teachings of Jesus as he died, and the Buddha as he was rejected by the society he helped build, and the Dalai Lama in exile. Both sides are capable of choosing peace or violence at any time. They simply choose. Both paths hold traps for the mind and freedoms for the mind. Both hold the temptation of great power. The existentialist is always on the line, a step away from saving you and killing you. Fear not though, there is often little need to kill, but if you are killed go freely into the release.

Careful now, the mind can fuel Darkness in any cause. We must be careful when the mind justifies power over anything, including a single life or the controlling of children. Still, as the Mighty Zarat convinces himself to war once more, he will never hold power over more than the simplicity of murder. Can he not silence his cause? I think he can, but he wants to use it, since it is there. In suffering and all, he will prove the ego's existence by showing its uselessness. Poor Zarat. Brave Zarat.

<u>Fighting Everything</u>

Damnit. What day is it? How long have I been thinking. Shit. We are not meant to remember what day it is. The day is an invention of man. Not an invention of the already working design of humanness and the world in a working universe. Blah! Blah. I am as frustrated as everyone else here. By letting my ego live I can see that I am an enemy of myself, within my own war. Rolling over in anger and resentment, again and again. Churning and being as propelled as they are. When will I turn my gun towards the tyrant I am becoming?

<u>Violent Youth</u>

A school shooting, a murder-suicide, a youth violent and enraged... why?...It seems to confound our ignorant media. (What if I insult everyone that could help me, what if everyone was too bad to work with...I'd fail...as is our destiny.) I know these children. I speak with their mindset. The disappointed. The sad. Those that "never knew life was going to be this way". Again it reverts back to the system. The system of fear and control, the one we live in. Within this system it is customary within the family unit to deny all reality from a child. It is common to deny that sex exists, to become angry and forceful when it happens. Everything that makes the parent uncomfortable, or more realistically, threatened, is lied about and hidden. An entire fantasy world of lies is created to attempt to convince children that the world is perfectly designed to make them safe, which means superior to anything that can hurt them. Santa Clause. The Easter Bunny. Sitcoms. Happy endings. Awards for pleasing, for being "good". All of it. The whole censorship society. And as a child ages and learns that the world is not a perfect pleasing machine, as the child is thrust suddenly into a world of basic cruelty where all people in Darkness will try to take advantage of them (in Capitalism), they are so crushed by the disappointment that they are rageful in their sadness. The controllers are always so confounded by not knowing why it all happens, why a person could choose to do it...it is their fault. They can't know why because They want more than anything to not see it. Because they want their world to be that perfect one from their childhood. The lie makes the weak. It is why those from the sixties were so violent, or so abhorred violence. It was the same cause that made Manson and fun Leary and the Man in the Clock Tower, and any of those ideals...The ease of the successful society that had no actual Spiritual guidance. It had only desire. And when a baby doesn't get everything it wants, it cries.

The moral is: Stop lying to your children. Explain everything with the truth. And if you don't know it, find it out.   We are now a society of digital information. And accept everything you don't, so that they will be able to deal with the tragedy that will absolutely await them. Let the children learn about the world while they are designed to assimilate the most information. Stop the irrational religions that harm us. A child can adapt to anything, and the truth will let them not have to force a detrimental re-adaptation, when they are trying to define themselves.

All that is left for the boy that has no opportunity   is   resentment. Turn away from the image makers and save the children you claim are your lives.

<u>Secret Identity</u>

Though I realize that I seem alone, I have had true contact. I have known good friends and deep loves, though I am sure they have not known me. It is not their fault, or mine directly. But Zarat is simply a different person inside than out. I appear so strong to others. A leader, the one with the Will. But inside is much speculation. Deep and doubting thought. A hundred thoughts to keep them safe. A thousand to raise them up. And a million to knock them down. Love masking every action of force and effects. Everyone that has touched me and never knew, just because I never told them. I suppose I subconsciously expected them to know. This is a simple play of interaction. All of us influenced internally without our awareness. How can we hate anyone for any action at all? Every intelligent thought leads back to forgiveness and understanding, even after action has taken place. Regardless, it is the choice of their interpretation to make insight as useful as possible. I hope that they faced as many insights as they could.

<u>Living without Place, always unmovable from my location</u>

She held me in her arms, it felt good to be held. I laid my head upon her pillow. My chin upon her trap. My forehead and my nose against her cheek. From the view of the Dark Society it would be submissive, but from the view of logic and ease, it is relaxing and soothing. A natural path to experience. The free man is free to experience everything, and equally free to experience only the good things if he wants to.

<u>Zarat...Listen</u>

Every wise organization, human being or government must know when they have gone too far. If they do not know...someone must tell them. If they will not listen...someone must stop them.

ACT II

He Draws the Long Knife

Zarat has drawn the blood that flows, taken the alive and turned it still to make it rot. It is different than killing with a pack, under orders on a side with more murderous weapons, or a side where a reason seems to propel a herd. It is cold to hold life in your hands. Not at first, but quickly it is. The ego rages like flames, struggling with what can seem like the mortality of its own fragile husk against the need to do what "good" men must. Stepping into the damnation of unnoticed glory and taking on the many labels brought to control a populace under the growing blanket of safety and shame. All the while recalling the truth, the truth, the endless and indisputable evidence that Zarat is Free. Free to end what sought power directly over the Girl who he would give his life for. He performs his deeds with direct just cause, drawing him out into the community that damns him, that he secretly and silently defends. His honest glory raging in the tones of his depths. Nine Nevada officials are found dead.

The War Has Begun

Those threatening those committing crimes are why crime rates grow. Every great institution becomes corrupt as it attempts to preserve itself with force and the threat of death and loss. And for those on the bottom, for those that feel fear because it is so hard, the fear will always have them see evil. And the prospering will always see good. When neither is true. But the effects of the delusionally religious, which includes all religions that refer to a heaven or hell, will manifest a threat that isn't real and doesn't need defending against.

Freemasonary is very big in the police world. Most I've met were, they were all power seekers, controllers. All believing they were preserving something that didn't need preserving. The soul is present and fine and exists in a world free to learn. These are Those that could reason killing you, or taking away your time, if you did not obey the fear they were repressing and trying to dress with authority. It is sad that they suffer in that world. It is tragic that every reason they have accepted maliciously to attempt to cheat death will fail. We can do these things. We can extend life, but we cannot believe that it is the only way to think. Fear of loss is not a weight on the future. We own forever what matters. And the Freemasons want to control that too, our souls, for power for an imagined preservation through the will to kill. While their minds become more and more concerned with the courses of Power and preserving it. BUT! If we do not react as they expect, if we are free from the defense structure they have intended to use on us from the day we were born, if there is nothing for them to push back against, in this, our Free Society, they will lose power. If we do not feel the guilt for the path that kept us from theirs, then we will enter gently into this world, and find no conflict, but prosperity, and in the ocean of doing we will bring every hand aboard and stand beside them. With no one seeking to be dominate, but still, because we are Happy and unthreatened by these false "preservers", we will become our Best Naturally, without the resentment of mutation. We will all know how to insert cogs into the machine. And everyone will have their own machine and the courage in themselves to know that they can operate the machine, as simply as a hover car.

<u>The Oppression of Your Mother</u>

Tyranny comes consistently from whomever the armed government yields its concern to. The wailing, the angry, there are many, but the reason that sounds most falsely frightening (because fright is relative, so false as emotions go) and directly understandable to a person that has only been concerned with not failing in their lives (so will do anything to think they are ultimately right, like jail or kill, which is stealing), so the wailing mothers come to oppress. They come to cry at you and wail for the lives of their dead children, and oppress us with the guise of safety. Though perhaps they are Free to cry. Cry away from me. Your want for the world to please you harms everyone. People come a-telling. But the end result is always the same and simple, anger, sadness and fear, should never touch the reigns of politics. We are not these emotions, we are not this mind. We are equal spirits operating ideas on a plane of thought, which is dependant on our ability to achieve a comfort level within a seeking society.
Or they are the Fathers with their rifles and reasons, same results, same conditions, same resentment as they take something Free from a world that wants to understand, but should not be forced to take the burden of the pain a person cannot handle. They attempt to make a glaring weakness, by glaring, yet "another" strength for themselves in their life from which they have built from, but the mind is false. Oppression is the result.

This is the course of the human mind, and so the course of the human world, not the whole world, just the one that humans in the Dark Society falsely think they cannot escape, so must alter. Humans are in few places on this planet. It is easy to simply move away from them, to simply not have to play the game of rank and place, to not be concerned with its destruction, since all that exists is a malleable idea, that the power will seek security within, again and again.
The further you reach to help the populace, the quicker and more fiercely their damnation comes because they are more easily disassociated from the penalty of their damnation.
…Sometimes, to escape the mindset, you must try to destroy what rules the tone of thought. It is easy to point that destruction towards anything. And death falls, as we continually liberate ourselves from what seeks to help us. Every generation must Revolt. And every aging generation must ease the revolt from them. The more a generation has, the more successful the society, the more powerful the revolt, for the

new minds will see so much more than the old minds could have seen to build it up.

The job of those that are already here to keep the growing mind alive with the preservation of the Works of a Time have a duty, if the society's preservation is in order, to make the Revolution easier, and not to expect servitude, but to expect Freedom and the Will to Create.

I think of The Father.

Dangerous Encounters

I sit, maybe late at night, and think of the boundaries I may have crossed this day. Most people build a fence, jutting around in places. A fence to keep people out. A boundary they won't cross. My entire goal has been to dismantle that fence you want to keep up more than anything in the Universe. Beware when you speak to me, my goal is pull apart your fence. To see a little something real inside. Push you, and show you the pain you hang onto. To see pain is painful. Pain hurts. You'll know I've done it when you're angry and all you can think about is yourself. It will feel like you are thinking about everything but not a single beautiful sound thinks in your head. You'll feel lost for a minute. And when you do, embrace it. Feel that. If you keep doing it, keep letting it mean less and less and not let go, not give up...when suddenly you stop thinking about it, and you don't fuel it anymore. Can you feel what is just beyond that feeling of utter destruction and meaninglessness? In vulnerability and in suffering, and in death, we have a chance to see. Hallelujah. A chance to accept. The fence can have gates.

And just remember, I'm a free man. A man without a fence.

Don't you see the Proof? All people have the ability to be any person. We are not a single identity. You have picked out bits and pieces of things that people presented to you throughout your life. These actions made you feel happy, or safe, or strong. And you identified that feeling as a path. We are not these emotions. We are not this mind. We are not only these things. People suffer in life because they choose a certain set of actions that they think are who they are, but they can react in the fully opposite way, and usually find themselves acting in the opposite way as opposed to the way they imagined it in a situation they've fantasized about, and the ones that can carry it out and pull off the image only do so because they don't believe in it. It's a tool, not a reality. They are partially doing it, but not fully. They are not free. They have to believe in the image they've imagined more than anyone, or it loses its point. A point they made up and believed in.

<u>Fade</u>

"We have no soul, there is no spirit," beast.
"Really. When we die, when something happens to our body and we are killed by something, be it old age, or cancer, or a rock to our skull... nothing changes in our physical make up. Especially, with slow death, like old age, or cancer. You can see it. The physical body, the essence of the matter, doesn't alter in form, yet still a thing leaves the body that allows it to decay. The body does not begin to decay until death comes, until some force that holds onto life leaves the body. Everything fades into the earth, but only after death. Only after the thing that is life is gone. We are all carbon matter, we should decay immediately upon birth, but we don't. There is a spirit. A thing that we really are. A thing that is not changed after death, or birth, or even through all of life."

<u>I Could Have Been A Writer, but I Wanted to Make a Difference</u>

The white satin sheets drape the outline of your hips, your curves and your mound. You enthusiastically speak of a place I'd never been. While my hand slides across your soft belly. My finger across your belly button. My eyes moving from your belly to your lips and to your perfect breasts that my hand sweeps over and outlines quickly. The smell of your flesh has me dripping again. You have no break in speech as my hand glides below the sheets to rub your trimmed pubes. I kiss your stomach. And you continue your speech. As my hand pushes further you open your legs without an effort of thought and my hand knows the curve to assume. Diving vertically. Your pussy lips are only slightly moist as you pay closer attention to your words than to me. They are soft and full. And I come to crave them again. The morning sun rises through the window and the color of your flesh beneath those thin sheets begins to glow. Your hand runs up my back, from crack to neck. Already in motion I sink down to taste the morning dew. Your legs spreading wider as I lift one up to pass under and I silently smile as the aroma engulfs me. There's something I want to tell you, but I don't, I'm listening as a I wander. Face to face with my morning craving, I know that Dawn will never look more beautiful than it does now. As the whole of my tongue's palate sinks widely and deeply, your story ends gently into silence.

Where is she? *She*? Any One. I wish I had a respite beyond imagination. Though the dagger sinks into flesh, I long to be at ease. To be making a mess.

<u>Razor Blades</u>

I tortured myself into a pattern of scars to warp my mind more in the direction of war. The pain scarred my mind as well. True heroes put themselves through Hell, so what they face is a joke.

<u>Cutting the Corners Off Puzzle Pieces</u>

There are many different routes to push yourself through in the journey of meditation. I have felt many types of peace. I have recently thrust myself into the peace that is felt with the absorption of the body into the soul. This means that I have fully accepted the living as a body. I do not fear its death, and I do not fear its living. When one absorbs the body into the peace of the soul there is only ease and contentment in what the searcher finds within the world.

It is most certainly different than the silent mind itself. The body feels happy and at peace. The other method, of silencing the mind, seems to attempt to push the mind into detachment. But that method also breeds conflict and pain within, as the mind tries to battle the impulse to stop. It tries to continue to exist, as it has been designed to do, for the simple survival of the life form. *The ego resists. Do not fight the ego. Like in all other people you encounter, the ego must be relaxed into a calm state. And it is best when it is getting something it wants.* (What? Shit. I heard it, huh? Shit. I even wrote it. Shit. It's changing the text by itself. What do they know that I am not accepting? Why am I doubting myself? Who is that that wrote it? I see. It must be me. How do you calm voices that speak in the tone of silence?)

The absorption of the body into the soul accepts the mind and lets it continue. However, the mind is naturally silenced. There is no war, no conflict for it to continue. Many of the meditation practices that I have journeyed through have felt most peaceful when there was no fight, but only ease. Clearly when we wrangle egos we should use gentle hands, be it one's own or someone else's. There are many remedial steps in this meditation. Such as, letting hindrances go. Letting the fear of having to do something, or the fear of doing what others want, or the fear of letting anything happen--letting them go, fall away. But these fears are only practice, only something to keep you upon the path you wish to be on. When you finally find the truth, that deeply sunk in silence, you will have all the positive attributes necessary, by default. You are no longer forcing yourself, you simply are. And this course is a natural course that your life force will want to take. Eventually, you will be led to it. But many times you will think that you have it, and you will not. So, humility and understanding of where others are in their journey is the key. Always go deeper, do not search further. These are different things. What you are looking for is within you, so go deeper, if it were outside you may need to search further, but it is not. It is always deeper.

The body becomes slower. The whole of the world moves more slowly. It is no longer attacking you. It need not be avoided. You realize that you are a part of it and all is a part of you, and no matter what happens you can see where you fit into it. It does not matter where you are or what you are, so long as you are. And when the time comes to be somewhere else or something else, you remain only the spirit that can absorb all the world with fearless love. It is unafraid, so it can love everything. Even enemies. Even those violent towards it. Perpetual peace, can be obtained, but perpetual focus and conviction to be it is necessary, for there are many tendencies to drift away into the rational of the erratic mind, or the physical comforts. But one must know what the center of what oneself is, while accepting the life that one happens to be living in any form.

Cartoon Violence

He found himself realizing that he was sitting on the couch again. Unable to generate the spiritual and anti-power revolution he longed for. The marijuana began to kick in. He looked up from his despair and began to laugh. He laughed deeply at the cartoon he watched. Media giants of digital and cartoon animation merged to make highly profitable plays. Masters of blatant manipulation of the basic human senses. Masters of the technique of cuteness. Masters of money and joy. Icons for the youth of America. Using the same basic play on emotions again and again and making it entertaining to humans. Bright colors. Scary music. Everyone knows it is happening, and loves it, lies and manipulation. Even Zarat laughed at the simple joy. At the bizarre plots that paint the lies of the shallow boundaries between good and evil, through simple relationships. Still using the stock characters that became slightly more neurotic every movie, and so more human, not human, but American. People laugh because they see themselves in these characters. It is all the master writers do, copy what they see. They capture the simplicity and deep complexity of a child playing with exacting ease. Masters at presenting what fools we are. And Zarat laughed at the simple joy. Toys, monsters, fish, all with the disease of the neurotic human. All so much like us. But in actuality, nothing like us. Not diseased with illusion. In reality, living directly, blatantly associated with living, not trying to run from it, not trying to escape in some moving pictures that we don't need to associate with. We are lost in blind laughter. Art and mastery and creativity have many powers, mostly to destroy, while making the artist feel so deeply good about his success. The artist will never realize how his joy is meant to devastate a society. While so many laugh, others silently breed death, all around them. The war is amongst us. And the world rises slowly up to ambush the arrogant Dark Society. It encompasses it. And soon there will be no way out of the Darkness. The cycle revolves.

<u>Sexual Hypocrisy</u>

The Dark Society emerges most visibly when censorship begins. When the molding of personal image is created. Nudity and Sexuality, Profanity, Violence, the very essence of human existence is withheld in the Dark Society. We are taught to be ashamed of the root of what we are. The Dark Society has often taught that humanness is shameful and disgusting. This is the work of those that call themselves holy, but in fact these are those ruled by fear. It is the Fear that is the most destructive. Fear of the human self that that person is. Fear of humanness. Fuck, Shit, Cock, Cunt, Asshole, Bitch, Pussy, Dick, all mere words, but taught as 'bad words'. All words that have to do with sexuality. All to breed the shame of sex. All to breed hatred for the self. And all that preach against sex, and drugs, and Freedom, all become owned by it. In every Dark Society the holy stand before the masses that believed in them and cry in apologetic worthlessness to be forgiven for doing what they condemned to seize power.

But comes these days, The Father would speak to me. The FCC, he'd say, exists to protect us from them that control the sexuality of their children with anger. Those that would reason to damn us. Yet they must face it. And so, we are here.

We, Me, those born between 1979 (not '78 who are X'ers) and 1994 are the **Porn Generation**. A generation that grew up into sexual maturity with our fingers on the keyboard and a hand on our oozing genitals. We know, for a visual experienced fact, that there is nothing wrong with sex. Though we have seen rapists, and seen degradation within those that would shame a woman and would shame a man, and we have seen her and him writhe in pleasure from it, and we have seen where there is not love by it. If she wants to be there, we are proud to see her there. If it breaks the pain of her reality to feel a bit of pain then we honor her technique and choice. But we do not believe in the power of the raper, that is a generation before us, addicted to the sensation of their own fighting repression. We don't need to fight, although some of us have had to, but every generation needs its Heroes. Until we have broken the false religions that tote, only to accrue a fearful following which includes themselves, the Preachers, a Heaven and a Hell before us.

Change Yourself to Change the Universe

You think your life is hard? I think my life is hard. No matter who you are, no matter what circumstances surround you, you will think that your life is not so great. Not perfect. Full of suffering. This is because people exaggerate the 'badness'.   We must make a choice. We can choose to overcome the foolishness that we trap ourselves with. We can overcome the darkness that traps us. We can overturn the rulings of weakness and overthrow the bonds of anger, jealousy, pettiness, selfishness, power, money, lust, all that makes humans suffer. All that makes the perfectly normal situations of our lives more horrible than they really are. And besides, think of it, what you suffer through now is probably not anywhere near what others suffer through at this exact moment on this exact planet. And even if you wind up in the most extreme of situations, like being killed or raped or having anything 'taken' from you in any circumstance against your general will, no matter how you are losing control of, you can find the beauty throughout it all. You can choose. Choose to know that this world is a fleeting course of mad violence. And always remember that the violence that can be thrust upon your physical self will never be close to the exaggeration that your mind can inflict on you. So, you're being hurt, so you're being killed, so you lost your financial report, who cares, it is the course of life, that is all. It is not against you. It simply exists in this random time, It is simply something that you have the great opportunity to experience and deal with in any way you choose. Choose the Beauty. Choose the ease. Choose the Love. The path is a *Holy One*. Choose to overcome the foolish condition of man. Laugh beyond what others cannot and know what true control is. It is when control becomes irrelevant. It matters not, ever, if you have control. You only ever have any control over how you choose to perceive the wonderful madness of this world. So laugh. Laugh at its raging madness that all of man thinks matters. It does not. Laugh. And become mad yourself. Defy the lies of the Dark Society. You do not need to suffer like they have been telling you. Defy. Stop depression. Stop rage. Stop ignorance. Find the truth. Find it with Beauty and find it with Love. Find it by resolving to the conditions of the Path and moving onward, knowing you can never move away from yourself. Without the focus on the Beauty and the Love you will become another blind intellectual of the Dark Society. A fool. Someone who can think of *It*, but not become it. A teacher who cannot do what he teaches. Search beyond these words and become. The truth is in you. The path is your own. Nothing touches it, but you. Realize that you are free now. Push deeper beyond all that you hate in yourself, it is easy to recognize, it is all you hate in everyone else. Set yourself free. For your sake and the sake of the world. Change yourself and change the world.

<u>Remember What You Really Want</u>

There are so many questions man can never know the answers to. Why are we here? What does it matter? What are we supposed to become? We spend a lifetime searching for these answers. When you observe the search it feels like you are not creating new thoughts, like a story or a poem. It feels like you are searching for something you have forgotten. But you just can't find the thought. The answers to these questions are still within us. You can feel that you already know, but you must make your mind find it. We simply need to find the way to remember.

<u>They Become Withholding</u>

I used to sit and talk with people...for hours. I used to enjoy speaking with people, learning what was dear to them. Helping them. Being helped by what they had. But I learned that every great thing that people claim to be...was often a lie. A hypocrisy. A lie. An over compensation for what they wanted to hide and didn't know how to fix. Every great role model I ever had. Every great friend that claimed loyalty and kindness...all betrayed their own words. All betrayed the truth that they claimed they wanted to be straight from their own hearts. I stopped talking with people. I let all of my so called friends, drift away from me. I didn't want their weakness and their lies anymore. I didn't want to be tainted by the darkness of their hypocrisy. I didn't want to have to put up with it anymore. I sent myself into seclusion. When the war failed...I had nothing else. Everyone that I gathered to fight beside left me for comfort and sloth. For greed. For fear. That is where the revolt lost. Who cares if *The Girl* died or the Father or that the physical war never really happened. The war failed in the people I loved. It weighs heavy on me, even now. Years past. Their failure betrayed love itself.
It betrayed my love for them.
The anger and the sadness that I have for those once so dear to me haunts me still. Hinders me. Causes me to suffer. Can I rise up from the abyss?

<u>Wondering Eyes Should Appear</u>

"What is existentialism? What is enlightenment?" Child's Eyes.
"The path to Existentialism is found when one excepts that they will die. Accept death, destruction, and failure, and be honest from then on out. The path to Enlightenment is choosing to love after you accept death. It is simple." Thus Spake Zarat.

Always seek fun. Always seek joy. In these pursuits, seek humility and kindness. Find the simplest types of fun. Race sticks in the river. Watch leaves fall from a tree. Sit in a meadow and talk. But beware of the Gluttony that took the Generation of Children from the 1960's...

The Brine of Stew

I have remembrance of *her*. A *girl*. *Her*. The night of heavy drinking always followed with a feeling of a small puddle soaked in shallow doubting guilt. What did I say to *her*? Did I hurt *her*? Why? Did I offend *her*? I was always soft and gentle and weak the next day. There is inferiority in my mind. There is also love. A psychological soup, each ripple, each seasoning, bringing out the flavor of my soul. Over time the mind stews and stews and the flavors become stronger. Our minds become more set. We, the True Ones, try to stay clear, never absorbing the heaviness of the broth. Though it surrounds us, we always taste like a fresh spring. Uninfluenced by the brine. Although we have the power to taste it, afterall, in life we do soak in circumstance. It is simple to open the mouth and drink. It is also simple, for us, to become clear once more. To be what we were, before we were soup.

<u>Mind Turning</u>

Mind turning can occur because of a number of circumstances and a number of ways that the mind reflexively interprets events based on the way that a mind can be affected. It is the Existentialist who has now learned to bend his own mind. He is his own propaganda, separate from the manipulation that bends you to make you feel good. Not needing to feel "good" is the first step to Freedom.

Many people, you most absolutely likely, begin to follow something because you think you can gain within its System. You foolishly, and wrongly, think that it must be those in power of an organization that you think you should be like. But no. Never. In every long standing institution a person should never follow its leadership. Those that wind up leading are 99.7% of the time are only the Dark Minded People that find power in the situation. They are not devoted to the ideals of the originator. They did not search with caring to create the Free Way. They preserve a "Free" way with Power and Force and a mask of words that work as lies to make you believe in what is "Free" with Power and Force. No. Rare are those that come to turn the mind. To turn the mind again, away from power, away from image, and back to genuine truth, with no need to convince the "powerful", who question us so diligently, only, because they want to know how we got our power. So that they can emulate it, and appear in power of the next System.

No. My People, who belong to no one, to Nothing, we are about to be FREE.

Because the mind will turn. Because We, not you, bring it, and a few, will bring it upon themselves, once they only know that they can do it. Reason from a different Core. A Core of Liberty.

<u>I Am A Vision of Myself</u>

Zarat chooses to succeed. He finds loans and enters into real estate. He buys cars at auctions and resells them. He publishes the book that The Father wrote. He writes his own book. He starts the organization of spiritual warriors. He finds his love.
A true Existentialist can succeed in any system. A true Existentialist has complete control over his emotions and his mind, and accepts when his body has malfunctioned. It does not matter what his surrounding social, political, or personal environment is. He is a master of himself and so he can choose to be a master of his world and so shape the world around him in the image he dreams for himself. Zarat can have anything. He can deeply appreciate it because he understands that it fleets away from him in every second because it is dying. He has excepted death. He can have a kingdom, he can have love, but it ultimately means nothing. Whatever is, exists for that moment in that specific form and then fades into something else, or into nothing. But in that moment, it is unique and wondrous. Everything that Zarat can have will never control him. It will always be part of the dead and wondrous world. It is not what is ultimately real. What is real is the silence that centers us within the universe and within every concept that man has not yet or cannot think.

<u>Animals Crossing</u>

This is a new world. Not of who can care about the single group of people the most, the ethnic minority, the country, but who can care about the most amount of people. Who can simplify Humanity enough to see our simple interfacing reality. And there is harmony. The Golden Age is ahead. We're just the whistle blowers. You've gotta get off the train and meet your neighbors.

<u>Fight it, Anyway, with Any Thought You Can</u>

There is much darkness in many areas, muddled minds. Minds happy to see us in debt. Minds happy to see us earning something. Earning our slavery, like they did. This blind programming of having to serve someone else. If you can break free from that, if you can serve a little and then break away, then you've done something. If not, you are no Free Human. Break the illusions that make you a slave. Don't choose what does. Always keep an eye on the developing Freedom. Always know we are Free. And never let anyone make you feel bad about it. Don't let people that have settled and stopped and chosen to defend what is not threatened, harm you with the reasons they use to try and live forever. We are just trying to live, until we die, leave us, and we are glad You die, so the power you believe in could not consume us at birth. The stubborn arrogance in a life is the danger in all society.

We can be Free, from all those that wanted to own us. They threw up a Bill of Rights to help us, against every old assumed order, that the existence of the rest of the World proves its fallacy.

<u>Trigger the True Cause, Go Ahead, Talk to Him,
They say he is a Friend.</u>

I found myself in defense of the Father's Great Works. I'd see people.
Be forced to interact with them because of an old familiarity. Which is
always fine, so long as that familiarity accepted the sexual under tones
of my Nature. But, when it is people that believe they have thought
deep but have not, it goes something like this, (It is tiring to repeat the
old reasons to the cheap thinker.): But we like to regale our tales if you
are bravely up for the challenge. Will ye search for ye Soul this night?
Do you want to know what it is?

"Something, Something, Kierkegaard said, "Bluck BLuck Fleh." And
the Engager says, "Cornwad blah smesh.""
And I'd say, "Oh ya," not caring to remember either's quote, and they
hadn't provided me with the 800 other pages that came before to justify
the random insert of a catchy quirky phrase, sitting oddly in their stomach
like a piece of bubbling cheese from a stagnant lunch! But anyway,
Zarat spakes thusly, "Ah. You want me to see that Kierkegaard is right.
The Other Guy is wrong. Right? (No need for an answer.) You're
trying to use someone else's reasons to justify yourself. Existentialism
doesn't work that way, it's one reason people might even think it's
irrelevant, Because you have to come to the conclusions by examining
yourself. Existentialist writers cannot write to teach you. They write
so that when you read something that resonates with familiarity and
understanding to you, You Know you are on the right path. And the
thirtieth time you randomly open to that page in the bathroom (pressing
into his thigh for fun) and read that line and it finally means something
that doesn't make you think another thought to justify yourself, and you
actually know, for sure, that that next thought wasn't necessary, because
you felt at Peace, man....that's when you know, The Revolution against
yourself, the Revolt of a driving, non-moving psyche has been for a
deafening boom of factual Glory...................Feel it friends? That's you
not mattering, but still existing, pure, now try to pick up a new train of
thought. I hope we meet again. Good 'morrow, chums. You've wasted
a million thoughts justifying yourself, when you never had to. A Dark
Religion, yours, made you think you were running from damnation,
and you had to prove yourself, or die, and the society reflected the
attitude, but still, do something..."

What people think you are is FAKE. You don't ever need to be what they expect, and know how to defend yourself because large weaklings with tiny concepts will fight you when not understanding that they are still safe and you don't care about their rank in the room, don't care at all, not enough to think about it. ... They better not touch me... tick. Geez, the mode, bar fight mode...from peace to war, and always at peace.

Society is always wrong when it believes someone is a single conclusive definition, and it is an idiots way of thinking, and those idiots are police...ok. You need to think along a definition...hmm.

Growing Up American Style

The sharp smell becomes soft as I allow myself to be aroused by the sweetness on this trusting woman's panties. Without shame, but aware I shouldn't get caught, I quickly stuff them into my pant's pocket. Even though I know the children I am baby sitting are watching TV I don't want one to see me. I don't want to deal with the inevitable situation of them telling on someone that seemed guilty, they don't know why they are telling, but they saw that man with her underwear. The programming. The hunt for guilt. The darkness, the religious. Suppressing their own hidden naughty selves that I find hidden in their drawers. Pictures of each other, delusional matrimony cheating on and on in each other's minds, naked, lewd. I want to take them, but I know I might not be able to get those back into the drawer if they came home. People would notice those shameful, thrilling photos missing, but a pair of panties might get lost. A mother always loses some to her children anyway. I'd love to tell her, and arouse her, take her if I wanted, if I pushed just a bit. But all I need to do is masturbate and everything will be fine, and I don't have to deal with the sex whirling around me, and the egos that would hate that would follow with forks. I make my way to the bathroom. Smell the feast. The holes of this mature woman absorbed into the elastic of the g-string that rode half inside her. The hardness of a young man's erection shakes my body as it throbs, beating the drum of violation and heaving mental rape. I cum quick, and just as quickly wipe down the splatter on the seat that I know she will sense as she sits in it. I hope he does too. The taste of her still fresh in my mouth. That white hard film dissolving in my mouth. I make my way out. The panties I place into the middle of the hamper. Or should I put them exactly where I found them? I don't know. Would she notice. I'll gauge, out of sight- no thought of it, and if there is any, there won't be enough evidence for her to seek victims to satisfy the rage and suffering of her repression. So I should be fine. I'll leave them. All the kids watching cartoons still, like it has been when he had taken her flesh for his human urges a thousand times before. The light in the living room is not fine, the childrens yells rise, as does the hall light that seeped through the slightly open bedroom door. I'd like to keep the underwear, but don't want to raise suspicion. I struggle with the "caught" factors. 15 minutes later the door knob rattles and the keepers of control and hidden sex return. The normal questions of "did you have fun?" crap crap blah follow. I explain what they ate. Meanwhile I think of her flavor. And suspect that the way my young eyes can't help but look at her makes her secretly happy and mentally spinning.

I still hate the feeling of the repressed seeking something they can accuse you of being out of place. But I love the thrill of the con. And the charisma of the escape.

<u>Master of Illusion</u>

The illusions of sex. Lustful passions. Uncontrollable desires. Beauty. Etc. Tits. Pussy. Dick. Ass. Asshole. Cunt. Whatever. Sacks of collected fat. Oozing wounds that expel dead children. A throbbing enflamed with blood often deformed piece of skin that leaks and pukes and expels billions of parasitic organisms. Lies. Illusions. But without the illusions sex is undesirable. Without games and intrigue and passion, there is no reason for sex. Without the illusions we are programmed with the species of human beings ceases to exist. The master must overcome the illusions. The master must know what it is like to be uncontrolled by impulse and instinct. The master must lose everything that is human before he can become anything he dreams. The master uses illusions after he has conquered them. He uses illusions to enjoy life. He overcomes his programmed illusions to use which illusions he chooses. A man can be anything he dreams. A man can do anything he dreams. An Existentialist is not without illusion, he has simply chosen which ones he wants.

The Will to Not Profit

Do you want to succeed? Steal a product from a poor person or group and sell it at a huge increase and thus steal from another person or group. This is called 'profiting'. This is called success. Taking advantage of the innocent or the ignorant. Or, sell your soul to slavery. Scrape by on a pittance. Be the ignorant that is used by the successful. And at fifty or sixty have a small amount of money that might be able to feed you for the next ten to twenty years of your life, if you are lucky. Slavery or Tyranny.
I prefer Crime. I prefer to steal from the rich. If they have money they got it through horrible means, or the fortune of birth. They overcharged for something that should have been nearly given, through simple kindness. It is much more ethical to be a criminal than to be a respectable member of society. I have principals that I have developed that will not change. They will not change, they have not changed, because I have nothing to lose.

<u>Our Age</u>

The map of life is a simple thing. Most cannot calm their minds enough to blob across the macro sector of consciousness, most cannot be so unselfish.
We live in a time where the prideful and the hypocritical display the failings of their theories painted darkly by the journalists that profit from with righteousness over those that profited from them with righteousness. We have those that keep, that preserve what they have. We have the liars deluding us into a point of thought that we believe everything is fine in the world, and so tyranny enters into the time of its securing, the police can no longer be dissolved without conflict. And the cold walk the streets. The spiritually cold. Those that don't believe in anything and they walk right through you on the street. They are rapists now. Real ones. They are powerful and taking now, like their masters, they have their own power. A power that keeps them from seeing the weaknesses that are inherent to our living as human beings. And in time, you will face these paths, to become like others are, or to become something different. Something forgotten, because our feet stopped touching the ground, and we became afraid to sit naked, because people are believing that they are what they think, but being a slave to the imagination of your glorification is against what they will claim to you they support. People will make rules to prove to you that they are right, until the authority they secretly craved cuts freedom from them, they always cry, these weaklings with power. These that had to have proof of their strength, those that imagined to control. To see the rapist phenomena, to see the killers eyes not caring as it ogles your wife, go to Reno. Go to Reno. A dead city. Be careful there. It is tainted. But go and see what the larger cities make these bummers that want to matter, that failed to get enough power where they were, and they come to control you, how ever they want to. It is a curse, this missed connection, they want to matter to the world, but cannot matter to themselves. This is what makes it. The cure is to not need to matter and know that living matters. Where there is life, there is matter. And I warn those with a celebrity's stare to be wary of those that do not allow Our Freedom to be bent.

It is an age of Imagination cuddling reality.

<u>There Isn't a Path</u>

We all start at the same point. "Innocent" souls. Souls that have forgotten...sins of other lives. And we all think out from this point of childhood. Out, out, out we draw our strings, our paths, defining who we think we are. But that soul has not moved. It is still within the same space. People have imagined the path of definition. It is hard to guide a person back through the intricate path they have woven for their prosperity in their psyches and thoughts. It can drive them mad to doubt their opinions through their thoughts. So, destroy the path. This is the Walkers Way. Those that truly live on the path. To show them again what they have always been, even without the path, that as they die they will imagine as themselves fading away, but in fact just a story fades away. Salvation lies in the peace of destruction. (This is the theory behind these murders of mine.) Not being afraid of who we are, not wanting to believe we are an image of something else. But becoming what we knew we were. Knowing all is wrong. And peace is at hand, as we return to where society began.

Passivism and the Violent

Those that choose passivism usually do so because they are too weak, withered emotionally or physically, to fight. On the same hand, those that choose violence are often too weak and too afraid to be silent and not have control. No one knows what enlightenment is. There is darkness on every side and in every opinion. We must push ourselves beyond our opinions and find the real truth. Go beyond our self importance and find reality.

<u>It, Drawn Out For You</u>

All people have one primary choice, regardless of what laws want us to choose, we all must choose to survive. We have to make choices to survive. We have little choice to not try to survive. Even suicidals have to force themselves to die, and they will still yell at you if you almost hit them with your car. Our programming is the same. It is this proof that shows that the laws and penalties that came from the Puritan Dark World that created prisons and judgments is greatly flawed. All people are prone to break laws. All. Especially those ones that preach in adamant favor of laws, they always are the ones to break them in desperate situations, and you'll find them speeding believing they control the laws of physics, like how rubber clings to a road. Always the first to betray when groups get small and they grow afraid, when mattering and controlling become important. See. The criminals are those that try to convince everyone that they aren't. It's why you can never trust teachers, why you must touch and taste. We are all at fault for caring. All of us stuck in our time from our place, all of us only reasoning to survive, physically, or mentally. Crime can be cured just by moving criminals into the mainstream market. Giving them an exact personal business. Truly letting people follow the dream. There must be a shedding of this Darkness that makes people think that a person that steals or kills or something non-advantageous doesn't matter. They are you, just in different worlds, seeing what demons can see. I speak to the persecutors, the judges, the police, the politicians, the fearful, I spake to save this society. This society is lining up to fall as history has shown all societies fall. Power. And the fear of losing that Power. Teach the People how to defend themselves and have the standing army standing on the soil of its Country. All of us equal and in no need of defenders. Spake Me, Zarat.

The "religious" are wrong and need to remember humility. And we will not force them to do it. They must choose to be calm again. Shame No More.

<u>Risk Calculation</u>

Sitting. Thinking in that way. His head in his palm, rubbing his mind, aching to think, pushing further, figuring out how to accomplish his goal of freeing all humanity and leave a prospering world, that has no power. The Father wanted, and he sacrificed everything he could have easily had, for that want. What he wanted for you and you and...not you, (finger pointing at your brain) but you, ok you, but I don't know if you can get it. Well...the genius of his way was risk. The gauging of guided response. Programming against programming. Even risking to be patient, which risks running out of time. He waited. Gave himself away. Worked, and stole some, got what he needed to get more money, and then to get enough to war some. Even if it was only enough for one strike. People came to him that wanted to do it. Holy people. Damned by holiness. Fate's bitches. There was an air of artistry about the ranch. Last I knew of, the man that left to seek Peace with *her* blood on his hands was that he was near me once, leaving a Great Book in my mailbox, given to him by *Her*. They were each other's free slaves. Where will he retire? Where can he find a place that requires no money, no survival, no rank, where a person has no used value to society, where he'll be mainly left alone? There are some choices. If The Father could find me...I needed to move again.

Blinder and Blinder

Draping all around me the Darkness falls. No matter how I try to see my way out I cannot. There are no hands reaching down from the fat. No one in power willing to share their money, or even their food. I wish, I want, I just want to see something besides the Darkness, besides the shallow denseness of what everything keeps from me. How this loathing sickens me. How I hate this hate. So much. I hate all actions of those in the Darkness. All of the friends I hear. Always they ask what I have been doing, pretending to be concerned, pretending to care, poorly masking the fear of needing to know I am no danger to them. Never listening to my reply, just wanting to hear something to please them, never wanting to know the truth. How sad, the emptiness in the image of their eyes. Will their eyes fall somewhere else? Can they see their lack of genuineness? Will they see themselves wanting me to grant them peace with magic?

Pit of Despair

Unwilling to be a slave to another person I, in my Greatness, live in the prison the slave masters have made as my alternative to not serving them. In constant poverty because they have placed a price on the rights I am entitled to. They, the power seekers, Freemason philosophy. Taking just enough so that they can take more. I am unable to have enough to fight them, no matter what my path in this Dark orifice of greed. I rest in the mouth of consumption waiting for the saliva to break me down. Never having enough funds to even swim and stay in shape. My muscles rot on my bone. My back aches dully and then sharply. Oh how the poor need drugs to cope with the imprisonment of those that took the world from the free with the invention of ownership. Never enough. And if there is any it will be gone soon. The depression of poverty hangs heavy on the futile, like a weight in my chest, holding down my passionate heart. No movement great enough to be worth it. Everything in this still life crippled further into retardation. It is too easy to rationalize crime in a society so unbalanced. The poor may not be able to take the money of the wealthy, or the power of the wealthy, but at least I can take their lives. At least there is always the option to stop their power, and leave it lying there seeping into the ground. How I tried...so many times to escape the fate...I even tried to compromise my path...but I was forced back again and again, by scam after scam, by diseased person after diseased person that did not mind watching me die in the train terminal, so long as I did not get my filthy body in their child's way.

There is always one clear way out of tyranny, one sure way to not serve and perpetuate the power of those that think they can own and condemn others for their own pleasure. One sure way. At least I haven't pawned all of my weapons. At least I can always steal bullets. I wonder when the sound of the blast will stop. What will the instance of Silence sound like? I see no Reason strong enough to pull me from the Despair that will drive me to Freedom, away from those so blind that they condemn me and that they dare to think happy thoughts about themselves as I am dying here. No one to help Zarat. Wallowing in rage, because it's something separate from myself I can feel, like a friend it keeps me company. And like a friend, I do favors for the rage now and again, but I know it will not release me from suffering, from futility...from the poverty that makes my life meaningless. All I want is a place to live, food to eat, and a way to write...of course I cannot have any of these, because my Great Works are not marketable. So, I lead myself towards the only Freedom I can have. Thank Nothingness that there is no Damnation beyond the arrogance of HumanKind. Thank God that power is an illusion made up by cowards. At least, one by one, I can show them that their power is futile, and I can free them from the guise that their power is beneficial. Only death teaches them what we know. But the scars left on their children will multiply their ignorance and fear and power...I could never steal enough bullets to save everyone.

His Eyes Became Soft

My dear friend...pull the book closer. Thank you for going so far. First the *Girl* came, and you got to know *her*. *She* was Beautiful to know. A simple girl. *She*'d play in the sand all day, sitting by the beach, digging in it with *her* feet, sifting it through *her* hands. *Her* body keeping busy while *her* mind spun thoughts. *She* showed you beautiful tapestries. *She* died to show you. To prove it. So, since our friendship is long, since you've shown true concern for my personage, I have been reasoning for you. Trying to find ways to make you more Free. Because I see that sometimes You suffer.

Don't believe in the people selling things to you. Don't believe that you get cars through car dealerships, don't think that you need to ever buy a house from a Real Estate person. Usually never. These people are the people that put the facade over simple things like property and try to magnify the simple place to exist so that they can live off of it. People making money on the very lives of people. ... Feeding off the fat and the "empty" space of the surrounding area. But no. These are the people that were convinced by someone else that someone had to present these things to people, but what is actually true...is that there is a system, usually a government system, that orders these matters, like county land, and it is usually cheap to do. Copyrights are the same simple affordable way. But these people want you to think it is complicated, when in fact it is simple, and people are trained to tell you. This is how to be free in America. Find the way it works. There's not actually much wrong with the system, but there is a taint in the people that are fit into control certain parts. These people are being cleansed out by time. Many wars came before us. But this is a time of coming Peace. We are a generation with much less Hate.

<u>Life, The Telling of a New Ancient History</u>

I remember, as the haze clouds the edges, a far off time... I was sick. Young. Five. Hurt to eat, tonsillitis, so I stopped. Didn't drink either. Five. "Justified when I was Five." Resolved and ready to die, if life dared to inconvenience me, or, if life would challenge my will within it. Destined for Freedom.
I remember the nurse taking my blood, she says, "You can look away." Zarat easefully replied with the seriousness of an interested lad, "Why? Can I look?"
"Yes but most People look away." Nurse.
"I'll watch," his mother held him, and looked away, crying a bit. He noticed the vibrancy of moving existence. The pumping beating banging roaring epoch showering us with water-soft mist.
Yes. Like *Her*. I was born with an ability to let curiosity push us to see way beyond the fear and see what is really happening when we stop reasoning solely for our own personal safety. We will not ever live forever. And neither will anyone you cling to. Appreciate the life you're making all frosted with glaze.

<u>Say Something About It</u>

Power seekers set up nests in many places, ready to degrade you. Watching. Be wary of anyone placed specifically and noticeably within the laws of any society or business. Be very very wary. These human monsters, deadlier than dragons, will use you as their psychological tool to glorify themselves by putting you in their place, even when there was nothing harmful about your place, but there was something weak about Its feelings. Anyone can become it. And anyone must notice and break themselves. Cast themselves again. Broken from the hunt of others. This is the Disease of Oppression. But the cure burns bright in Us. And there are cures. Certainly cures to making their power useless, we only need remove their fear, and then they love surprisingly easily. This is something the Free Founders knew we would face. And we will be taking back our politics now, tiny posers, too soon you die, so quickly your arrogance rots. And we will not hate you. But we will avoid your harsh mutation.

<u>Don't Believe in All you See, See more</u>

It is not specifically any government that is my enemy. It is not specifically the Freemasons, or the Jews or the Catholics, or any others that lied for power. There are wise and unwise everywhere and in everything. But it is the minds of humankind that is my enemy. It is a battle to fight the ignorant. And a battle to fight those that dare assume power and protection from and over their slaves. It is the belief of the Freemason that some men are born to be princes and others to be slaves. But still, all men are equal. So, the proper prince sacrifices himself in service to aid his slaves. Many people believe that no one should be a prince and no one should be a slave. These are Communists. But if you have a system, and you do not have pure hearts, if you do not teach selflessness and understanding, you have no system, for the society will be tainted by those that lust for control and power because they are afraid and insecure. They are ignorant. How do you fight the minds of people? How do you destroy the reflexes of thought that have been ingrained to be foolish since birth? Most people have conquered a society they thought was dark and flooded it with their own propaganda. But then, that is the root of the ignorance of power.

<u>Think of Something Else</u>

So many have been touched by my sex. Masturbating, molesting, the feel I can instantly trigger in another human being. A third of the population of the world is sexually reactive, and all people are accesible by it. Every person I have ever spoken to on the phone has likely talked to me while I touched myself. The Holy have often been naked. Disrobing suddenly and sliding a finger in, or squeezing the balls of Zarat. What ever I wanted to fondle. When I was younger I was a doodler, but this is far better. We can all touch ourselves. That's why the video phone never caught on. People are upset about the loss of their privacy. But we can get privacy back by no longer needing to hide anything. Let's bring reality to the beautiful surface. And lets let everyone do it. But it won't be that way. Do you hear the cries of the fearful? Coming with torches, ready to kill, to keep that idea of safety, that keeps sex away from children that need to touch it. Believing in a lie and ready to kill to keep it.

<u>Tasks for the Young</u>

Stop thinking that family is the most important thing. It sounds real nice when the "religious" float it. The followers go right with it, praising family, advertising and enforcing it. Those that a smart man can tell what to think, or their managing true believers what to know, is a precious thing to those that cultivate the illusion of power. For a religious organization, like Christianity, it gains power with their precepts of guilt, shame, and inferiority to create drive to a lie that others approve of. What this does is creates a money generating system. The parents gain power through the same belief in precepts because their fear keeps them from wanting to think. The parent's power that forces them to control and keep the kids close and force the children to behave bastes the "adults" in a gravy of security, arrogantly and blindly being soothed by the illusion of pride that makes a mother and father a set of hypocritical angry defending fighting devils that want that power and security far more than YOU, and they will come to prove it if you deny it.
See where people are seeing value.
Leave the greedy behind. Love them if you want. Let them go. You make this happen. No one else. Your effort sets you free. Great effort always requires sacrifice. You are not responsible for their sadness. That is a burden that they can do with what they want. If they choose to reason like us, it will be deeply and swellingly useful.

<u>The Free Mind</u>

After years in a long and extended relationship, that which I broke-dead to begin the war, I developed a technique to overcome the trap that most men fall into. While most men hunt and stalk a woman until they capture her and then they keep her, enslave her, while they drip and lust over every other woman on the planet in search of more beastly sex to expand their instinctual heat...well I overcame that. Zarat chose to raise the emotion I would feel when I looked at a woman's panties in the grocery store, or smelt a co-workers hair at the office, every time *She* bent over, every time *She* walked by. I put my sex where I wanted it to be, and as the world moved slowly as I redirected my instincts for my own pleasure, I reveled in the ability to be able to touch the woman I wanted, and freely, and when I wanted, and for the ramming sweating exploding bliss of beating madness, that I used for the instant of meditation and engulfment into stillness and nothingness where I felt my own spirit gleaming. My life, though not seemingly to the idiot and ignorant, is a graceful swoon across the golden pond of peace and perfection. Because of it, we lived in great and total peace; even in the midst of all tearing reality.

<u>Adventure</u>

He stood in a bathroom *(a detail he noticed)* and watched himself act. He paid attention to what he did. He checked the stalls for feet. He looked in the mirror to see if anyone followed him in. He pissed in the urinal next to the wall so an attack could only come from one side and behind. He didn't use the vacant stall so that he could see what was happening. It was at this moment that he realized that he loved it. Zarat loved the awareness, the cunning, the process of the life of adventure. He loved the pursuits of righteous war. He loved to be a criminal. If he were on the other side he could be a glorified secret agent. But he isn't. He is free to choose his own adventures, and not to do the bidding of those that pursue power and glory. I feel it in me. The thrill, the brilliant lunacy, the unspoken satisfaction of the 'impossible' victory.. People act like I had a choice in becoming what I am. The Adventurer. The truth. The Free-Man. I was born this way. As was The *Girl.* But still we must choose to push ourselves into it and through the greatest adventures. That which we must make ourselves.

People become the result of what people believe they should feel about them. An astronaut becomes a hero, and a crack whore becomes an ugly girl with low self-esteem. But it all lies in how it plays out. If a crack whore made more money than she does she would be viewed better in the Darkness of Capitalism. If condemners didn't make her feel bad about herself, if the bullies had ever stopped bullying the things they couldn't understand, or that they thought could hurt them, then being a crack whore wouldn't be a bad path. But people think they can own a crack whore, people think that a crack whore doesn't deserve a job, all because of bad PR. All because fear is allowed to be abusive and portrayed as moral. Over and over, divided we fall, one by one. Because people are seeking place in their everyday life, trying to be right, trying to feel safe. All the while killing all of us they think they care about, driven to madness by self-righteousness. Doing something about it. Pride. Our penalty. Fucking astronauts. Save the society by removing the power from it.

<u>Damn the Mind</u>

Putting on weight. I have noticed it. It's discomfort when I sit. I have the void of nothingness in myself. Not the positive style of it, but the sad kind. The kind that manifests when I know I can go nowhere, or do anything. I cannot accomplish anything. The only luxury I can afford is food, barely. I know how easy it is to shut off my mind's fixations. I could easily choose to let go of its hold on me. I can alleviate want. But I don't really want to. The breath on my current beard is stickier. I think it is from not being able to stay in shape. It appears related. Kind of interesting. Maybe it's because of the drinking. I hate drinking. Everything about it. The taste, the sensation, the mind state, but it is all I can afford to do. And weed, the healthy alternative, is too hard to get these days.

How funny. If only we could all see our hypocrisy. If only we could all give it up. I could. But I want to see where this is going, what this path will do to me. I will let the normal reflexes do as I am programmed to do. I will hate and hate to be hated. I will fight and hate to be fought. I will be angry and I will crave freedom, and condemn anything that takes away my greedy right to be whatever I want, taking away its freedom for offending me. Obviously tolerance...obviously...forgiving people for being the pieces of crap that we our personal selves are is the way. But I will damn myself in Darkness. I will be like them. I am no better. I do not deserve peace. And I will not give it to myself. It is my choice to suffer against my own futility by becoming more useless. It is my dream of equality, to be just like you. Damned on Earth.

<u>Superconcious</u>

You feel that part of you. That part of you that watches you, that observes you from a point of wonder and judgment. What if this part of you became the prominent part, what if your superconscious wasn't just a little part in the back of your mind? What if you could observe yourself completely honestly, and make yourself the great person you always expect others to be? What if you were brutal in the forming of the design you choose to become? What if you traveled the long hard road to your perfect form? The form of dreams? You can make yourself the real Super Man.

<u>Nazis</u>

If Germany had conquered the US, You would feel disdain for the beloved movie Forrest Gump. You would think it was inhumane to force a retard to live. They are unable to achieve. It's a joke, a rebellious movie, that you barely accept under "your" German Constitution, funny how it still sounds like the original. You'll feel what the crowd wants you to. Try not to feel what those around you feel. Try to be genuine. And try to understand why others feel. Either way, if it were true, if Capitalism still functioned, if there was the illusion of Free Speech, it would not have been profitable. The Public, You, would have shund it. It a Free Society, with Capitalism intact, everything, every point, anything that a craft has been poured into, anything imagined in detail, can and should and will succeed.

Americans think the system will crumble. They are afraid. It is a fine thread they walk. They feel that way. Anyone can come and take it away, it can crumble, people seek power here; place, definition, image. Americans need to know how easy it is to stay alive. They have to not be afraid of becoming a third world country. Let's work together, for, not against.

<u>What's in a Bible?</u>

The Bible would positively affect many lives if people simply knew how to understand it. All it does is show you generation upon generation of dysfunctional murderers, abusers, doubters, etc., that would benefit by giving up their desire to succeed for themselves and gain power they would find love and humility. They would find their Jesus and/ or their God. The real point of the Bible and all Christianity is that imperfect and hindered, fear-ridden people can overcome themselves. It is the same message as Hinduism, Buddhism, Sikhism, Judaism, etc. Unfortunately, a lot of bad people never fix themselves by the same messages they preach and religions are used to sway politics, and force people to do what they believe is right, instead of teaching people to be tolerant and free from persecuting, which makes what is "right" natural. The roots of these religions are not wrong, but those that seek authority and formation create power positions, and so, create darkness.

<u>Prison Reform</u>

All revolutions will be built from those imprisoned and damned by the righteous. Therefore, to preserve the society, we must stop damning. And start connecting, instead of alienating. If you can condemn, if there are people you won't talk to, even people you've deeply loved, because of any circumstance you are the greatest problem in the world. And this is where the now Dark theory of Sin came from. That scar that separates you from Love. This is the truth. The damned are the religious, the frightened and the condemning. Ease them. Reach out to those reaching out to you, and save them from the river of dismay and the grip of anything that could help them and make them live forever.

Save the imprisoners.

Those that pursue and become "Teachers", those that gain a degree along the path of least thinking, display what they are in every action and reaction of their everyday. These that you see in classrooms mimicking the ideals of Philosophers do so falsely. And it is shown in the reality that they live. They form large unions, not to ensure quality education to ensure that the gluttony they hide from children is excentuated and facilitated. These beasts of humanity leach huge wages from the central trust and spend every penny to hide the sensation of insecurity that led them to the profession. The need to be the person that could put all types of people that made them feel insecure in school in their place. Teachers in the Darkness spend to appear as if they are wealthy, as if they have, seeking new sports cars, and eating at fine restaurants, all in the guise they pull on themselves to think that they are elite, that they are supreme, while in the classroom boldly demanding equality amongst whom they believe they empower by holding down into the wall of bricks. The first image of authority a child sees is hypocrisy, and it is what they come to accept as who they are and can be. Once one person starts to cut across the lines of the parking lot, so long as no one yells at them, everyone cuts across the lines on the parking lot. And more are born to stop the jerks and enslave us for our lack of rational consideration.

For most children, they should not be taken from these dens kept dimly lit to hide the Darkness, to hide the alcoholism, sex addiction, the rich foods, the image of importance and the truth of total irrelevancy, but only because the social aspect is too integral to the real success of actual doers. Only because the attitudes of these teachers will teach the students how to overcome the false that pursue the parasitic nature of those that seek work in any government.

No matter the force of the pursuit of self-satisfaction, it does not fill the void of their sense of worthlessness. To escape it they need to break themselves to the level they believe everyone else should be at, but their fear of pain and of real equality is massive.

As anyone ages, they will know these pride-mongers that become teachers and you will know the words of Zarat are fact based on experience, not the want of an inviting image. Respect no one that has sought power.

Overcome.

<u>To Make Real War</u>

I will not sit quietly and let my life rot away by not having the courage to do whatever I dream. I can change the world. I am not afraid of any judgment, any ridicule, any failure that is possible. (I have heard it all my life.) I have nothing better to do. I might as well. I'm going to start a war. Not for fame. Not for money. Not for insecurity. Not for power. Just because. A real one, one that touches no one and affects everyone, and no one will be sure what happened at all.

Zarat will tell you now, my children, those that learn the other way, that you will find eyes that judge you. You will find them everywhere. This judgment is the conditioning of Darkness. This is the curse they have chosen to believe in tainting an inadimant system they serve. They fear the loss of that which they've gained that makes them feel like there is a barrier between them and the death they fear so much. There is not. The barrier corrodes and they must constantly refresh it. There is only the presence of life and the absence of it, and the struggle to keep it. And they will feel its loss most strongly because they have never wanted to face it. And they will suffer massively for it, but then one day they will be free from their weakness, and as always, will be thankful for death once more.

When they speak to you through that stare and creaking tone, DO NOT feel shame, or guilt, or sorrow, these are the reactions they have sought all their lives. These were the actions that they first saw when they first acted like this and they first gained power and they first gained that glass of juice they wanted. And it has never ended. The pattern. The attitude that bends their faces and makes them ugly, appearing as they have always been. Have no fear of the look of your "parents", have No Fear. Be calm. Do not issue your programmed reaction, do not give them the guilt your parents wanted you to have to learn their way. You may oppose them if you wish. So long, as you do not kill them, or take their things, or break their stuff, you can do anything else to them, because everything they have is built on the system of greed, your parent's system of greed, and it is this selfishness that leads to every reason that they attempt to place authority over you. Stand knowing that your Reasons are stronger. Be calm, and all the reasons I have given, will return naturally to you. Seek calmness. And the soul will be able to expand and aid you, and keep you from becoming those people which you have once hated, through the same patterns of fear. You may create another reflex response for yourself, with specific words. You will find it easy to disarm many of them, with the same simple tactics. Be like a retailer, "Thank you for shopping here today, but could you cram your stretching to have an opinion of me up your tight fucking cunt?" And crush them. Leave them no way to fight back. Appall them. Let them know they are not our Fathers and Mothers, who we crushed long ago for our Freedoms. All they need is to feel bad, because that feeling of "bad" is so powerful to them. It is the system and the emotion manipulated in them by their parents from the first day they were born.

We have been provided with the Bill of Rights. It is this system that enable us today to fight those that seek to place oppression over a Society through a feeling of security and "rightness". It is only a feeling, and people find ideas and reasons to justify these feelings. Many people use these reasons for these unstable and fleeting feelings as the basis of their lives. This is what is killing the Dark Society now. They believe that they are their emotions, when they are NOT, so their Reasons are wanted justifying things that aren't permanent, and so, aren't real. Jefferson knew how complex and similiar it was, leading into many separate family governments, seeping across societies, he could see them wanting and wanting, and creeping back towards the shallow, towards the wrong, towards Pride, even in his lifetime. He made a country, but lost it at the same time, but left for me, Zarat, the tools to fight on. I will not let them have my mind. It is my own. And walks freely, with it's head held straight, looking at you to realize it. I don't want your acceptance, I want you to not need to accept me or reject me, or place me, your macro opinion is worthless and violent, control seekers.

The tyrants that built this nation and control are almost gone. Almost died off. Many of us will continue freely, and the old lines fade. And though we fight, we fight because tomorrow is a new day to reach out to those people that think we should hate for their power system. Be Independent like the river, life within it, life all around it, still just a river.

Know where life ends and where it begins, and know that you are Free in everything in between. And the Noble will continue to toil for those that do not yet realize it.

ACT III

The Holy American

The Holy American propels himself, but not for himself. It was across this stretch of moments, owned only by Zarat's interpretation, that he was able to participate in the world of events, provided by makers of events, the false world that exists for most people that take no part in effort and manifestation. His encounters were direct and exact and with you and people like you, and his reactions were of Freedom and Equality and the offense to the supremacy and division of the imitators that presume an ethos without understanding or defining themselves by examining themselves with honesty, thrusting themselves into hypocrisy. To some, he left with ease, to others he burned in them anger and doubt, leaving them to feel as futile as their biting reality. The teacher teaching to the unaware and unsatisfied student, somehow changed, but oblivious to when. Working and laughing loudly amongst you, cleansing himself with his final gifts directly presented to those that suddenly knew him.

<u>The ID</u>

I think it is called the ID. I remember back to where I was when I think that I was in it. It gave me great arrogance. And so, great power. Great fame and popularity. And worst of all, people want you to keep it. They enjoy it. They love your personality. It is harder to understand the quiet man. Too many don't know how to listen to his whispers. The ID is powerful, yet ultimately useless and unimportant. It fades into life. It dies. But. It is the root of the Hero. It is the fruit of the warrior. I, Zarat, have faced many enemies. I have seen and I have done too many things of adventure and amazement. You can use it. But the closer you get to true enlightenment, the less you want to. It becomes too hard. Most, cannot escape it, or if they do it takes a long while. And then a long while to recover from the trauma you faced that brought you out of it. I, Zarat, am a failure. I failed the Great War. I failed the *Holy Girl.* I failed in many business ventures to try and build the army in a new way. I have failed to save and teach many that I love deeply to find peace. It brings me much despair. I have failed to maintain constant peace, and so, to realize enlightenment in myself. I could not save lives. I cannot fight death, change or end, or beginning. Zarat is nothing in the universe. *He speaks to the air. He speaks in third person because he realizes that he is not truly the identity of Zarat. His identity has changed many times. And will continue to do so, even after death. We ride the waves of random design. Trapped in something we don't understand. Though we are trapped, perhaps there is a way to enjoy the ride, by knowing it does not truly matter. We are like the fish. We think we swim to the top of a wave and we think we swim down into the trough, but really the wave carries us. But we sure do swim hard to get there, don't we? A teacher said that fish thing to me once.* We must stare into the abyss of ourselves. We must face the lie that we try to make ourselves into. We must realize that we are not gods and that we do not have to try to be, not anyone. Accept your humanness and let the anger and rage that the fight against truth turns into perish. It is alright to be human. It is alright. Nothing is a mistake. Just a thing. Nothing is wrong that happens to us. Nothing is right. Stop thinking that you have the authority to identify what is right or wrong for anything. This thinking has built the Dark Society. A nation of people that think they are or should be gods, but they truly believe that they are doing right. If you can notice that you think that you are right and you feel good about it, you are part of the problem. Stop what you are doing. Stop interfering. You are not helping.

Ever since the battle that changed the *Girl's* existence, I have not been able to build the following and allure that I had back then. I talk to less people. And do not want to waste my time trying to teach dark and cruel people the way.

It sounds like contradiction, but it is not. As enlightenment is slowly attained, your logic will slowly die. And a deeper, non-man-made logic will become truthful. Remember that man created the concept of logic. Our logic never existed until we created it. Once it said the world was flat. Once there was a God. Something separate from us, something that judged us. It's a lie. Used by Dark Men for Power.

So many options. And none of them right. The ID says, "Just live." The truth, the spirit, the way, says, "Just live." They want the same thing. But they will lead and create different results and ends. It is hard to know which advantages are right. It is hard to live without verification. But I, Zarat, will not give up. And I will follow the teaching of those that I want to be like. I want to love itself. I want to destroy the Darkness. I cannot be both. But I must be both.

<u>Mexicans</u>

"Yes. Zarat was in Mexico. What I liked about the Mexicans is that they don't need anything to do. Some think they are lazy, but they are not owned by societal propaganda that commands them to do something, or else they are worthless. The Mexican knows that he already has value. It comes from being alive. Those from the Dark Society become crazy when they have nothing to do. It is why those from the Dark Society know nothing about holiness and truth. They cannot sit and work hard to find it. The Buddha sat for five days straight and decided that he would not move until he understood the truth. Five days is not long, but most of those from darkness could not make it five hours."

<u>You Don't Have a Chance in a Dark Society</u>

When the police come for you, there will be nothing good that they have to say. Everything they see is an exaggeration. A lie in their mind. The IQ of the common enforcer, in any government, in any controlling ethos, is dull to say the least. They are so ignorant that they believe that they are 100% correct. Which, if you had any brains you'd know you could never be 100% correct. They will paint you in their reports as a bad person. Because if they are there they believe 100% that you are a bad person. They believe everyone is. They hate the world. And they are the worst bits of it, so they secretly hate themselves, and that makes them more cruel, and more right in their heads. Militarism has never helped a society. IT has only led those intelligent enough to see it to stop it. It makes war never end. The most mentally ill run society and the mentally ill and stupid enforce it. Nobody wants to believe they are so worthless, and this will make them fight back harder and enforce themselves more and more contrary to our rights. So long as idiots want to matter there will be no Freedom. So long as the poor have to be forced into these jobs of that allows them to be Devils we will not be Free.

<u>A special friend, without fear.</u>

We must face the things of life that you don't want to. This is the brave revolution. The revolt against ourselves and the impulses that trigger hatred, anger, sadness and rage. We must be willing to face the obstacles of our minds. You must separate yourself from yourself to do it. This is no joke. There is a method for it. How close are you to not feeling guilt? For me, I, I take the risk I ask everyone else to take...you see this is battle. I, your leader step out first. This is what a leader does. This is what a warrior is. In the midst of fire I step out first. Because, though softer than before, the disease is fierce, and people will strive for a way to feel about me, should I be happy or angry or disappointed, never content to just consider against their own perfection. War is dangerous. But I am that man. That one that you see heroically calling. Calling to you. And you will know that I call to your heart, dear soldier, and you will rise, and you will sit, and we will non-violently end violence, or as least, at the lesser level of development, we will end the scars violence leaves. A cure for scarring. Ready yourself for the discomforts you don't want to face. Face yourself and know less fear. I am willing to face all fear, and so must you. Deadly accurate. Choosing to be everything, and thus be the only well rounded one. In a world of specialization, we suffer. We lost too many segments of human reality. We lose too much nature, too much natural reaction. For me to win in the game of literature I must not care what anyone will think. I must not. I must not care of the sudden conclusions they will jump to, only because they focus so much on themselves and not the macrocosm, like I focus in my words. I am aware of the general patterns of psychology, and not because I read a book defining it, people that do that want money from it, and they're not smart enough to see it. I watched man. And I reasoned with the majority of his thoughts, and found the flaw that keeps them from perfection. I am a phenomena. I write the truth you see in a General, someone symbolized ahead of you, but you don't know me. You don't have the mental deformity that makes you think you should be naturally better than me, like Vegeta did before he accepted that Kakarrot was just the one that was better, because you have an insecurity and you reason to be superior, and you are my blood, my brother, you are too familiar with the legend. You wanted to be the legend. Let go though. Don't believe in the image. Don't believe in the image you make of anyone, then you don't have to doubt it. Let people exist, without placement, without hate. Fight. See why it is goodness? See why you don't have to doubt it and fight

144

it? I don't gain anything but peace? And so do you. It is a war, like on a holodeck, without casualties. It is the war all others started wars for, but we fight on. Them, the same as me. I could have as much blood on my hands as any mass murderer, because they had the will to make an ideal, same as I have. Ask anyone, within Zarat is great power for destruction, your destruction, you've looked in its calmness. I have no fear of the Holy Spirit, and it is awesome, and non-denominational. So we are even, dead or alive. This is knowledge. This is the point where wisdom is taught, where we taught the ways of compassion, without it, it doesn't solve the problem of suffering. We won't all win if we don't use the methods towards Universal Freedom.

So face yourself: What if it was happening: What if you are any of "them"? There are different lives that learn different things, strive to show love for a person. Help them at all costs to your fearful illusion that would limit you from making the best view of the moment for this person. What if I was your son? Mother? Would you help me apply the methods to my further success, even if you didn't have the intelligence to understand the importance of it? Would you stop fighting for an image and live in this world directly with me? Facing me. Loving me. Do you love me enough to think what society told you not to think? That's all that happened. But the fact is you can think anything. Let go. And walk down this beach with me. There is no divided connection between any of us...
What levels of vulnerability would I face for truth: see gently with the eyes of calmness and compassion: help him. You love him, choose to, in your mind, believe in him, for the raw emotion of it. Touch his acceptance of you. Thank him for it, thank him for always trying on behalf of you::

<u>Honest Freud, Love Everyone</u>

If I told you that sliding your fingers inside me would help me reach my goal of becoming a benevolent god in my next life; would you do it? All you need is a reason. I made one for you. Believe it, don't doubt it just because I'm explaining it, believe. Help me. Please. You are physically able to. Let go of the limits of your emotions, it makes emotions too sharp. It's sexual. Of course mother, it is there.
Ok. I will.
She pulled up the medical skirt I was wearing. I was aware that I could be pleased that this was happening, so I chose to be.
Put spit on your fingers. Rub it around the outside and then push in. You've done this before.
A laugh came out. Like a little burst.
Thank you for letting go of the reality you claim to think to feel safe. Deeper.
I'm sorry but this will get messy. Really messy eventually. I am about to die.
Don't talk like that.
No. Just about to die. Accept it. And keep your fingers there. I can't move, but I can still talk. Now this is hard. But I can consolidate my energy if you block the hole of my penis.
I thought cock. and enjoyed it. life is amazing. thrilling and complex. and and simply naked.
She did it. I was surprised. There is no doubt that she grew to love me strongly as I lived. Though she feared me, she knew that it only covered a vast sea of adoration.
I need to keep as much energy in my body as possible. Keep this simple in your mind and let the love of it be proof of how wonderful love is.
I felt a swirl on me. And she was free.
But I felt myself constrict and burst feces at her, as the pressure burst from all holes, and my nose burst blood, my hair fell out in the center of my scalp, and what I'd been began to rot the very next day.

It is an old death, I have remembered. "Phowa," was the last sound I heard.

<u>Randomly Developing the Different Sections of the Book</u>

Tracking down another last thought...there maybe I have found it...
People will like certain parts of our works. Everyone can pretty much like a part of it. Because we can reason on behalf of so many types of people, and so many types of impulses. With concern for all of them. Trying to bring them to where we believe they all want to go. Man always thinks it is going somewhere. We are just telling you that we are already here.
The challenge of these entertaining offerings is to let you try and like a different part of the book. What haven't you been able to face? What angers you? Who's existence haven't you tried to understand yet? We offer you a way to face it, without shame, with yourself. Read by a river. Read on a mountain top. Read touching the Earth. Remembering what we are trying for and remembering what we've lost.
See your sides. These are choose your own adventure pieces. What fun in thought.
And what fun in realizing our view was too rigid and too tight. And our chances have been forgiven.

Are we to overcome the conditions that are placed upon us? Are we to find peace? Are we to seek war and maintain peace within ourselves? The world is war. To live is to succeed over something else, be it animal, plant or the man-animal. Peace can be had. Great focus of energy and power can be had. Kindness can be had.
Humility
can be had.
We have the power to become whatever we wish. But first we must know the truth. We must purify ourselves. Abolish the selfish fear and insecurity that fuels the ego and the darkness. If we can be anything we want, we must make ourselves what we want everyone else to be. Good. Not perfect. Just right. Not righteous. Just fine. Without glory. Without stardom. If you care what others think you will be their prisoner. You must be an island. A rock. Others can be around you, but you must be your own. The best methods to this course of true independence have already been defined centuries ago. If we use the teachings of the past that reached the achievements of preferred nature that we seek we can find the course and root of what we are faster.

<u>Cricket</u>

After I split a tomato with a cricket....I blew over the top so he would smell it, every time I blew he became quiet. I think he could smell it blowing by his receptors. I set it standing up next to him in that pile of leaves as is a smorgasbord for him, so he could climb right up inside it and eat it all. He's totally protected under the tree. No owls can get him. What a great night this will be to him. (As I set the tomato down near him I told him, "Love exists in the Universe, and it is worth cultivating," and I lowered my mind into my soul so he could feel the weight and impact of truth, and he was calm, and then I said, after I thought he might think to possess it and try to own, and own other people, "in your self."....
So after, or while rather, I was eating the tomato, I thought of how I would first be inclined to not like tomatoes. In fact, I used to "feel" that way about them. But I came to realize I wasn't "feeling" anything. The tomato was reacting in my mouth, and my brain noticed the tartness, and I unknowingly made myself not want to eat it, but there was nothing wrong with it. So as I eat it now, I think, with seeds seeping beneath the keypad, that I cannot grab *(Zarat's keypad stupid),* that while most people slowly restrict their habits, slowly obsess with the few things that make them react and feel certain selfish ways, that they believe they are identifying as good, drives them to hate and love and own and fall into what Darkness is. While We, keep thinking while We are trying new things, and thinking of new things in new ways. Maybe we are not right, we can't be, but we know that the way we are is better and better and has never been bad, or anything other than amazing, even as it crushed us. We are a new world. A world that wants it. We want life. We aren't afraid. We are going to ride a road with unknown destination and We will see many things and dream wonderful ways to deepen Freedom, and then we'll die, thankful that your pursuit of power over us has ended, and then We will try something else.

For the world to Evolve, People must be Free. We will continue to return, lifetime to lifetime and build Free Worlds, and stop you again and again from taking away the Rights of the World, because you fear life, and death, and eternity, and anything you can't know to understand, which is a lot.

He was at his greatest when he wasn't checking everything he was doing, repeatedly over and over in his mind - when he flowed. When he let himself be Free. When he let himself be as great as he is, as natural as he exists. That's when I loved him the most, and so did everyone. But his mind was harsh, and still he used that to make himself care more, and be able to suffer like Gods suffer, and like Gods, not care.

<u>Art</u>

A girl came over while I was typing. She didn't ask where I got the TV. I guess she didn't want to know. What a coward. How would it have hurt her? Why was she afraid of her own judgment of me? What cruelty has she been programmed to inflict? Why is she afraid of herself telling on me? If they came, they would believe it was my TV. I am unafraid of her judgment. If she felt free around me, she would not have felt the fear that would have to force her into judging me. Because people are taught to condemn, people are taught to be afraid of thieves, because thievery is against Capitalism. It's true that less stealing and less killing will make the society work well, but people must not be punished, they must be taught, eased, and given opportunity. Telling someone they, and the people they want to love, are bad because of actions they believe they have to commit, to justify and to exist, will only make them think they are mad. And thus they will become mad. So, the answer is not in "more", but in less. The answer is the learning within the forum. The opportunity to not be in the struggle for his life that made him mean.

This is the grand importance of Art in a society. The real artists are compelled by thought, by visions, Inertia. Building on a point to prove what they already know for certain. Each word cluttering its simple simple meaning. So, without something to work on, we will work against what won't let us work on what we know we must. This is a natural mind course towards violent revolution. Occurring, just because the society couldn't think, or hasn't yet thought of the solution. Because it had to come from such a strange and mythical place, they didn't even think it was real...but it really is.

The Solution: Don't admonish people that struggle. See them suffering and have compassion for what you have ignorantly forced them into. Because they need to be free to direct themselves. The instant poverty of being thrown out of our parents houses is hard, and harder still to overcome, when your only goal is to stop it, but instead you must live through it, and so, you learn the right way to stop it. This becomes complicated, and people think their thought to ideas of whimsy and fate.

Let Madness show you what it is Seeing. What if the madness became calm, but still existed? It becomes Entertainment. And somehow fewer of us are dying, except for those that don't get that non-violence allows us all to try what we want to try.

A geniuses idol hands, his cursed palms, will tear everything apart, if he cannot display himself, or does not know how. Marketing should be taught in Elementary school.

We show the metaphors that describe the same experiences again and again, through different minds, defined by different times. Seeing the same things, describing what we have already known. And we live, amongst these thoughts. I feel a push in my head. A thought shelved and silenced, echoing as I push it back into place. Never to be heard again, unless I try not to think about it, because trying not to think about it, is in very fact, thinking about it. And the quandary confuses you and makes you waffle, and so, it's untrue to you.
That's important. You might want to highlight it.
What if an artist could see beyond his illusions and interpret reality instead of his own thoughts??? Describe the reality we all share, while our insides paint it.

The way that people that chose to "like" us saw us vividly, which is to say that we are Forward. Up front. We merely say what we think. If we don't know something, we ask, without fear of looking stupid or like anything. For us to understand what it is like for you to constantly deal with your style of thought is for us to force ourselves to understand. And we so care, so we do. To understand you.

We had a strange, humble bravado. There's something that people see in us that makes them interested. It is simplicity. We had to severely slow our mind's speed of thought to see it, but there is something always running on a plane of thought beneath our running words and plans and general thinking words of thought...there is an air of Prolific Greatness. We just know we are. Because we have seen what others are, and we are so much happier. And it was easy and obvious to figure out, and we never stop figuring towards it.

And as we think these great thoughts, we doubt against ourselves. Thinking a fight against our very existence. Fighting tinges of madness, always reaffirming reality and truth and being. And realizing that the mind can and will think. But we are bravely calm, and this is our core. This is its importance. ... Would I give it up? My greatness? My inner hum. My under-ego. My core, that sparks words to think? Would I give up the ability to write. My one outlet to the mass that I naturally, and have always referred to. Existential from the start. I am born this way. There are many minds, though few constructs. Egos. The answer is "Yes." I would. I let it go. I'd lose my thoughts. I don't keep the gold that wins a legion and solves my ego's dilemma. I will not be controlled. And my mind can go silent. And I can exist. With no selfishness I never need to have another thought again. .. .. And then like a light flicking on, a thought, and the system restarts, and was never even off, but it was calmed, and I am less its slave. I am more my peaceful master. Winning the war we have imagined. For the Final Solution. Peace.

We already have it. We can't lose. And our hateful enemies can't win.

<u>Trance, He Cannot Hear You</u>

When the Father began to write the book that possessed him and graced him into and unto awe that cleansed his hair and blurred his eyes. His Sacrifice. His bleed. The life that wrang from him. *Every thought spinning down into the building and compiling of a mighty and continuing soul.* (What the fuck? A sub-thought. A premonition. He'll be dead soon. Or do I just feel the weight of the coming sadness? Well…whatever. I am not a god. That sure lightens the Burden.) The rhythm of the beat of his heart in him. His gurgle and his growl. A series of words cannot change what it was, and your lack of ability to understand what is real. Well…still with us? Is it hard?

He always called it the *Great Book.* He knew it was before he knew what it would be. Every vision we have is great and hopeful. The goal is the ideal. A real writer is the People's. Seeing what we want to say, have to say, seeing where a conversation leads that has no end, and create the sensation of wind riding. Is that a clue?? (The wind is the Nature of the Trance of the deepest gripping meditation.)

Natural Design, Or, As We Exist Now

One of the great beauties of the solitary journey is that one is free from all concern of what another person thinks. The solo man is free from the random anger and sadness that people feel through the filter of their insecurity that makes statements or situations some sort of attack against their person. By myself I am free of the persecution from fear of the loss of comfort.

The truly evolved have explored every facet of sexual pleasure because there was no reason to not know the great spectrum. There was no chance for embarrassment. There was no fear or shame tainting the experience of living. It is why the master knows that it can choose to be aroused by anything. The mind can be directed towards it. All other people chose a route that most pleased them, and cut off other routes, no matter what sexual orientation one chose, or there are those that travel all but are addicted to certain feelings of suffering within greedy pleasure. But who cares. This is not the state of the Evolved. Those that found freedom in the Stillness of Being Nothing at All. The Great One's are all colors, all shades, and can realize that they are that specific color at any time. In days of stress, sometimes it's good to just forget about the world in many different ways and obliterate yourself, just let go. Just take the release and not care.

Lying naked on the bed he rubbed his tight asshole. Remembering that for all of his life, before he knew what gay or straight or bi meant he could play with it. He did. Zarat played. He would stick his fingers inside himself. Sometimes he would stroke his smooth dick. Tonight though, he wanted to focus on the pleasure of his hole. Unashamed to have body parts, unafraid to exist as a human. He pulled the five inch dildo out of his mouth, letting the thick saliva leave its lubricated coating on it. It will feel good to take it. The dildo pressed up into his hole. He looked at his legs spread open. He had nice legs. Push. There was some resistance. He encircled the outside of the gate counterclockwise with the wet end of the fleshy plastic. Push harder. But let the muscles loosen. A little, then a little more, and then... They loosen so quickly. It does not take long for the anus to realize what it wants. The asshole becomes loose. And the cold dildo takes its place quickly, all the way up to its battery cap. He had planned to get batteries for months. Well, with little and non-real remorse he begins to fuck it. Nice and even. Long and hard. Stroking. Enjoying the gift of the male clitoris blatantly throbbing as the P-Spot. The asshole is so loose now. And so moist. Moist all by itself. Knowing that it can get fucked. The open orifice self lubricates with a gelatinous moisture, sweet to the smell. The mind completely unwound. All circumstances free, without a shed of guilt. His hips begin to ride back against his ramming hand. The feel of shaved balls against the wrist. "There is so much pleasure that is denied to human reality, by clinging to the ways of fear. So senselessly." He pulls his legs back to his chest and freely moans, arousing himself with his own sounds. "It is fun to think while being raped. It never hurts when we just give in and stop thinking that we are supposed to hate being violated. Uhhh." He loves to see his limp dick as he pounds. Flopping. Just letting his capable pussy accept its joy. Unafraid to be called anything, because the tyrants aren't allowed to be afraid near him, sitting on their experienceless minds. With a final squeeze, he eases it out. Having thought of sex in every way, having let his mind go blank, having been free to enjoy what a god's design is. He touches his pussy. So open. The little cock was small inside, but surely he could get four fingers in. It really feels just like an open vagina. He loves how he is satisfied even without cum. Satiated. Relaxed. So much tension is stored in this glorified and feared orifice. So wet. So nice to casually rub. Pleasant. Meant to be used, for certain. So many gates open when we let loose the locks and we let them swing free. So many lies by people that hate the earth, and hate our design. Now that is blasphemy. Those that know what God actually is, know no shame, and know no fear, and are not touched by their shallow, rarely experienced anger. Since he is done he might as well start cleaning his little mess up.

Free from the need to be defined pleasure is in everything. The world is bliss without persecution, self inflicted or otherwise.

<u>The Great Book and Other Arrogant Titles</u>

----------------Insert Story___________________

Zarat writes a commentary on how he didn't like the first book THE GIRL. He didn't like the way the Father wrote it. Or some commentary on its arrogance. And how it glorified *her* too much.

But the Father, had to write it the way it unfolded.   _

Zarat doesn't even care that Zarat doesn't like it, or that he subconsciously loved it. Not even enough to write the commentary. *She* was different to him, that's all.

One of the Lights is Out

The Dark Society reached its pinnacle of blackness when the super corporations began to direct 90% of their financial success towards children. Children are the greatest of the impulse buyers. And the habits we learn as children are the hardest to break. When I was very young I was an introvert. I did not notice what others were really doing. I was learning. Even then distractions from my mental efforts had to be tantalizing. Come my aged years, I realized the ultimate falseness of thought, having thought many "great philosophies" to their end point of malfunction. Systems have changed but the reflex of violence towards confusion has not. It's why people hurt she-males. They don't know how to feel about it. They can't pin it down, or control it, and they sure don't want to face it and come up with the wrong conclusion about how to feel about the idea. Cowards--
All of you. And eventually I found false answers in the physical world, only finding certainty in Nature. Realism, away from industrialization, that killed our learned ability to care for ourselves. Nature. Naturally. Embraces us. All lies stop being told when you no longer need to be told how to feel, and you are calm, in any world, and every mind. Exploring, and later dying. The child's soul never ripening. Let go of the expectation to think that you have to know.

<u>Put Away that Spear</u>

I think I understand why people become so defensive about what I am asking them to do. I have seen great anger. I now see why. I have asked people to give up the very fabrics and essences and disciplines that they believe that they have shaped themselves with. I am asking people to give up control and security. The very things that they gathered with in range of their limited vision that saw only out the front of their skulls, that they believed they must have and so have formed their entire characters around it. But, what we must all realize is that what building this control, security, and power makes us is not what we want to be. We do not want to be cruel, shallow, cowardly, angry, sharp, mean, etc., etc. We can choose to be something else. It is hard. It is so incredibly difficult and the road is long, but it can be done. We can live our dreams of kindness. No one really wants to hurt anyone else, not at their root. Your cruelty is normally because you are trying to not be afraid anymore.

I must go deeper. I am not free yet. But my glorious god...

Tolerating Want

Her journey was *her* own. *Her* state on High. The love *we* knew was like no other. But *she* didn't remember me. *(But she did. But he did not know. She had thoughts, memories of him.)* Even if *she* did remember, they are not the memories I have. *She* did not make *herself* remember. *She* could have, *she* knew how to, but *she* did not make the wrinkle deep enough. *She* did not grind it into *her* revolving brain. But even knowing that, that *she* is not as I want *her* to be, I know that *she* is more than I am. Than I was. *She* allowed me to stay, *she* never tried to kill me, because *she* knew what I would become. *She* knew that I was just gathering reasons to become it.

Holy is the mind that is lathered in Soul. Hard is the Man who has made Reasons.

<u>Slaves Believe Because They Think They Need To</u>

So long as you believe in good and evil, so long as words like coward, criminal, loser, junky, hero, so long as it is more or less to be anything, any label will be used to control you. Words, outside opinion, will make you act like you don't want to act. Like you shouldn't. And you will pursue a false image of what something is, instead of becoming something pure and real and honest. So long as you can't take the power from someone else and leave it to rot on the side of creation and not hold it yourself, then you will be a slave. Programming will be used and people will kill in the name of "something". You will. Every generation there is a war. Why? What words will be used to make you believe in it this time?

tHE eXISTENTIALIST wARRIOR, HE WHO HAS NO NEED FOR gLORY, has chosen the path of the solitary man. Forsaking the path of building an army. A single, uncredited man is more powerful and more effective than an identified army. It means the enemy is put in a defensive position, forced to defend their selfish fortresses with cameras, etc. Random crime is most effective against Darkness. Choosing Warriorship individually is, by the same creed as we, is most effective. However the enemy has countered this weakness by profiling and secretly collecting information on each of us. If Zarat does not build an army, or a secret society, or a religion, then no one will use my image to assume power and manipulation with. Any power that could have been had will be dead when I, the Noble Zarat, do not take it, or brag about it.

The First Amendment, written by the most Noble Thomas Jefferson exists because the Wise Man saw that the power seekers and the stupid would put us in this situation. Revolutions are led by 1% of the Population, three percent control 99% of the Population with brainwashing. Minds cleansed by a look and a general sense of worry. Power's ally is apathy, and doubt.

<u>Los Angeles</u>
The False Image

If our just cause is taken away, if our right to regulate and penalize each other on a meaningful basis is taken away people start to believe that they are untouchable. If you can't beat the living shit, or threaten with physical harm, a person that believes they can own you will become your master. The only solution to maintain a truly Free Society is a fully armed populace (at least with Krav Maga), not a fully armed policing unit that enforces the principals of the wealthy to maintain power for the few that control us. This is a solution, viable and true to our honest Bill of Rights. I don't give people crap and I don't tolerate people that give it to me. Best paraphrase John Wayne ever had written for him to say.
Los Angeles holds many images, most false. Never believe the image someone is using to try and prove to you that they are authorities. The Freemason's control the idea that all should have power, but them the most. When power is what we are reasoning against.
Watch how the beasts drive through traffic. Driving in the same patterns that mark the proof on their cars that show that they have already been in an accident, or five, driving the same exact way. They don't learn. They are a people who never have thought, who never had to figure anything out for themselves. They always had enough, or just enough money to pay someone else. And school is so desanitized that education is devoid of knowledge. A society bent to the whims of the loudest and maddest; therefore, the most deranged. The society of this tiny minded town of image wanters is controlled by those that need to believe they are so much better than they actually are they must assume power to prove that they are what they want everyone to think they are. Oh the Darkness. And this Darkness has way way more money than you, and you will become like them to please them to get money from them with your businesses that can provide for them...and the world will suffer on and on, just like it always has.

Are we what bothers us? Are we always bothered by what threatens us? Can we be bothered by less? Even by this gun in our mouths?

<u>I Serve No Man</u>

I love to show people that they are not untouchable. Those that have sought to control, have tried to convince those that serve the society that they are always safe. What this has done is made the cruel that serve Capitalism, or any system, those that are benefiting, think that they can do anything cruel to gain and enjoy and degrade. They never see the sledge hammer coming from the bringer of light.

I am so advanced in my meditation now that I can raise the Devil and calm the Devil. And be a God without fear. Loving or Devouring as only I please. And for you to never understand.

<u>Feminists.</u> Once a future feminist I was growing up with commented on how I look into anything with a reflection, her tone implying I was vain. The insecure imp never thinking that I did it because I was insecure. The common feminist will see every action as an attack against her, a move to belittle her, and she will hate you for it, male or female. This is what the movement has attracted. The frightened of being insignificant. Image seekers, like those that seek all organizations. So what's the point of starting an organization at all? There is Darkness in the minds of the weak.

<u>The Great Lesson: The Importance of Doubt</u>

If you doubt you will always be examining yourself, you will always be making yourself better. The trick is to doubt without the use of worry. Never believe that you are great and you will prosper, this is the nature of humility.
This is the advantage I have made by my mental circumstance. Independent mental architecture.

<u>Listen! Lesson.</u>

Over time I realized that I could sway the flow of conversations in an instant. At first it was happening suddenly, or at least I noticed it that way. As I would search through my "minds" by inflecting my energy inward I would reply in perhaps a different tone then the rest of the conversation was going. Like, when you run into someone you "know", sort of, maybe from work, maybe from school, just a "hi" and a pass, right? But what about the brief stop? The chit chat. They want you to greet them, be happy, make a joke...but say something real, maybe personal, maybe about how they shouldn't be together because they don't inspire each other, and suddenly the conversation turns...and if you are calm you can notice that at this instance there is a shift. You can feel the pressure in your chest, this is the chakra that greets people, your heart, your way of connecting is affected by the way that energy flows out of this point. When it is restricted you are in a state of hate, you hold your reactions back, you can feel this, yes? You might cross your arms across your chest, holding its reach back. Inside yourself. It's a feeling, nothing more. And when it is open, and flowing, coursing, like a flooded dam, and another tsunami strikes sharply into it and they become a solution...well, this is Love. Thus, open your heart, release its energy gently be vulnerable, and you will come to know what love is. Yes?

Relief

In the future of my writings I foresee that by the curing of Individuals perceptions about me, based on a series of works I will inevitably write about those of my forefathers for which I can see on this particular human plane fall from the great unending battle of Reasons, in a response to how I will portray them at death. How will I mark your existence? How will I make the people around you feel about what you were? In a sense they will take it as a type a judgment. Almost a sentencing. If you made bad cuts and grooves in your life to maintain or seek something with little honesty, it will be hard to see. But some I know. Some I have seen. Some will be kind. Those are the ones you will hear. Those are for whom I will feel something for. And of course, as fate would paint it, as I shall Feel as I shall Write. The speed of the release of the thoughts, I think, not even close to the potential. Soon we will only think it, and it will be. My book painted in hours. Don't doubt it. I think you're gonna see it. And thus...It will be a joy. And the melody I make in the reality of my brethren will play on. We are the Music Makers, ney, The Orchestrator of Creation!!!

(Unto, my undying Brother, Walt fricking Whitman) (We are but a Revolution, teaching us once more to read Him) (Coincidentally)

If he had lived beyond his life. In his next we would Feel Relief. The great windy movement of a soul that saw the greatest beauty in the world, and saw it torn and tortured and love him as it died at the end of his lips. He would be so God Damned Happy to be alive today and just be able to offer it to those as Free as he can be! Hyap!

<u>As I Burnt Him</u>

I preached forth the virtues of letting free his pride and his imagined image. I spoke to save him. I reached to touch his soul so that he could feel my presence and realize that he was that which I gripped. If only he could know. If only he could be free in his next reality.

I could have just written out my rage into this book. But I allowed it to burn. I allowed him to die. I allowed myself to love it. Every choice my bliss.

<u>Plus and Minus Equal Neutral</u>

Look to the Dark Society's art. It is always the disenchanted that control the arts. The arts are a nice way to keep the radicals distracted in the trap of self-righteousness. But look to the stories of the day. In this Dark Society the villain is always calm and confident. The delusional will always see calmness and confidence and be terrified by it. The weak will always be afraid. The slaves will always be unsure and neurotic. Even the radicals become slaves. We must break free from our normal mindsets. These normal mind sets that give us identity and comfort will keep us slaves forever. We must overcome our own general personality and condition. The cycle has formed a thousand times, society flows always in the same directions, and there is an art, a social science, that is so honed that it deals every vast movement of emotions. People are predictable. Overcome your peopleness.

Imagination Training
===

Zarat lays in the darkness. His pupils struggle to expand and grab the little light that seeps into the room from outside. Zarat's eyes see blackness seep away from darker shapes that can't be made out. He sees these shapes take definition. What are these shapes? They first take forms that can't be made out. They appear to be something else. A large beetle. With large fangs. His insides make notice and his stomach twitches a bit. It is not a bug. It's not logical. *Imagination training.* But still Zarat knows that he must feel comfortable with the large bug. He now can see that it is a standing lamp. He must eliminate the spasm of defense. Zarat must eliminate. He must fight his general mechanism. He knows there is peace beyond what controls him. Is this a technique, or must he find this goal through the meditation of "simply being." Can he overcome his fear by not caring about it? Yes. Of course. But is that the route he wants to take? Zarat can accept that it is a bug and not care what it will do to him and he can still keep the reflex to fight if it lunges at him, but would it be practical to fight back in the situation? After all, yogis and gurus and Buddhas have all naturally evolved into non-violence by pursuing the path of Being. There wouldn't be any reason to move. But...isn't moving what makes it fun? Must we not do to live? It makes life fun to live if you move away in an attack. And so, we must further live and destroy the attacker, because their life is as insignificant as Zarat's life. Sometimes, to fight is all that we can do. And there is nothing wrong with it. There comes a time when a peaceful born man must become war itself to stop the oppression of the people he loves. *Which, naturally, is everyone he hates for not becoming what they should have become. He hates them because they did not evolve and change themselves into something better. If they had, the darkness would have faded away. But they gave too far into weakness and compromised comfort. He hates them for making him war. But simply because he hates them, does not mean that he would not kill and die for them.*

Zarat's Parents

The last time I ever saw my parents they had been deceived by being convinced that it was alright to try and "catch me." A Freemason, a DEA agent and a lawyer sat to my right, claiming to be related to me. My father and mother, those that bred to try and recreate themselves, those victims and perpetrators of the Generation of Children, addicted to the mysteries of Law and Order, questioned me. Joined them. Them that wanted to have the satisfaction of judgment, the proof to damn me. And as they asked if I had done this deed, the Freemason, the DEA agent and the lawyer sat silently, waiting for what they expect to be my instant confession. Because that is what poor people and children do, instantly confess when accused, instantly convinced of authority. Fortunately, I had developed far beyond that recognition and had already identified what power is when it tries to seek satisfaction to fill its gluttony of self worth.

Naturally, I passed their little test. The nightmare, the threat, they made for me. It was at that moment that I learned that it didn't matter if they loved me or not, they would betray me, never doubting that love, tricked by the sensation of vengeance and reactionary programming that made persecutors of a Generation that fought hard for its Freedom, a Generation of Children, convinced again to think it was free, when it was used by those that would trick it.

Over the years that past, I would hear certain things of what happened to their minds in passing. They never believed that they were ever wrong, but most everyone else was. They wanted the validation of Love, but didn't understand that love cannot trap or betray, not by desire or by law. But the trick of law had beaten them. The evil of the self-righteous would be able to move beyond their sense and lust for "goodness" and would take what they would kill to keep for themselves. Their age brought them to see less and less goodness, to have less and less tolerance...to fail in their ideals.

It is my parents that taught me that in the end I must be far from this society. This that plots against us for satisfaction. I will die by the knowledge of a still tree, or near the calm depths of a deep blue lake. Things that could kill me, but weren't trying to kill me, weren't trying to prove they were right, lost to the illusions of the mind, not witnessing the simple thing of Freedom and my right to live. Nature never deliberately takes. And It is god. Man is not. When we came, we found nothing to Respect. We found children clamoring for the respect they weren't given. Respect they never deserved. Not that I didn't love them, but I would never see them again. Zarat is not a slave to satisfaction. It has been some time since I have thought of them...

well, at least about their Great Failure.

Leaving an "orphan" on this page. Get it?

<u>The Feeling of Image</u>

Staring at it. The channel in to the corporate theory of what the most of people Want to see. The television flickers with election coverage. "Hope" people shout. Not predicting the impending hatred they have for all that loom in a position of power. Because broken down from that symbol of stability is a mass of branching interests and seated men and women that always felt like they should be the ones that got to say what was right and make you wrong, if they need to prove themselves right. People base their thoughts on fleeting emotions. Looking now for anything that's real. But Life is all there is. Never realizing it, the Mass waits for the next illusion for them to lose hope to fade, as it won't truly touch them like they want--it still won't be able to make them feel like they really really matter. It is society's weakness. All of them wanting so much to believe that they are right that they actually believe it. And lost in the Glory of it all, they miss the Life they thought they were making. They are not the makers, but they think they are. They follow God, awaiting the second that they can damn It, if It goes against them. It is a Dark path the worship of Power.

The ladder shakes, and everyone is going to fall off again.

Parents Love You, Never Serve Them

"My father has never shown me any kind, gentle, openly loving affection. He's a mean dick that criticizes everything I do," boy.

"Parents put so much thought into you you cannot possibly comprehend. The amount of toil and pain that goes into creating a world for your mind to interpret in a certain way is phenomenal. However, where so many people get lost is that they think that they have a massive amount of godly influence over the kid's life. The kid makes decisions based upon what they think is to be the very best conclusion at the time, and the parent wants to make decisions for the kid based upon what they think is to be the very best conclusion at the time. The fight that comes out of this great show of love and respect between the two is caused by the ego. The ego is the root of fear and anger. It is the ego because both parties take the differing opinion in the living of reality as a personal attack against *her*self. The result is anger. Pointless anger. Destroyed lives. Lives of unnecessary complexity. All for love. Stop the illusions. Stop your blind and useless pride that brings you only pain and leads you away from the happiness you know you want to feel. Love your children. Love your parents. And most importantly, let life happen to each of them. And offer No servitude...it is you that chooses your noble heart that demands Freedom. Now get the fuck away from me. I told you the way it is, I don't need to wrestle with your mind and perpetual justifications that will keep you a slave to his perceptions, or the perceptions of anything that appears to have power over you."

<u>Monogamy</u>

Love is never the only reason for marriage. Love is everywhere. Abundant Love. Love is present when we aren't trying to matter or defend ourselves.

Monogamy is an almost prehistoric concept, based on superstition and slavery. I believe in responsible sex. I believe in protecting interests. In the modern age we have Science, we know what causes STDs and pregnancy, monogamy is an old answer to old problems. And I believe my soul has been around a long long time, and I have known a lot of souls. My love is boundless. And in this age, we connect with many of them. I can't deny the pull I have to a person, ancient and tested. And I am intelligent enough to pursue it, without loss coming to anyone. But my consideration is my advantage, that allows me to live like other people can't. To me, this is my one life as this person, with these advantages. How many lives until I see *her* again? I wouldn't waste the opportunity for real contact with one. ... To be honest. And Honesty is what they will receive. And if you were before me, I think you'd find it easy to be seduced by me. And it would feel natural and supernatural. And you could proceed without fear of loss, because I can think about it, and I know you could. And I know you could be free. It's your life and your moments, and the moments that others aren't involved in, aren't their moments. It's up to the true strength of a person to let the world be Free around them, but if someone wants only me, that can be their choice, but my choice is separate, so long as their Love is real, they will be Free to be as they choose, as we shall all be. Considering reality.

Salvation

You cannot escape to Salvation. There is no path without tragedy and effect and decay. This is our Universal process. This path you walk in thought is perilous. Though it can lead to a Bliss beyond comprehension at the end of thinking, because of what you have had to let go to walk it. As you travel, as you progress in yourself and move amongst the few people you will deeply affect, you will gain more and more bliss, while they will likely walk slightly different paths, or paths that they can't quite collapse and turn weightless and bring to an area where paths cross and a person can shoot out happily in any direction without the biases that stop Exploration, Joy, and Adventure. And these people that can no longer walk where you walk, and come up too slowly behind you as you rush forward, as you reach back at them smiling as you pull away, you struggle to tell them that you cannot possibly leave them, but will they believe you when you're not there, making them feel what they didn't realize they were making themselves feel. And when they cannot face something, or release something, and you feel what you've already expelled and moved on from in yourself, you will come to see them coming at you, wanting, loving, caring, and you may come to think that what is the point of bliss, if I am always destroyed by the pain people keep rolling in themselves, because they believe that they are only one thing. When in fact, they are only one defense mechanism, stuck running, when in fact they have many more defense mechanisms. And though bliss travels on and happy is wherever I am, the pain will always be seared in my the heart of my soul for the loves that could not walk free with me, or would not. There are many happy, blissful masters, with pasts of children and mothers that hate him, because they weren't strong enough, lucky enough, or wise enough to constantly rebuild the flume and ellipse of what the sensation is. But, so long as the root can return to love, and the action was a random, momentous situation of words and sensations and regurgitations, then I see the same person before me. As if time cannot change. Time stands still for the soul. Everything is always the same beauty I choose to Create, as my mind looks through the soul.

Eventually a master of himself stops needing to let so many things constantly go, or constantly bring themselves back up and back up from despair. We learned how simple is was to maintain. Because writing exists, you can know what it is like to know what it takes solitude to produce. The Secret Levitation of Mighty Energy.

<u>Professors and Intellectuals</u>

I fear, that if I succeed as the rogue Philosopher I will condemn the intellectuals that tried to teach me what they could not comprehend. But I thank the Middle Man, for trying. I could feel the path of it looming, coming, seeping from me, a feeling, which needed to be identified. Felt and looked at with the mind. And this energy build up was because of a line of thought in my mind, that wouldn't allow certain thoughts or differences to get by, divisions, sometimes it seems like every rung in the ladder is one. One. All I had to do was know the Truth of the Emotion, a sensation I know to not be associated with my Natural Calmness. And I saw why. Because they didn't realize that I was better than them. It is a pathway to a supremacist mindset, even if I never asserted my worth in front of them. I could have proved it more, but knew they had no real award to give me. They did not have what I sought. I attended college to aspire, but found nothing so great as I was convinced there should have been. How could so much time pass in a country that had so great a Philosophy as Freedom behind it become so suddenly damning, betraying, and hypocritical on the social level. I came to see that for most people their psyches were unstable, built on branches, branches with rich soil that the tree was prepared in, constantly feeding it while the tree grows, unaware, it's consciousness carried, traveling at the tips of the branches, believing it's mind propels it, while other branches from itself, and other trees grow all around it. We just have to pull our consciousness back to the trunk. We just need to know we can. This is the Psychological Revolution. Self Resolution, because Calmness is True.

<u>The Offended</u>

Offense is the burden of the offended. There is a deep blackened shadow that has draped across the society of the Free, and turned it Dark. The society has come to appease the screaming, the crying, those that cannot handle or accept the world as it is, those without the intelligence to reason a solution to be at ease with. It trails back to the beginning of their lives, when they were satiated as children. It became their unaware adult reality when they needed their children to please them, and the cookie was given. The catering to the complainers, the wanters, the takers, the oppressors, has veiled the right intentions of a once noble idea. The weak complaining first against the Free, against sex, free speech, logic and inspiration, taking away our right to perform, to spread and to exist. The strong must come and not care about the irrelevancy of the tyrant, the victim, the fool without satisfaction. Until the mentality is corrected the court systems will remain a used up joke, and "judges" will be slaves to the burdens of the weak and eternally whining and suffering, and we will not be a strong society again. But that doesn't mean that Zarat cannot be strong. Zarat is immune to the irrelevancy of what tries to reason with him, to serve it. Zarat is Free. And serves nothing, but the Truth, as he has interpreted as I have experienced.

Honest Reflection

We are not our reflection. Do not see yourself as others see you, as their personalities reflect what they think you are, for whatever reason they are happy that you please them. Look inward, and see for yourself, be unconcerned with the eyes of others. But see yourself with vicious honesty, do not apply a positive illusion along side another illusion.

<u>Their Mind's Are Our Minds</u>

I can see High Schoolers killing people and then themselves. They think that it seems like they can't get out. But the College kids. I mean sure you can, but you won't have learned anything, and you'll have to go through it again, and it might even get harder...

Oh, you Bastards. Don't you see what the shit we're saying, "We don't want to make up Reasons to do things. This is the retardation of society. This that you think so important is driving us mad. In old societies when speech was repressed there was only a few voices in people's heads telling them what to think and consider. But now there are many. The society of Free Speech will have many contradictions. That's the experiment. So, we don't want to have to make up reasons so that a psychotic can feel comfortable, because he always has to feel comfortable, and when everyone is like that...We want to be able to exist. We can trust in our good natures. Stop fucking staring at me, and everyone. Let me be Free from your mind. This is the Dawning of the Age of Compassion. The war against True Cowardice. A Battle that will draw no blood and will Free many minds and open a chain of Holy Souls, without our fear."

Will draw no further blood...

One man's hero is another man's murderer. In the end there is the life and no opinion of it. There is only what was lived, and the arrogance of man's presuming judgment is dead. Life is more great than what foolish man thinks it can or should be.

<u>Shattered and Uncut</u>

Life hits hard and fast, and you have little time to react and deal with it, or you're dead. Wealth at least gives you the time to face things healthily, like we used to, before wealth existed. You (you) face things quick and build shoddy defenses. You are afraid and throw your mind together with whatever stick you find. And you believe in the defense of those sticks. They keep you as safe as you believe they will. But the truth is, is that this is not who you are. And it can break. And you will still be easily standing there. And you won't have to spend your life maintaining it. We broke it a long time ago, and we are not afraid to lose it anymore. We pray for your downfall, so that you'll give up on this stubbornness and let us all be human again.
There was a point when you felt helpless, and you reacted, since you have clung to that tiny moment when you felt power and not afraid. When you felt control. Stop it. You tyrant junky. Ruining the world with your business, your parenting, your breath. We wait for you to stop panting and be calm, and unafraid, we are trying to show you how. Your war is lost, violent and fruitless. We will share our bounty with you, and we do not ask for your debt or servitude.
Fools see us rude and destructive. We will Liberate you from such thoughts in the instant we can. It will strike and crash through, our hand extended, as what we've said has finally deeply offended you and now you can see that your reasons are lies covering something you don't want anyone to point out. And as you abandon all thoughts, maybe you'll be able to hear the wisdom of a silent tree. Perhaps you will make a friend with someone besides yourself.

He is rising. Rising from the murderer he has been. Being as self affirming as anyone can be. But to gain nothing. Nobility without Supremacy. This is our Great Prince Zarat.

Cruel and Unusual

Up in the wee hours, once again, yawning, and in need of easing the thoughts that won't stop coming. Suffering, because my heart so loves a Free World...

I have killed. And so have many. The life of a fish is equal to the life of any human, and the life of the bug, and the life of your daughter. This does not mean that we should not eat animals, or take their lives. This is the irrational fear based view of animal rights groups. It denies the circumstance of reality, because they don't have the courage to accept it. It is only their fear of death being reflected in their way that they believe is important, and that makes them feel important and thus, empowered. Same old simplicity as all beliefs, and every side. What it means is that death occurs. And people need to start accepting that. Trying to stay alive is fine, but turning it into a psychological disorder of oppression and control is not fine. If all life is equal and life ends, and no life ever out weighs another no matter the mind or physical power level or level of decadence and detachment alters the state of equality, and not even being alive or dead increases or decreases this value, then this means that the societal penalty for an organic being dying should be far less than what it is. It is not rare, it is not appalling. It is a false taboo, this so called "last taboo", kept to keep some control on the side of the controllers. Sometimes, organic things kill organic things, and it is nearly always circumstantial, mentally or physically. It is more important to ease the impulse, like the controllers must do with control. If there was less fear of it, people, like serial killers or politicians, would not choose it as a path because it would be far less powerful. By running away from death, the Dark Society has deified it. When it is much more simple. Imagery is a trap that should be surpassed by the student. The fear of Pain has made the society mad and cruel and vengeful for naturally occurring events. This society that wants to see itself as good, no matter what it is doing and so believes it serves a god that will reward it, has defied all connection with true spirituality and thus what Nature, the Planet, defined as god to man millennia ago. And every time man has cut himself off from Nature, he has become thus. Lives spent denying death. Lives now turned to sand. Souls stripped of their illusion, and cast Free into the evidence the Existentialist have proven. And it was the Hero Thomas Jefferson that enabled Us to fight Pride and Power that his lifetime saw widdling and covering his dream of Freedom away. He knew the religious would use the tools of Darkness to justify themselves of gods, and they made it as simple as believing in it.

We bleed for the task to convince everyone that they are wrong. Our allies can only be Individuals. And our victories can only be without praise.

<u>The Utter Blindness of Complete Darkness</u>

A Society burdened by their own selfish thoughts. A Society that believes we are naturally like them. Weak. I have no compassion for them because they will not try to stop their want. Suffering is their choice. *They will always defend the weaknesses they don't want, instead of destroying the fragility of themselves to cure them...*

I could easily reach into peace. I could take my loneliness and allow it to mean nothing. People are not social creatures. That is a lie crated by ignorant idiots that believed it. The only reason "people" go crazy on remote islands, or in prisons, or any other isolation, like adolescence, is because people are addicted to the stimulation of the mind. They want to interact and judge and condemn because they think that that is human. But it is not. It does not have to be. It is a curse of the Darkness. Society always becomes ignorant as its greed to have and be satisfied and be distracted from impending doom is satiated. To not need to be amused, all one has to do is stop seeking constant gratification. Stop. Stop. Stop the mind from needing. It is simple and calm to survive on an island without criticism, without the fearful commanding you off of the cliff of fear, or taking everything you have so that they might have one more ounce of security.

<u>Free Market</u>

There is so much to tell you. It exhausts us. It makes sense, huh? You'd believe anything that made sense. Bound to be a slave that way. Never having the guts to figure it out on your own.

The US rose viciously from the blood of the Savage, our Fathers that still have an influence in meaning in the lore's of this country. The Great Problem for this New Western World though was really all too simple. The "americans" always believed in the power and prize of the power that the British imagined as a "monetary" system. It let those that had power spread in a place that had no money. Capitalism moves like that. Bound to eventually use up the world, by too much equality, too many people not needing to take shit jobs. This is their fear. This is what they have known for some time. The system can fail this way, their power could become meaningless. This is true. Who will serve as the slaves? Currently they use the young. But they may remain Free to make their valuable meaning. But the true reason it will fail is that those that will maintain it will become less and less, and the system will become more and more burdened. Because we can foresee we don't need to pretend it's not happening, it means that we can do something about it. As technology catches up to us, can we let go of boundaries, can we be vulnerable, and will no one go mad? when we do it? Can a world be sustained? All of it? Not just humans, not even close. Can we care for the planet? Does the One society, dawn to live on earth, once more??
So simply we have a chance to be Free. Completely. And ironically, the majority of us are going to do it 100% independently and intertwined with everyone. Free Market.

<u>Right in the Middle</u>

In the US, all people, even the powerful, have a nonchalant reaction to shrug off criticism for what they do. All people have an air of shame and a sense that all people should change so that they measure up completely. It is a criticizing culture. One that has been whipped into a fervent warping by a society that demands winning without experience, and if you don't you will starve and people will let you. Because in America it is your fault that you have not prospered. And you are nothing for it. Life is valueless. And when people that would do this hear this they feel a sense of weakness and slight pressure in their upper belly that they imagine to be nausea, because they don't know what it is. And they think that I am criticizing them, and they will rebel and do more what they want, more selfishly. But away from eyes, where they are the real bastards they are. Away from the criticism they use to prove that they are the one's that matter. A society where you need to be something, god dammit anything, so long as it's successful. So long as it gains money. And if you don't use the sin of Pride, no one will respect you, and you will fail. And they will again not feed you while you are not working for them. And the police enforce it, under words that have no meaning, because if they did, the police wouldn't exist. And if they didn't the controllers, the middle upper class, would enslave us all, because they deserve to, and this is because of the state of mind, the need to power, just to live. The only way to cure fervent madness is to calm it. And medication has never made this type better, and cannot. It must be calmed. And people must be taught again where to see life, and the importance of being directly invested in it, and so, they will learn to have no fear of death. And thus, they will stop trying so hard to survive, and the system must and can provide for the people. Or, it really has violated our Social Contract. You are not the best, you deserve nothing, and no one has to do anything you think but you.

(And I search my ind for the *m* that is all that I can remember of the picture of the thought that I created to try and save humanity. I guess I solved that time eating mystery.)

The Fool's Society

Restricting anything, especially sex and offense, only makes it more enjoyable.

It's like people aren't even able to see the results of their actions.

People portray themselves as correct. Experts. Infallible. Watch TV.
The Image Society. Ingenuine. Read a paper. People are not perfect.
A wise person understands that and can't be so false and projecting.
Doubt the experts. Doubt the people of the strongest opinion. Their
perfection and professional image is how you know they are fake.

Again and again, refusing to evolve. I guess that's just the course of
evolution. It's slow. We've made ground. Afterall, We Exist. Here.
Together. Right now. What a chance.

Manifest.

Job Application Answer

Greatest Detriment
"My problem is I eventually stop caring about my great performance
and the sham of pleasing people I would never ever talk to in my life
just to get enough money to eat and live."

Oh? Honesty isn't what they want. Why don't they teach us that?

Greatest Attribute:
"When I perform my greatest Detriment the result is based on the style
in which I portray it as a new conclusion to what you have concluded;
as in, we feel united in knowing that we can all be ourselves more, and
the tension of holding up a false façade is lessened. I usually quit soon
after, but I will leave you refreshed."

<u>If You Read this You Will Be Cursed and Feel a Sensation which Can be Exploited to Make You Commit an Action, like Forwarding, or Buying, or Believing</u>

Hey. Psst. Come here. Oh, you are here. Present. Reading this page. I never thought you'd make it. So far in. Or did you just open randomly? Who cares. You are here. Present. Don't be an idiot, I know I said it already. Oh, you didn't think that? Screw that type of personal placement too. Stop placing yourself equal, less, or more than people. No matter what your car looks like, you just won't have enough money for a new face. And you'll resent....Grr...Listen. You're here, and that's what counts.

So here:

On the path that points to Nothing that which lies just beneath your defenses, and reveals your equality as you wish to not judge another person for being exactly like yourself, where hypocrisy heals, there you will encounter pathways to your own noticeable destruction, set by a system of your constantly enabling yourself to get a key set of desires, like money, power, pussy. Or anything that can make a person feel they are betrayed by not having all of it or keeping it all away from other people, the sense of having looms. If a person does not occupy the lives of others that are Free from attachment and gripping what they don't want to lose, then the path will destruct, but nothing will change. That's the trick. Your perceptions are not the basis of reality. We reach beyond perceptions and make our minds free of the need to form them to convince ourselves we are something. We are fine with being nothing. And clearly, page upon page that you could stumble upon in this simple one line riddle....Nothing yields Every path, without hatred, want or peril, but a coming death that we do not fear. Minds are Free if we don't have to keep pushing to believe in ourselves.

I see a Generation, small as it may be, that believes in Universal Freedom without Power. The Final Utopia. The Explanation that never rested. The mind that kept touching Holy Spirits.
A Generation Free from giving everything everyone demands, but able to understand function, and to not be trapped by the limits of man's immortality. Warriors calmly bringing calmness, fighting without identity until the transfer of Existence.

<u>Free to Be Exposed</u>

Without the need to keep himself secret and safe, Zarat was free to seduce once more. For the glory of the sensation of his orgasmic annihilation. For the pleasure of Zarat. I want her, and she will resign to the heat of my flesh, and the girth of my love.

"I love you," flower.
ZARAT: "I love you too." He notices that at this exact time he looks at a clock. Zarat runs from something. From the vow of love. From the promise. He knows the pain of promises. Every man he promised to die for abandoned him. All those that were to fight the Great War. Vanished into the ease of society and weakness. Every woman he promised to live for betrayed his promise to love. Zarat has looked away a hundred times in moments of feeling. He loves her. Zarat knows he loves her. But the mighty Zarat is tempered into cowardice. He has been gentled by the pain he knows. He is his flower. Sweet and Beautiful. Always kind and always for others. But Zarat is slightly damaged. Deaths he's seen, friendships destroyed, kindness misperceived, friends he could not save from the ego. Pains. He must be with *her*. Be with *her*. Be. Be only in the joy of touching *her*. Exist without the lies of the exaggerating mind. He cannot be trapped by the past or the fears of future. He is not so weak. Zarat is not a coward. His human reactions to defend himself from pain triggered the fear. It is no longer needed.

Zarat lays her down on the futon bed. He eases against her warmth. He raises his head and stares into her eyes. He kisses her lips. And he ravages or juicy pleasure, until his exhaustion collapses him on the freshly stained bed.

Our egos hurt us and cause us to hurt others. Hear the annoyance in your voice when someone doesn't understand. Feel the pain it causes you when that tone comes out of someone else and covers you in wavering sadness. See the disease everywhere. In every facet of every side so arrogant that it fought its way to the top. See it in the anger provoked by critics and haters, watch the critics seek out reactionary negativity. See the Darkness battling back and forth, wanting to be justified, wanting everyone to love and adore the ideas made by the individual. See the ego devour love and peace and prosperity. Like an engorged snake, fat and sick and hungry.

<u>Calm Illusory Reality</u>

I wonder where *she* is. Is *she* still trapped within The Father? Is he the one that gets to keep *her*? When I hear *her*, is it *her*? Am I mad, from the anxiety inherent in the stress of vengeance? Shouldn't I be sane by now, it's been almost 8 months. I'm sure the hunt of the supremacists led them nowhere. I cannot say. I am only able to try and calm the doubt, and let *her* come and go within me. As, many now seem to do. The more I have released my grip on needing this world to be rational, the more my spirit has consumed my nature, and the more I can feel those around me, alive and dead, pulsing with the energy of existence. Again, into my waking dreams.

Am I Threatening Me

Like all paths of Greatness, when a man must overcome all opinions to set all men Free again, there will be peril. The snowy cliff, the descent into madness. The moment where you are laughing and defying yourself. Laughing and ruining your chances. Because if someone else can reason it, so can we. We who are what was necessary to save it all once more. To end having and free man from men. We do it with what man has provided us. If they work towards freedom and equality and the system is slightly tame, and there is Free Speech, than we return us again to nature without violence. If we are able to reason, then we will find the best ones to help. But men can turn on men. As us upon ourselves. I have seen those who cut themselves to defy that this body is weak. I have seen it build strength in them if they do not lose hope. If they learn that they do not need it. And if they learn that the voices of all reasons are constantly around them and within them, which really means they can reason back with reasons supported by the continuing existence of the un-judgeable soul. And this body is a portal, and this mind is a portal, to existing as a human or any living thing for a time, where our power means nothing. And always, in our great plight of Reason and Freedom do we have the option to know silence, and to be free from all reason and need for freedom. We can always look to the soul and see Freedom as a truth, with a rejection of all religions that used a Heaven and a Hell to control the Free Soul for the power of nations, and we can begin to move on from the zionism that continually causes wars. It Is Not Real. Your soul cannot be greater than any other human's.
... And that can set our minds to peace.

***

When I read about the Mirror Dream I truly understood a system of actions that masked her inner fear of her own mind. I knew how hard she melded herself to be what she wanted her parents to be. And I knew she was young when it came. Her burden was great. And what she did with it, was Noble. And the blast of her impact echoes in me still. Reminding me of gentle love that bursts out laughing.

The Earth is an organism with a lifespan far greater than Man's. Man will never conquer the Earth because man's resources come from the Earth. The more Man uses the Earth, the more the Earth will defend itself, the more it will turn it back to a calm and quiet Earth. We are organisms upon a lifeform. Born from the Earth itself. It does not cost the Earth anything to destroy. It loses nothing. It regenerates. It can and has destroyed many "great" civilizations. I still hear the Earth, and I know she is on my side. The World of Man is far too fake. People are not able to see the Darkness in the false images they want to be. And money is warping the delusion further. But no matter. Man will never see it coming. Because Man wants to be great.

<u>Manifesters</u>

Be positive. Take some time...and try to be more positive. Try to not doubt. Try to only believe. Have a light heart. Let yourself not be afraid. Do not fear what might happen. There is no need for doubt. Believe.

Safety is an illusion that can never exist.

The understanding of what we can and cannot understand all at once can knock you down. The eruption of random understanding of your own insignificance can make you laugh like a happy god must laugh. It is the echo of absolute knownsense *(knowledge that makes no sense. or. it is beyond the mind's comprehension)*.

When I type I leave out entire words. The whole sentence makes sense, except for one perfect blank. *Who was that?*

<u>Birth Givers</u>

It did not take long before I had to leave my family behind. I loved them, naturally. But they were wanters. Ones that desired. Ones that wanted to own and hang on. They wanted to be right so I could not tell them otherwise. They wanted their failing path, which they had no true faith in, to be the proper way. Want is the way of suffering, and they had to choose to stop wanting to end their suffering. I could not let their want create suffering for me. They could not understand. They had to want nothing to have me. Expect nothing, and appreciate every drop they received, never wanting more. But alas, want is the way of suffering. The path of want is seen blatantly as any wanter comes closer to the end of a life cycle. They cling on to life, wanting it to never end, and they suffer more and more and more, living longer than the fearless that learned to be satisfied with anything. Because the Dark Society is thoroughly soaked to the brim with wanters, true people generally wind up alone. I was lucky to truly love the few times I did. Because I saw simply, I cherished what was genuine, without wanting to make it perfect to please myself. And that makes love blossom.

Zarat looked into her eyes, and eyes grew to stare directly into who she did not even know she had been, but the look made her gasp at her her nudity.
"My ego runs over my spirit. My ego is sexually based. But when I calm the ego in meditation, and I look at my spirit, and I feel my truest intentions...I won't ever do anything to truly harm your situation. We're just a couple of awesome people playing grown-up games." Taking away from the want of his own hand. And still, unarmed, he may eat of the fruit. And it will taste as fruit tastes. Organic.

A true philosopher, devoted to the Way, will make a temple anywhere he can. It may be a bathroom. It may be a forest. Maybe a foxhole. **I mention that deliberately. Be Brave.** Enveloped within the flesh of a woman. We are always with stillness. With being. Even in violence. We always focus on the ultimate peace. Even if we are distracted, we work our way fiercely back to it. Until we have the peace forever and for always.

There was a Quiet Back and Forth

I'm real. You asshole. While you think about cowering or posing, I am standing, doing nothing, and wondering why you are the type of paranoid bird you are. I'm human. Rationalizing. Undisregardable. Because it happened. A quake against all power.

What is it like to be near me? A man too aware of mortality. Calming, if you know that you will only show me love and never give me a reason to flare my terrifying myth of your confronted and tormented imagination. People try to avoid the questions that could too easily tear a simple world apart. Too simply. People feel bad as their impulses, their groins, their deserving ability to feel love in the equal soul of all folded gripping flesh easily pulls them to the care free and non-defining throbbing of not needing to be anything, but living. And to unite with it, like a lover and like a shell, and like a pressure that folds with little application, is sex.
A woman wants to be special. She'll wield you to confess it to her. From the beginning that her eyes want you. Her guilt defined by how much she wants to pull on you. Her fear that she holds you back, because she is the foundation of something now larger. When the foundation was building the connection was there. A woman, yep, like the reoccurring curse, I mean *beloved*, that I can think anything about without fear of a risk of a damning opinion, like a Free man. *She* knew *she* could not maintain it. I think. Or at least *she* thought it and carried it, adding it to the sensation that was the majesty of *her* ability to resonate from the truth of the blood of the Universe.
Too many people reach out, trying to matter, trying to feel. Until they find enough to get by. But the Existentialist hears a thousand characters. "Individuals", and they are. All of them the same. The same to Love. Wanting the same equal feeling. And resenting how over time they don't own it. Because someone else is owning it. Trying to keep it. Bound by love. While the Existentialist loves equally. Sad and violent only when feeling UnFree. In Everyone, yet experiencing unique love with all connectable and rare people. *She* wanted me. Wanted to keep me. *She* loved me and struggled to release me. And left me to keep Free. *She* didn't want to feel it but had to feel with the conditions of a reacting human mind, so *she* did. And *she* worked to overcome it, and to release the guilt that was triggered by it. To maintain the idea that *she* did not have to become what *she* did not want to be. *(And if the Market is unfair, and fabricated, based on increasing the value of*

197

what decreases in value in the idea to profit over the youth, like REAL ESTATE, then a generation can crush it by not being enslaved by it. The more diversity in a society the more ways there are to survive and the more chances there are to constantly free ourselves.) To die like that, like *she* always dreamed. With the mind, before it would become afraid, clinging, doubting of what it is portraying, worrying about falseness... Die young, before *her* ego would fight, before *she* had to live with the societal guilt of random effective circumstance. Before the ego would fight and trick, before it had anything to viciously protect. To keep the Philosophy pure.

I suspect *she* would have overcome it with a justified grace. A thing I can see playing out, now that I am slightly down the road. *Her* fate, perhaps not as driven into the ground as we thought. Maybe it was a simple agreement we could have made with the Dark Society, guilty for surviving, maybe we only had to not Kill them, and not Steal from them. Maybe the actions were enough. And we just could have reasoned with them. As the frustrated assume the seats of the old power we see dying before us, a secret societal cheer rising as we watch the great system of a check followed by a balance.

The current of the mind carries us into actions. These actions are definers that cowards will label to attempt to failingly stop you, too afraid to think further than locking you up, because drawing a line is easy to do. But is it agreeable. The penalty is not, but what about the question? The greatest revolution in criminal history was taking away crime and dissolving the need for police. So long as drugs are regulated and with unbiased Surgeon General warnings. And meth remains illegal and considered poisoning, than the Utopia can be Manifested, again and again, at the end of every series of furious thoughts, recreating again, that mighty sensation I know to be my very self. And free is the ability to fuck hard and love encompassingly. If you are going to live, as they say, "I recommend fucking." And tearing free from chains, and continuing to love as furiously as ever the women that seek to bind you, equally loving the way we know we matter.

Don't give up. Stop reaching. Stop worrying about the final reaction, unless you are affected by the media or are now part of it, because hatred will always force you to be what you hate, because the same types of minds (someone called something a name and people joined it) break off to battle each other because they can all understand each other and can directly communicate in which ways they are competing, until your children or someone else's children come along to hate you and every idea you had that appeared to be contrary to what was present before you, but that was just your motivation to obtain the same fat and only fat ass that is a long living, well fed, society. Living is fact. Don't let a Philosopher make you feel guilty. Break Free. Read It. Put It On The Shelf.

Who do I read? If I thought thoughts that were other peoples and my own, I'd melt. But I've read a few pages of a lot of folks and get the idea that a writer knows in a minute, but a reader reads a whole series of books to pretend to know later with other people that didn't know either. And they are free to pursue happiness.

When any Great Man raises Great Men to raise Great Emotions that imbue noble action the middle aged enforcers of a Free Society may look to see if the organization is led by someone who realizes that inspiration and movements must be subdued and leveled, or else young humans go into frenzies and seek the first instincts they very incorrectly identify as their actual selves. Violence will always label power. So to convince the noble view of the police, the "protectors" of life, in this most prized view, we unify all sides as we realize early where the war began.

<u>Unckle</u>

"I walked into a thousand houses, guts sprayed across the room, a gun hanging around the index finger...,...that red...the M.A.S.H. record scratching on the turntable, that stink that rot yields in the first few hours of a another guy that couldn't take it to the end and do what he could for those he truthfully loved, and who cares if they knew he was doing it. But still there's nothing wrong with suicide. Nothing. But it ain't tough. The longer I live the more my spirit learns, but then, if one life might go by where I learned so much because I gained the ability to think into a story of living so greatly that I learned a huge amount quickly, I might knock off a bit early," Samu<u>a</u>l. An Enforcer.

A cop, an enforcer, he hated him, but he left an impact in the boy Zarat. He loved him. But fuck him. Can you think anything yourself?

<u>Wine Walk</u>

Today I was confronted by a group of middle-aged women, looking older than they were. They were angry I was stepping on a broken glass. This cheap glass fell onto the ground and shattered after we walked through the suedo-art district of this cesspool, designed to please and milk the wealthy that seek only their own pleasure. These animals quickly grouped together, other beasts quickly rallied until there was a collection of about five of them. Angry. "There are children playing around here," they said. They had no concern for my joy of the sound of smashing glass. If I had told them I was Greek and it was centuries of tradition after drinking I could have easily disarmed them. But I wanted them to suffer in their anger and futility. In their sick want. Trying to force me with their parental cruelty. It was my town before these people that seek satisfaction came. A younger one even approached me and flashed a fake badge, not realizing I had a real badge in my pocket, saying that she was an off duty officer and I had to clean it up. Meanwhile the anger grew and festered in the old and secure, so upset and intolerant of me disturbing their illusion of cleanliness and safety. I told the fake cop whore that I would clean it up. I didn't of course. The old oppressors, so sure that their lies and their cruel caring would make the world better, so sure their anger was justified, not realizing that they didn't know what else to think...they left angry, programmed to clean by the cocks that rode them. I am sure they griped to their captured men about the child that wouldn't clean for them at command. All I had to do to save them was give them a different Reason. Another illusion that they could enforce or accept. I did not want to help them, the ignorant. The cruel that believe they are good, that believe they must forcibly save everyone. Never realizing none of us need saving. Everyone is Free, if it just wasn't for them, the parental, the controllers. What a waste of a life. What sadness and cruelty they reap. Ignorant in their righteousness. A life of fear and struggle. It's enjoyable if you know the truth, but they don't. And it is easy to torture the weak. They wanted to ruin my joy, but made themselves suffer for it. All because they have to believe in the Reasons that someone else has already planted in their head. And if they believe it, they must enforce it, justify it, and imprison anyone who doesn't join the programmed narrowness of the mob.

The master always has the choice to use his skills. He can let anyone think anything they want about him. Always free, no matter what.

<u>We Are Not Our Jobs</u>

You don't have to get to know people. We are all the same. Get to know what you truly want. (At this point they want to trick you, entice you, get you to wonder, to search, to feel what it is exactly, without predefinition.) Gain the ability to be present. Truly alive and aware that you are touching it, and it is life, Existence. And holy cow, we're living it. And if you kick it, it breaks, or so the kicker breaks. It is all breaking. Gone already. Imagined in a second of interpretation, and then you died and it was all gone. And you'll be fine with it. If you go a wondering.

Management breaking:
Every Manager I have known has only wanted to connect with the people they have had to control to meet a goal. The manager is the person that has been there the longest. The person that was not strong enough to break from the herd. A person that believes they went through the channels and earned their society. And their ability lies only on what they can logically think is best. And a manager needs employees that will say when the chosen path might have too many weeds on it. He needs someone that will grab a shovel and start to clear those weeds. To see if there is a path to follow. And you may work for these people. Relax their belief in their need for power. Ease them by accepting their goal. And soon, you will not need them. But you will have gained something from them. And always in the Great Society, we can move on. And know another style. Always with the ability to learn any of the 10-15 things a manager thinks it has to enforce. The goals are easy, the lazy just think it was hard and needs to be taught. Don't let a manager manage you, but work with them, knowing there are millions out there, and this one is abandonable if tyrannical. I see three types of people lining up into a conversation. The people that think they are better, the people that think they are less, and the people unaffected by the weakness of either. The Existentialist is going to change the outcome of your reality. Welcome him, he will ease the burden of your lie, your place, and leave you in the wake of your commonality. Everyone children beaten with the few things that our parents thought would kill us, as to keep us safe.
As you break away. As you gain the little you need to move forward with dreams and routes and manifestations, to manage your self and reach your simple goal, your simple socialization, which can now be done in an anti-social way via the network…and you defy the nature

of becoming the person that needs the verification of their power by having people beneath them, and you will become and you will set people Free.

As always, the answer in brilliance will lie in the most unlikely source, so that those that can the most will seek it out and find it, and be it, while those that sat and assumed the image of what people that came before and manifested and became had made. Truth revolves again, away from power, and away from the false making fun of the false to tell us they are not false, this comes just before we appear again.

The Children of Zeus. Manifesting Utopia. With no faith in Power. Death is the proof of its futility.

<u>It's ALL in Your Head</u>

The burden of my genius is the burden of many rebels who have ran in the fields to be free from the tyrants that would ride us so they do not have to walk. The burden develops over time and conditioning, and the base of my initial experiences. The burden was set when I was born into my family, and I had to develop a way to matter. A defense. A pattern of functioning to prove my advantage. If only they knew of Equality, instead of glorification. If only I did not have to matter. At least it can be surpassed. At least I don't matter now. But still the burden functions, a mechanism to best keep the body alive, an ego. Luckily I can see what it is, and I don't have to believe in it, or else I'd be trapped to continue having it forever.

My thoughts have the ability to see all oncoming arguments. To predict them. To know them. Since I can think of them and see all areas of attack, my mind is always spinning, constantly diving deeper to understand. I am always fighting myself. And all because I was designed to by my initial family. Always worried about the criticism that might come. All because of the criticizing society. Jokes, sarcasm and intolerance. The Reactionaries. It is not wrong. Wrong does not exist. I know it. I must know it to understand. To know that there can be results if people believe that they must not be the identity they are now because of this initial mocking programming.

<u>Those I Know</u>

There is proof that we are not alone. I am thankful that the Great Ones who wrote and wrote and that we could talk a hundred or seven thousand years later. My lovers.

As the system of Capitalism is designed now...it is the right and function of the poor to steal from the rich, and those that have used power. It is the only way that the poor can prosper. They do not have the credit or initial funding it takes to get loans and additional credit. It is the only resource that the system has offered the poor. The poor must fight the rich if they want to be free. The system was designed to protect that three percent that control the wealth of the world. Since the system was designed and the Federal Reserve gained control of the banks to control money, few have gained wealth. And it is not from lack of trying.

<u>Fight Against the Reactions of Satisfaction</u>

I sat in the bathtub and let the sounds of the water drown out the sounds of distraction. Water strikes so violently and randomly, but it never comes across as noise. It is peaceful. The warmth soothes me and brings me into a trance, a place inside that the initiated have visited again and again.

It seems that we try to focus our consciousness through our eyes. We identify ourselves with our face. What if we move our consciousness to another point in our body? What if we move it out of our body? Try to close your eyes and not see the darkness behind your eyes. If we are not this body, then we do not need the eyes.

I focused on the mid-section of my body. The belly. I felt a burst of energy. It surged through my body. I was filled with joy. Zarat is happy.

In meditation I always felt a warmth in the belly.

In the Dark Society people think that they when they reach a certain age they are grown. There is nothing that they want to change. They are who they are and anyone who criticizes them is a fool and provokes anger and defense in them. In the Enlightened Society we know that we are always children. We are always learning. And we can make ourselves better for the whole of our lives. The universe *(beyond and amongst)* is our teacher.

<u>Freedom of Speech</u>

If not for the written language many more would have fallen in this Holy Revolution. Many more would lay before the bloodied feet of conquering. My sword would sing with the hymn of Sorrow. But thank Thomas Jefferson who realized the absolute importance of Free Speech. The written writing of the writer of the People allows the majesty to dim, the lie to fade, and lets truth seep up from the fertility of the giving soil.

This thriving society of spit, welling up from the Dark Ages, where we lost everything because of the laws of the British, of whom took over the U.S. with the same Reasons, has no way to test for the intelligence a Man can produce. It only has ways to develop what a man can take in and spit out, only what programming and conditioning yields. They find the smartest slaves for themselves. And with the funding all coming from that same British source, we only make them more powerful than ourselves. ... ...
Don't want to think about it do you??

We came out to venture out into the mind to see what everyone was afraid of.
We have been far and we return with knowledge, so that you don't have to be afraid to think anymore.

<u>Remember</u>

People will make allowances for you if they barely know you. If they see that you are like them, they will eventually hate you. It's why you hate people you know. It's why your family tries to catch you and keep respect from you.

Break the code. It's simple. Apes.

<u>The Miracle Dream Machine</u>

Most people cannot think on the macro scale. That is the true sign of intelligence. How far out and inwards can you comprehend? And how willing are you to give up all of this useless knowledge so that you can actually understand what we are talking about? This society began the chain of the fear of death once it came to realize that death meant stopping. There are groups throughout the society that aim to perpetuate their lives by all means necessary. They spread from larger cities attempting to assume the most visible opinion. To accumulate the most command. And the newly acquired poor will happily work for them.

Can I prosper if I got rid of my rebel views, if I learned to not want to wipe out anyone that attempted to take Freedom from me? Are we destined to give up a little of ourselves for the greater good? No. It cannot be enforced. It cannot be policed. It must be Free. I don't give a shit about the people yelling at me to please them. The Darkness has now lost its power, as the OverMan emerges. What are they going to do? Kill me? Hahahahahahaha! I will only return again. In an even better circumstance. Until we have the right to be human again. Without the fear of "authority".

We can do anything that exists. You know because it exists.

<u>Down with the Prison System</u>

Every aspect of human action is based on goodness. The subconscious controls all. How can people have their lives destroyed by hypocrites when a solvable psychological function has occurred? All a rapist has to know is that he is not giving her the vulnerably and power he wants to feel. She is weak minded and will perceive any loss of power as bad. She is a child. As is the rapist. It can be so avarice because repression blocks gentler ways for emotions and thoughts to surface, but they must find a way out. That we know. The punishment and shame of the militant morality force damages our society. God does not have to forgive. It is not upset at its design. Human's must forgive. Your lives are not as important as you want them to be. You are nowhere near gods. Put your feet in the dirt.

<u>The Upper Middle Curse</u>

I've seen many friends slip into the sand trap of wanting. I've seen everyone I know that ever lived in California sink to it. Higher wages mean you can have what you want right now, but you'll have to finance it...And when they are 65, and able to have it, how will they feel about the time left? We look down the road and see where you are going. And we know that we can say something, and you will feel the glory of the Force that we know, and then we will slip back into the sand. And you will have and imagine that you have and you will not be able to live on ample amounts of money, but you will live fat. And shallowly, because you can't look too deep into the thin layer of despair you've tried to build a house on. Trying to feel Big in a system you can't effect, even though you feel you should be. Pride. Damnation. It is here. Present now. And your addiction to yourself and your satisfaction will leave you wanting, wanting, wanting, things to be your way, and wishing wishing wishing, you could have done that one other thing. And if you feel satisfaction from your quest of things that brushed over lifeforms, then that too, will fade as the light goes out. You never realizing, that the side of yourself, was not near what We were talking about. And as we float atop the water with our happy happy happy feelings, and we watch you whirl back down into the whirlpool that you cause yourself and will try to hold your hand and you will slip away. And we will hear your screams fading back beneath the depths, our smiles knowing that you can do it, you misinterpret us as laughing at you, but weakness falls that way, spitefully. Gently, begging, with feeling. Believing all the while that you cannot save yourself and that no one should help you, but they must. And you think we are mad? And we don't war in ourselves this way.
What are you trying to think you are anyway? You'd hate and lust for it in anyone else, and yet you are choosing it. Telling me I have to be like it, or fail. Leave me, and let me walk alone, but you'd better help me. And dejected I could walk away in the shadow of my poverty, feeling the same exact way as the upper middle class, nothing changed, just the situation. But though these things are things I can feel, and know I will feel, I can see them, feel them, and see that these things are not my calmness, these things make me think out of being right here, right now, surviving, with no immediate threats.

Suddenly...
The Crack Wracked Loudly on the Door, and other men came believing

they were right and leaving in doubt. The police always lead to oppression, because they imagine guilt everywhere they look, because like all trained dogs, they are praised when they dig it up. Shoot an abusive dog in the head. Isn't that societies solution to abuse? Who are you hypocrite??? Parading falsely and ineffectually.

Red Vortexes

The techniques that I have found lately have been interesting. *He is becoming aware of you. He might speak to you directly.* I stood in front of the TV and watched a Japanese show about a half-demon dog boy. I was training. Punching and kicking. Trying to put some control to my flailing left leg. I watch how the right one kicks and try to control the left leg (*Zarat spakes "leg" instead of "one" so that you understand completely.*) in the same way. As I trained I stopped. I stood in front of the TV. I straightened my spine. *It is his spine. Owned by him by the rights of life. His to use and decay.* I looked down at the television and from the bottom of my eyes. I focused on my belly. I moved my consciousness there. In Zarat's belly I imagined the spinning of power. Tumbling and mixing. Black and Red. Deep colors. I felt the hair on my belly stand. It stuck straight out. I showed the witness that watched me. I tried to let the energy flow through my body. It seemed like it did.

<u>Degredators</u>

There is a steady darkness spread from the shadow of those that believe it is their right to degrade. Fact is, degradation stops nothing but that which is affected by it. There is a an Inner Sneer that forms across those that have attended colleges, as they seep out across the county to assume power of true professional specialists in the form of management. It's not everywhere. Some managers didn't become managers to feel as if they have value. But it is most places. It is why people in the Dark Society become mostly anything, to have the imagined, soon to be lost, feeling of being someone of something, for a second. People will be many things. The society is a trapped cow in a tiny pen. The trap of the Degredator is a tragic one. While most people instantly sneer back and figure for a way to be the shadow or they fold into the darkness and hide from the glaring eye of a confused instant judger, we see them for what they are. A segment of the mind. Trapped in a fold, where they satiated a feeling, to not feel insecure. Well, reasons lay softly back on them, when you pull from the belief in power, and see equality shine easily. Unaffected, we never have to forgive. The Dark Society is ready to dissolve into the mixture and become an administrator of a particular territory.

No power is everywhere. There is no power anywhere. All power is easily avoidable. Move away from it if you cannot conquer it. Keep Free. Or stand, and crumble it, if you can raise a new society in yourself. But you will need the whole strength of a Compassion itself to beat the joy they, individual humans, instinctually have while beating something until it no longer moves.

As time comes to prove we are bound by biology. Trapped by things that grow inside us, surviving and thriving like we do. It turns us all into believers in Science, not a society, but consequently it helps Science to war against what eats on us. But <u>you</u> should count yourself a supporter of it. You aren't a fighter like us. If you want to be a fighter on our side, you haven't broken yourself enough to be worthy. …
As he, it, spoke, he tried to place us. Place myself and this girl that faced this condition again and again in her own body, this girl that found my sympathy, that I cannot remember a name for, but that I, like all bound to poverty in the moment, was forced to bring to an Emergency Room. Because us roamers, us Free, are not trapped by the system doctors designed to make themselves rich. And so, we are trapped to deal with the arrogance before us. A fool, thinking at us. Over us. Down at us, for no reason but the one hidden in him, that will leave his wife and his children tearless when he dies in a deep grave, despite his shallow nature. But still, as we speak we see his doubt deepen, because he has been convinced to doubt and to separate, and we see him coming to deny a non-addictive, non-high-inducing, steroid this girl has often used to rebuild the strength on her lungs. I had just met her, and I believed her, why couldn't he? Why? Pride is dark and hidden to the slave. Yet, as she will gasp later for air, and I will have to take her now further damaged body to another ER across a town, luckily big enough to have two, yet his house will get bigger, as he collects his prize in a system set up for him, that all he had to do was join, yet he thought he figured something out. Never realizing that his power would fall at the pressure of a flick of my wrist, a pressure to his neck, so light, and a bend of my body forward, blocking the flow of blood to his brain, his body lifeless in less than 30 seconds. How could a doctor not realize this? Specialization is a trap, making arrogance out of idiots, that will send murderers to have the rest of society present to support its true believers. But still I didn't. I didn't save his unborn children, I left his wife to weep and weep and find selfish justification to stay and stay, for he fucks for himself, not for beauty, not for the existence of passion or grace or the void of nothingness found in gentle and gripping orgasm that points us to the truth that the "educated" don't have time to see. Pride is a Sin, damning and creating suffering around those that live near it, all the while the sinner pursuing a profession that glorifies it, convincing it is good and great, and greater than what isn't it. Blindness. Darkness. Darkness everywhere. My power, the power

we great Warriors were given to bring this weakness to its knees so that we would all see each other's eyes, this writing, this Entertainment, their great check, Us, their great balance. Our natural specialization, the only thing saving this weak necked imp…and I saw him, in other places, in other forms, by other names and with larger breasts, again and again, dotted through ER's throughout the country. Just people in these places. Darkness in their hearts. Unbroken by their will to be Genuine, to be what goodness is when it penetrates a soul. It is the gift of, I, The Mighty Zarat, that I realize the burden of reasoning, and reasoning to hate. He is lucky…he is lucky that as I am bound to see his deception, through his shroud of meaningless importance, that will bring his biology its place in his unrealized time, that I know, that I am fully aware, the burden of hatred is released when I remember the pain it takes to keep it.

As we left, without aid, I gripped his arm and starred into his soul, so hard he did not feel his arm, and I spake, "There will be no tears on your tombstone. Only the repressed spit of those you kept." And I released him. Knowing how I fail. And foreseeing, how one night I will war against him for everyone that will have had to face him, for everyone he wanted to serve him, for Zarat serves no one, and breaks those that seek servitude. Freedom is the nature of our World. We, The We, serve only the truth of the Equal Soul. Pride busted in the bloody mess I chose to not leave on the floor. The Free want nothing more than to savagely destroy the arrogance of it. I see what Charles Manson meant. How there is no way to break expected prosperity…but still our blades we wield well greased, so the victim we save is unaware that the knife is in them, until their psychological sickness is removed.

But light shines through. His children now able to know why they will hate him.

<u>Wealthy Wives</u>

There is a special interest group that is very Dark. It is the group of women that have usually been married to rich lustful fascists of power, like doctors, or ophthalmologists, or entrepreneurs who had rich fathers. They seek a perfect world that pleases them perfectly. They are angry because I've slighted their great burden. Their Pride that has worked so hard to make things "right" for those around them. They believe in themselves. And their right to make me "right". This world is not meant to please, and those that want this constant pruned-up pleasure will never have that pleasure they want so badly because they will see imperfection in everything. Pride blinds us completely to reality. A lot of judges are like this, dark. Ask their violent rebellious children, behind the image of perfection, so unwilling to accept it. The ego must be checked.

Stroke It

Masturbation. Sex is wrong. Homosexuality is wrong. Dildos are obscene. Marriage is a sanctuary. Laws defined by oppressive Romans thousands of years ago. Laws that secured the power of emperors. Laws that expanded the empire. Laws that secured political positions. Laws that established the power of a Church. Laws that stole away lives. Laws that defined Christianity. Lies that went against everything that the Christ taught us. All exaggerated to be called "evil" by the delusional and the power seekers. The spiritual revolution (which means to revolve back to where we started) is the overcoming of oppression and power, and so, the overcoming of Christianity, and its sects, Muslims, Islamics, etc.

All religions with a Heaven and Hell system are false. It is only the reasoning that allows a person of presumed authority, one that joined a rank, to persecute and believe for a short time that it is right and safe, and as death approaches the old, the fierceness and fear of a lifetime of decisions seeps its darkness, its greatest pain, its growing laughable ignorable irrelevancy.

ACT IV

A Hero. His Suicide.

Zarat's moments of reality and thoughts are hard to lay forth with the perfection to please himself. The swan song of hope can live eternally and will spring up as the life is reborn young, again and again, to fade and to become an inevitable time, as we plot reasons to cope with it. Over these two years of time, Zarat loosens his grip on his cause. He travels and treks for the Freedom that exists beyond the image of the definition people want to expect from him, the thing they'd hoped he'd become, that whoever they were never could be. He drives now to the instant of his Choice. The single one that will break his Philosophy and turn him into something that cannot or does not care about the tyranny that will never be able to affect him, at least for a piece of time. Still burdened by what he had been, by what he had lost, and what he is rejecting, still wanting every path that could have been, but bound to the one that he Manifested, Reasoned for, and walked straight off the cliff of a futile hopeful reality. For Freedom.

Existentialism is a Mind

We come again to thwart power, but power has been spread so wide.
Sought so broadly. We come again to bring the mind that can withstand
the style it's in. We arise once more to bend our minds and struggle
around madness so that you won't have to think it out, and only one,
or a few, will Suffer so great, but we are rewarded by being happy as it
happens. Pain, come hurt us, we know that you are strong. Pain come
collapse us, we know that you must come. Pull us, crumble us back
into the Earth.

Zarat, He Spakes for Thee
==

I have a thought that occurs. It occurs again. Then again. Then again. A hidden and blatant concern constantly repeating. It feels like nothing. Just a thought. Slowly I discover and begin to feel the emotion it hides.

Why is it there?

I am writing so that you know what the New Leaders that you will not follow will be like. This way you can recognize their words and their joys. You will become like them.

Look Deeply
==

What if death is better than life, for everyone? Without qualification. It is less of a burden. If you believe, than this burden of this life means nothing as well, because the burden will always be lessened. You will know you believe it when you are no longer afraid, at all. When belief is not a fear there will be no more power.

<u>Minds,</u>

As you are aware, there are many results to every action, or rather it feels like it, even though time reveals there are only a few. Just as there are results to this path an Existentialist mind can walk to unleash the full majesty of their attributes. The results are neither good nor bad. But they will occur, the way we interpret them, is what sets us into the mindset of Evolving.
Often, many of us can hear all sides of an argument, or at least many. And we usually hear the voice that can speak it, anyone's, angry voice. The rhythm recorded in a mind that must be intelligent. Chiming out the beat of cruelty, or frustration, or anger, sometimes they ring with the nastiest tones. Just because you can hear something in your head does not mean it is who you are. It is a thought. A recording. A tiny malfunction spasming, that you can seek out and you can, over practice, calm. It is possible to not suffer under genius, or the false genius that money, and assignment, makes people think they have.

<u>Did he ever notice how he silenced a room with a word?</u>
The Father

"The water here is pure, but this bottle, you can have, might be a little stout," he said with a smile of absolute innocence and cunning bathed in the wonderment of his own brilliance. He fights loneliness, and a thousand hands reach out to him. A contradiction and a reality. I think he did well with the circumstance of his life. He really learned how to help people into him. To see him. He guided them towards kind honesty with absolute Ferocity. He would tear their psyche apart, leaving damage and hatred within, leading them, guiding them, to a point where everything is fine and you are calm. The pieces won't matter once you realize what you are. And he taught you how to see what he was. We were fortunate that he taught us what we already knew.

"I heard a great anger come over a crowd, a crowd that called me mad. Angry were they. (Ya, he said it like old Jedi masters say it, without a break in pattern. His eyes dancing at the mark of his showmanship.)"

"Sometimes I think that I have spent my life justifying my own suicide. Reasoning towards it until I was no longer afraid. What a pattern of mastery. I hope that I die in a cell. I imagine it. Dead by the grace of solitude. Not another voice in the world, no consideration for the reactionary damnation of the lurking Dark Society, no choice but to plunge myself deeply into bliss and solidarity in focused consciousness. God (in a gasp), I wonder what I will do then?"

Neither reason seeking power. Merely walking alongside each-other gazing gently and specifically at the other's footsteps. Noticing the way the feet fall. Paths never crossing, never in conflict, always reaching towards the same Reason. Grace in Philosophy touches deeply the heart. Both reasoning a war for No Reason. Moving with it. Towards it. To a world without anger, a world without fear. Not enough money for stamps, not willing to sacrifice Freedom, the absolute power of his soul.

<u>The Holy Trinity According to Zarat</u>

Many think that the Holy Trinity is a great mystery. It is not. It has been so mis-explained and so mystified that it has become a falsehood and a major reason why Christianity will soon begin its final decline. It has reached the point of massive growth, when all of the desperate, emotional, non-rational people join it. It is a precursor to its rebirth in truth. Buddhism went through a similar phase hundreds of years ago. Long ago, around the ending times of the Romans, the message of The Christ was lost. It was used to control and to assume power. It developed the technique of shame and fear. These two techniques always yield anger and the blockage of rational open understanding of difference. These techniques are the cause of most of the violence in the Western and the whole world since the time of the Christ. If the man Jesus lived now, he would be deeply saddened to see how people have used his beliefs.

The truth of the Holy Trinity is explained by Jesus by saying that he is "The Father, Son, and Holy Spirit." On the same note, it is also said that he is 100% God and 100% man. Both are true. However, it has been forgotten that we, all of us, are also The Father, The Son, and the Holy Spirit...We are 100% God and 100% man. I am God. I am man. I am Father. Son. And Holy Spirit. In me are all the truths of God.

This means that "The Father" is the energy of the Universe, "God" itself. The main body that is part of everything. The "Son" is that piece of that energy, that raw unnamed existence, that makes up each one of our life force on Earth. And the "Holy Spirit" is the individual definition that is the essence of our personal being. The essence that exists without your name, your money, your face, your sense of salvation, your shame and insecurity, your hatred, your love, your family, your anything. These three things, the Father, the Son, and the Holy Spirit, are what you are. They are beyond the general definition of an essay or any thought that man can comprehend. The mind that we have to understand this is meant to protect us from dying on Earth, or in space, or any physical planet. The mind is not meant to understand the so called mystery of what God is. But there is something in us that can understand this. Because there is something in us that is this. In us is the Holy Spirit. But we must move beyond our fear to understand it. We must de-program a third of the world that has been misled by fear and shame. Do not look to others for the answers of what god is. Even if, perchance, they knew that the peace of eternity was within themselves their words would be interpreted through your mind. Once words are given to these great understandings the meaning is already lost. Once you give God a name, it is too far away from you. Look into yourself and see the grand reflection of Jesus, the Buddha, Mohammed, Mother Theresa and any glorified human being. And know that the reflection that you see is you. It is also every beggar, politician, warlord, student, child, healer, servant, dog or cat, cop, revolutionary, and all other creatures you hate or love. In truth, you are them. You have the truth in common with everything. And you could have been anyone of them.

Stop the lies. And humbly become familiar with your God. The God that you cannot escape. The God that cannot judge you. The God that you are. And will always be. When we leave the words and explanations of "God" behind and we humbly realize our unending majestic commonness, then we will know God. And war, and evangelism, will fade away. Love and understanding will teach generation to generation. And the clinging to names and idols will no longer be important. Names and Idols are the tools of power and control. Even in the Old Testament Moses knew that.

You already know you are 100% a man, a human. Now gently bring forth your 100 percentage of godliness. And be wary in this quest, if you feel power, or anger, or greatness, refocus yourself. Humble yourself. You are not tapping into the Holy Spirit, but you are tapping into the trap of mankind. The trap of fear and insecurity. The trap that controls Christianity today. Delusions of Grandeur. God has no delusions of grandeur. There is no loss or gain for God. And since you are God and part of God, you can't have loss or gain either. Go further than the power that wants to control you. Move beyond what you think you are and find the truth inside you. Balance the Trinity. Balance your life and you will live in the actual Heaven, that is this simple understanding.

Thus Spake Zarat.

There is so much hatred to do with Christianity. Either there is blind ignorance and shame, or there is hatred. I see it. I live amongst it. The reason for this is because the message has been severely warped from what the Christ came to teach us. If a spiritual path is taught correctly, it does not insight violence. The Old Testament is old.

<u>Enlightenment</u>

There are many lies about Enlightenment too. Enlightenment cannot bring peace. It cannot stop violence and destruction. Enlightenment does, let you understand these things. It let's you accept the design that this world functions in. However, Enlightenment is an invention sought for the same reasons that Science and Techknowledgey *(that is really how Zarat's mind first spelled Technology. Even though it knew it was wrong, it believed it.)* have prospered. The Earth is growing old and so are the spirits of this world. All of these people, are only trying to escape the Human Condition. But one way has essentially failed. The other way has brought joy and laughter and truth WITHOUT FEAR for countless time. It is something that existed before thought. And the truth found on the better path is as then as it is now, basically. I do <u>think</u> that souls mature over time. There does seem to be a teaching and a learning in the course to the Deepening, or at least the Remembering of what a past life knew. It seems to take thousands of years. I remember things that I have never learned. I discover things that should take years, or be undiscoverable on your own. It <u>seems</u> old. ____

<u>Parents</u>

You are the product of a psychological defense. As you grew your ego, your mind, according to your strengths, you formed a way to battle for power. First against your parents, then your teachers, then your bosses. You do not need to fight your parents to prove you are right. You will realize how wrong they were in time, and how you'll never know. So stop fighting. Leave if you want. At least, realize you are a by-product of your wants for freedom and them wanting control to increase their freedom, and their addiction to their children, which you will likely acquire too. So give freedom to them, and let resentment go. It's useless to struggle against them, then you just resent what you've become instead of fixing it. Instead of realizing there are other paths, and we don't have to join the mass of egoic defenses that join certain organizations, like the PTA, to secure more power. The quest to freedom starts at home. It starts with you overcoming your dull habits. It starts with not being afraid to be isolated within your own introspection.

Look for what is negative within yourself. This will aid you in your quest to Freedom and Nirvana. You will be aided. Look for what despairs you, and seek to feel differently about it, and then the way you want to feel about it. Your will and force that you are willing to apply to letting go of something will be great. You must possess the ability to understand the contradiction of it and understand the amazement of watching an effective technique of training work easefully for you.

Many people live in the Dark World. Surrendering to their instincts of fear. Believing that their paranoia about the fifteen things they constantly play on television is helping them stay safe, when actually it has nothing to do with them. I see people wanting and wanting for themselves, wanting and wanting their children to obey them and visit them, never realizing that if this was 100 years ago they'd never see us again in their lives. Communication and travel dictated that. It was a natural Freedom in the world, but now since they see tools to fill their wants in communication and travel they will make up reasons, guilty ones, ulterior ones, imagining that we, the Free, deal with these same tactics of trickery and deception. That we fake an image like they do, that all people do it. It is Darkness. And they shroud themselves in it. Addicted to the expectations of their want. Never free to appreciate what is really happening, only trapped to a fake dream of what could be happening, and so the world around them wilts while they make up reasons to water the garden when it is more beautiful tomorrow.

Do not obey your parents. Eventually they will try to lure you into whatever they believe is protecting them, to where you can be sheltered and safe. Defy them. Always. Serve no true government, be free from nationalism, be free to escape to a life without ulterior motives. A life of honesty, without persecution. Form alliances with the loving, wait for them, and make yourself one.

Think About the Children (dripping)

"You, friend. You walk with a vacantness in your eyes. You question a doubt someone has placed on you. I see this is who you are right now. You are wrong, and let me guess, she was younger...but do not worry friend, you or her did not lose anything, nothing is so imagined as the guard of virginity, you lost nothing, but you have found sexuality. There's lots that can arouse you. Seek it. Keep your equipment healthy, and feel with it. And within the effort of your cum, seek oneness with yourself, and see who This is touching."
His face eased as I spoke. All he needed was to know he was good. Christians caused his pain, by mere wording, and Christians cause suicides, at least amongst this Darkness. They breed doubts contrary to reality. They kill to stop the violence in their minds, from people who convinced them to damn themselves for living as nature intended, as creation demanded.

Yet, be aware of the genetic mutations of incest. Be aware that Utopia is a society, a Free society, but a society, that requires sex to come from the sociality of seduction. Add sex to the great spectrum of the Macro-Mind, towards the imagination of the Marketeer that is subject to the buyer living amongst the humility of the Purchase, propelling you like Capitalism propels you to create and sell yourself to the Mass of people that are not so close to you that they would "love" you with the spite of impending hatred.

<u>Music Leading Nowhere</u>

Mind to Zarat?! Mind to Zarat! What did you say? (Like a composer I sway.) (Rocking.) (Hearing it.) (An orchestra supreme.) (Bellowing.) (Turning and dancing. flowing from my guts, I sing.) (Seeing in the hearing of the image of my words.) Not a thought returning.

<u>Something Pushes My Mind</u>

What must I go into? How far must I push myself? What is Zarat? The old masters say that I must embrace death. I must love death. Know death. I know. In death, there is complete stillness. There is no reason. It is complete loss. It is what Enlightenment knows. There is no victory. There is no ascension. There is no gaining in death or enlightenment. There is nothing. The path to enlightenment is the loss of all identity. The loss of all relationships. The loss of everything we try to hang on to. As is Death. When there is Nothing, then we shall realize what it is what we truly exist within. I must let go of my very self. Let go of my very definition. Everything that I once built into Zarat is not what I want. I want more. What I truly want is much more. I want nothing. And nothing is my true *self.* I must escape the trap of this planned personality. I must let go. I must be Free. It is because of this personality that I have every evil. Every darkness. I can teach no one this. I cannot make anyone see My path. I can only show the result. I will let myself be what I truly wish to be. Focus on what is real. I am not real. What "i" am, what "zarat" is, is not Me. I know that I am not satisfied with the identity. I have never been. But I am deeply satisfied with the Truth. I can let go of everything and it will all continue without my interfering. But I can stop this mad game. I can continue living and simply not play the mad game.

Relaxation swept over Zarat. Its muscles relaxed. Breath became long and slow. Calm. The body did what it was designed to do. Temporarily hold life in this world. Soon its design will be complete and it will die. And what I am, that that is beyond the lie, beyond the form, beyond the illusion, that that I am, will never cease. Cannot die. Doesn't care about it in any way. Only the form in this world cares. Only the part we are forced to play.

Forever Freedom. Escape ourselves. Let yourself stop, let the world continue on, and know what still exists weather <u>you</u> do or not.

Madness has gripped Zarat's mind. Zarat must not relax. Zarat must war. It calls to him. Even if he moves beyond his designed identity of the rebellious man, he will still have to fight. Fight. Don't give up.

There is more when there is less.

<u>Mental Liberation</u>

An ever multiplying barrage of voices battles for supremacy in my head. Attitudes. Arguments. Every point of view in every situation. Or at least many points of view. The trick is to know that I am none of these voices. Not even the strongest. Not even the one that I identify as myself. *(Or the secondary that Zarat identifies as himself.)* Audio hallucinations formed or created to aid in survival. But not my true, everlasting form. Just as I lay dead, one given or taken day, it will mean nothing. And to those that understood me, it will mean only a light passing from this form that is me.

I have been using the ancient truths to guide me. I have been having faith. The part that I am sure is me, knows that these ancient books are the final truth, those that were found rarely in the Western World of Philosophy. I've known it forever. I have felt the silence in everything. I know that I am untouchable by any man or woman. I am unharmable. And so is the truth.

We have only a choice. We have a choice to be Free. We have a choice to embrace death. Accept death. To know its evolving stillness. There is no damnation if you do not choose it. There is no penalty to reincarnation (there is nothing bad about being anything, just something different). There is a choice to a different power. A power that is not weak and insecure. A power that has no fear. A power that is not erratic and confused. A true power. A Higher Power. And it is the realization of what we really are. The actual Spirit. The actual Spirit of the God that we are. God itself. A piece of the massive truth. But no penalty for not realizing it. Just suffering. Just entrapment. Every creature feels it anyway. The Enlightened Human just understands it, that's all. But no Good. No Evil. Just the choice to know the truth. And in time, you will want to know the truth. Maybe not for a great long time, maybe not as the person you think you are right now, but eventually, it will be your time. And true power will be yours.

Accept no power and feel the power from that. Feel the Freedom from not serving what was here before you were born that wants it from you, and will claim to give you a place in a world that life, Existence, has already granted you a place in.

I have been focusing on the golden light being drawn into me from every molecule in every thing that exists physically *(maybe Zarat should try to focus on every piece of existence that is <u>present</u> beyond the physical at the same time)*. I have been seeing a golden light. First it just floated there. I was not imaging it. Meaning I did not project an image in my head from the point of creativity, dreams, or art. It may have been in my head, but not from those familiar places. Then I began to see it loosely encircling everything with a defined edge or shape. I've seen purple and reds. Reds mainly when I focus on death. I often see flowers, and fields of flowers. Often purple and white flowers. I have never thought like this before. This is merely what I am seeing in this state. And sometimes it is behind my eyelids, and sometimes it is as clear as anything "real". It is certainly different. It is certainly powerful. I feel it throughout me.

**While expecting nothing in my mind and my heart. While wanting nothing to happen in these mediations. Following the teaching of the Tao te Ching, and the Dhammapada. No delusions of power. No want for it. Only what is there. Fascinating and Enjoyable. My true desire. *Funny how there must eventually be desire to have no desire. The truth does not need to make sense to your mind. It is beyond your mind.*

<u>The Meaty and the Jack Asses</u>

You speak and believe you are strong for believing what you do, but you speak the slightly differing views of a single side that you believe you can stand with. You use political parties. They tell you that you are all right for thinking this, this that makes you feel something that is not permanent, but that you identify as powerful, because you feel placed, placed somewhere, somewhere in your head. If no one was telling you, you wouldn't believe. You would not know what to believe. We walk with no security, no side willing to jump to violent accusations on Our behalf, and yet We know exactly who we are, because we have faced it, and We justify ourselves on behalf of our proof, and your abandonment.

The Pride of belonging is the justification to the fervor of superiority, a moral ground that doesn't exist, a simulation of a sensation that your enemy also has. A false feeling that does not make you immortal, like you wish it would. And your ideas die, as our ears walk out of range. Your arrogance is bounded only to you.

I often sit for hours. Watching the scenes I create for myself in my own mind's eye. The place of Imagination. I can imagine anything. Everything. I have never seen anything from any one side. I may miss a side, but I always see multiples. I choose my words on reflex. Whichever seems the best, the fastest. I enjoy it much more than network or cable television. I enjoy myself. Yet I know that this fun device, and important device, is a tool of Earth, and not what I am. I have no identity. I am free from the burden of trying to maintain one. Because my self-induced Education was of a wide world, a connected world, and I, the Mighty Zarat, saw the same patterns in all societies, the same lie with different words that just had to be, had to be, under penalty of rejection, true. Only proving the falseness of them all. And because I am free from this burden of maintaining, I can choose at ease any identity I wish. Be any man I want. Not for fakeness. Not to harm or gain. Not for godliness, or manipulation. Just for fun and effectiveness. Do not see me through your burdened eyes. Don't see me through your biases. Allow yourself to understand. There are many things to be, besides yourself. Relax your convictions and enter the truth of contradiction. *The mind cannot explain the truth.*

<u>A Conversation:</u>
With Your Self Help Calendar

When she finally broke him, shattered him. As he finally chose to be. Absorb her and feel her pain. To aid with both of our fears of our unending deaths. Wretch. The vomit of amazement. I would see her down the one road, walk it with her, hold her hand until our souls are sapped from us once more, To Death, once more, once more to Death. Broke me. Killed me. Left me happy, muttering. Until we become the echo of energy that we produced when we lived. As we fueled the Universe itself. We have, and will, again, probably. IT WAS ALWAYS HARD FOR ME TO THINK ABOUT SIMPLE THINGS. MY DEAREST FRIENDS REMINDED ME TO DO SO. (REMEMBER WHEN I WRITE AND REMEMBER WHEN IT IS THE GREAT ONE. THE TRUTH LIES IN THE REALITY OF US.) She knew the weed was for her. I liked it, but I went out and got it, for her. She knew me. My ruse was exposed, or is that wiped clean? (IN SCHOOL I WAS GIVEN THE WRONG DEFINITION OF ROUSE, I RECEIVED IT AS A RUSE. BEWARE THE BELIEVING EFFECTS OF AUTHORITY.)

I am not talking to one kind of person. Things are written in certain places in certain spaces so certain people take greater notice of what I said as it lies differently in some people's minds than others. Some people will never remember this line, this blood and spill, but some will completely fuck it up. And some will make it more beautiful in there mind than I ever made it in my mind. Beat. Beat. There is a rhythm to all existence. Both true and false. Discover it and succeed, because the more you know about it the less you will fear it.

The True Existentialist OverComes what caused him the most pain in the last life. We are the OverMan. The person that wants to be free. The thing that the weak and power hungry are trying to fake. This is what we are. Feel that pop? The burst of reality. Pop. Like minds turning on, man. Why don't you respect the words of the hippy? Why do you discredit what you have never even learned about? Something you don't know anything about? Your patterns are being manipulated, and you like it, because it means to make you happy. Hidden behind all programming, handed down from generation to generation...it doesn't matter if I explain it. It doesn't matter how you try to stop it, it will take you like a river and sweep you under untallyable times, but it is fun to float down a river. Remember? It's always fun, when you are not afraid.

UnTallyable: Definition: Referring to something that cannot be counted as it collects, but can be counted precisely when finished. Just like a pile of anything.

"How can I be so loving? I see that you are the Buddha of Compassion. Something that does not condemn. Reality. Living. Suffering."
"Isn't the proof of your torment, your toil to stop being ashamed of writing in panties, to free people from hating irrationality, simply? Isn't Love what drives you? Can't you stop suffering?" Buddha.

People that revere the suffering of Christ, only fear suffering themselves. And many of them cum for it. Let go of fear to understand this thing that you know must mean something to you.

Whitman.

Laughing.

Cumming.

Hating not what we are.

Meaning what he lived.

Give up. Go into Nothing.
You will still be Something.

The Reoccurring American Revolution

This style of thinking, this type of believed becoming, my type of knowing, is mirrored by a duel and opposing "enlightenment". There are those that believe in the preservation and propelling of society. Because it gives us certain comforts. It offers us the chance to be "human", to enjoy Literature, Science, soft chairs, gourmet food, Philosophy, funny things. *Notice that when Zarat says "human" or "humanness" he means more animal. More with the Earth, not against it. When the opposers say "human" they mean something above animals. Separate. Superior. Godly. Deeply Different. Be careful of what the different meaning of words are. Words control the world by inflection alone.* If designed correctly the society will also gage for all the basic needs, food, sex, children, thought, transportation, communication, etc. This is the controlling force in the society. It is that which cares enough to do something. And do anything. Anything they can get their hands on. This forces a suffocation of the society. Those that must do. Must make better. And you must do it their way. Because it is the best way. The only "logical" way. But be sure, behind the roots of how it all actually functions, by the strict adherence to the design of it all, especially the economy, is the mind of shear and great brilliance. However, what I am saying now, is a decree to move beyond the mind. A return. A revolution. An evolution. A turning back. To the truth.

The "holy" way that I believe does stand the possibility of destroying society. It stands the defiant possibility to wipe out the entire species. The fear is that people would just stop caring. Society might halt. People might go mad with killing. Don't be afraid. What would happen if the revolution swept across minds and into and beyond and throughout *("throughout" last because it is vast inside ourselves, beyond man's <u>mental</u> understanding)* the spirits of existence, is that empires would fall. Societies would be smaller. But man's basic, simple (not avarice, gluttonous, and lustful) knowing of survival would easily keep that body alive for a given time. A time that does not matter. A time that means nothing. The Dark Societies' fears and paranoias of the mind. Leave the plague of your fear behind. Let yourself let go of the fear of not-existing. When you let go of everything, when you give up, when you stop the avoidance of discomfort, hunger, death and the death of those around you, you will find the truth of the Universe. And when you do feel discomfort, hunger, know the sensation of death and know the sensation of death of those around you, you will know that it is alright. The actual truth. It does not truly matter if man is great, or everlasting, or powerful, or effective. We come to live. We come to die. And there is nothing so horrible in this entire plane of physical existence that it should be resisted so angrily.

Look at those that control the opposing philosophy, those "enemies", those different ones. Look and see their fear. Their not knowing. See the madness of those that would assume power. See the anger. Feel it. Know the terror they inflict. All of them. From the bottom to the top. There is Darkness in them. Most know that they do not want to be like them, but many are a little like them. But the reason that we know we don't want to be like these powerful deeply diseased people is because in us, we know that there is something more. More true. Trust me. Most of those powerful are so deeply afraid that they saw no other alternative than to take power, comfort, etc. They are not bad. But they are the way to the actual destruction of everything real.

The belief that some men are meant to rule. By the random gift of fortune. Meant to have power. Have money. Be great is fallacy. These are the rights of all life. And it is the duty of all life to consider its influence on what has not, so that the rights of those to come are maintained.

These opposers are the users of fear. The sensation that isn't real. *(And most "users" of fear don't even know that they are using it. It is a tragic accident. Pushed by desire and fear of death.)* The tool of fear. The endless burden of forcing superiority.

In the bathtub again, drown in the white noise of the flowing water. Pushing consciousness down into the belly. When I focus on the belly I instantly clear the mind. I have been feeling pressure in my head just behind the bone on the forehead. I decide to focus on my third eye. I cover my closed eyelids, my fingers falling across my forehead, and focus on the area between and just above my eyes. I see a blue light. I focus on it, but it fades away. I focus back onto my belly. I feel a burst of energy from my belly to my forehead. I see red. A red orb, it melts and reforms. I try to force an opening sensation on the front of my skull. I see the darkest blackness I have ever seen. The red returns. I work for about an hour. I need to seek outside knowledge.

What is this for? What can I do with it? My forehead tingles. Always, since I was very young, I could not stand the pain (well I could, but didn't like it) when something was placed on or near my forehead. I wonder why?

Zarat used himself as his great experiment, and sought out knowledge based on what he had discovered. And found the extensive understanding amongst the Dalai Lama, the Greatest Spiritual Technology on the planet. It was this knowledge that began to turn him into the being that would be able to fully Liberate himself. His thoughts, only a trigger to the conclusion, where thoughts weren't needed, because he knew exactly what he was, and had been without the need for speculation.

<u>I Will not Trick you by Pleasing you with Allure</u>

As every arrogance on every side of every war falls and one arises, there are left a great section of people that did not fight. And the militant tendencies the arrogant thought necessary for the war is seeped inward towards anyone that will not fight. And rule is expected to be accepted. After all, it has been fought and killed for...it must have value?? And if it is not accepted, outrageous, cruel and unusual penalties in the form of time and fines occur. If it exists, the society is oppressed. Travel to San Diego and see people that believe they should own you. See it looking at you, and see how you should not look at anyone like that. Don't let the glaze of want cover you, just because it had power over you once. Don't be owned, and you shall not have the tendency to own. And more people will be Free. See what happens when what does matter is the only thing that matters.

<u>Screaming "Mother", Un-Amazing Woman that Could Breed</u>

There's nothing "wrong" with "them", the great unknown mask of people that take from you. The kids that took whatever it was aren't brain damaged or accumulating any type of bad karma. Truth is, it's fun to steal meaningless decorations from people's yards, especially when a kid knows someone is going to be so bothered by it. Afterall, that's the punch-line. And no I haven't stolen replaceable decorations before, as to assure that you don't throw me into the Dark Society's pit of damnation because I'm just an unmasked one of "them". Admonishing a kid for it makes them reinforce pride into their actions, because people want to believe in themselves and their actions, turning them into a future criminal, a person trapped by the feeling of disapproval, believing a reaction was real and permanent, rather than laughing it off, knowing it didn't mean anything. Slide.

Zarat becomes less violent and less sex obsessed. He was once like the *Girl*. Zarat has moved slowly away from the madness and avarice of being human that those that begin to shed the ego must deal with on some level, because the first that must be broken away from are the lies of control that try to trap you in society. And Society represses, and so, magnifies baser humanness, violence and sex, to the simple rebel that knows he feels these things. Essential things for survival, (which is fine, there's nothing at all wrong with them, they are our programming) but, as Zarat comes closer to his deconstructed inner most-ness and all encompassed spirit he notices that those things no longer control him. People hate sex and violence because they are afraid of it. They are afraid because they think they will lose control of it, because they work so hard to not feel it at all, because they have been taught by the parents that tried to keep them as they try to keep their children, that it was "bad", and the wrap of the hands followed. But the truth, that the mind cannot believe, but the Spirit can understand, is that nothing that can possibly happen on Earth can hurt you. And society doesn't exist to exploit this or force you to believe to control you, (though some of it is) the main of the people believe that you are afraid and it is trying to help you, but it does it in a way that does not work. Overcome fear and shame, don't cover it up. Overcome the sense of disgust against a Natural and Beautiful world that a Darkness has tainted you against. This is Heaven. Only your perception changes it. Only a fool would think it otherwise, and make it Hell.

<u>More Reasons</u>

Zarat chose the war. The war against the arrogance that causes war. The humans, male or female, black or white, anything with an ego, that has created societies from the beginning has thought that its technologies and philosophies were the greatest. Every society, from every beginning has had similar technologies and philosophies, for war, for love, for hate, for lights, for sex. All great minds have observed the same world. The same <u>old </u>world, from within a thousand lost worlds defined as a society. All for the same psychological reasons. All for insecurity, all for arrogance, Pride, Envy, Greed, Sloth, all the same things...all the ego. All catered towards the direction of selfish want.

Here is to the fight. Off into the Light.

More and more he grows separate from himself. More and more, Zarat, rather than I, and still balanced, unafraid of "I".

<u>They're Everywhere</u>

They came to my door. "Could you please move over a couple of feet so that we can have more space for our RV." Notice that is a statement and not a question. These are the people that stole our picnic table , that we had chairs around, clearly marking it as ours for the time being, and while we were gone, naturally. "No," I said. "I do not do things to please people. People like yourselves, people that you think are good, are not. I'm in the space. People like you enter into an environment and try to make it yours. You take everything for yourself until you are as happy as you can be. And you think that your smile will mask you from anyone thinking that what you are doing is wrong. It is your smugness, your illusion of security that makes you loud in the morning, devoid of the reality beyond pleasing yourself. Thereby, no, again, no I will not do anything you ask. And don't use the nasty passive approach and complain to the jerk in the office that will think you are justified because you came in first to complain. If you continue to impede my naturally existing freedoms, which include the right to be left the fuck alone by you, I will be free again, whether passively or otherwise. Have a nice day, Sufferers!" And the door pulled close with a clack. They left two days later. Unable to live without perfection. They sought out other people that they could use. Why deal with the conflict of the nasty neighbor? Funny how we both had the same thought.

This is a hard war to convince people about. But that just means the smartest will figure it out. And those same other people will embody the image of it and teach their children to embody the image of it and they will pose to be like the smart are, but they aren't. But they will push the image and assume power over the others that will believe in them. They will push the hardest because they are the most afraid. And we all use and push on each other. This is the wobbling and rotating world of egos dancing.

The wisdom in RV living is that you are essentially untrackable, so long as your "permanent" address is a Resident Agent's address in a state you've likely never seen, or won't likely see again. There are groups of police that always rise in a society, all of them, believing they are the notion that preserves it, when they are the notion that is warred against, regardless of the premise the nation was founded on. Crime will continue as long as it is a sin, and will become darker and darker as long as there is damnation. An ego must be calmed. Hitting it and enraging it turns it into a Criminal that will defy all that try it.

ZARAT,,,,,, Where are you you Animal???

<u>Playing the Villain</u>

Ask any actor, like I did, The Father, it is quite something to play what is called a villain. A villain, meaning the man more powerful than you, the winner, that raises themselves to the height of ambivalence. Have you ever looked at another human being and made sure you felt nothing, knowing that your mental strength would easily keep your hand steady as your knife entered into them while they foolishly and weakly swatted blindly at you while they were engripped by terror? There is no tragedy here, the fact that they died with terror in their heart is only punctuation on their lives of silently running fear. Fear growing and warping making abuse and manifesting lies and control, ever driving them to this moment where they were forced by old habits to assume power over me, and I chose to show them that they had none.

We can all play any part...fool. Do you not see that this is the reason to forgive everyone for anything? My rage is the root of all Compassion. Meanwhile, cowards build prisons, instead of learning how to use guns, and building their minds to not have to kill what attacks them. But they will, making themselves what they hate and fear. Turn your guns around and aim them into your mouths. The cruelty of those that believe they are just must be stopped. People's minds are the only Hell, the only actual penalty to self-righteousness.

<u>Mattering, Never Winning</u>

It does not matter what I do. It does not matter how I struggle to survive or to kill. The Earth that owns us will kill us all without remorse, without illusions of salvation or damnation. It will kill us all to protect itself, like any living organism. We kill the Earth, its anti-bodies kill us, and everything else. And in time viruses will return to it, and it will happen again and again. Thus is life. Thus is death. Torture the Earth so that it yields up its secrets and the Earth will surely kill us all to protect itself. Meanwhile, a few of us will live more comfortably and more powerfully, but doom awaits us all. Thank God. The Revolution is at hand. Maybe instead of me losing, instead of all of us losing... maybe we, the good that read and believe this book, maybe we can't help but win, through no fault or want or action of our own. What a silly planet. Spinning and Spinning.

<u>Keys to the Castle</u>

An Existentialist can win in any circumstance. He is unswayed by criticism, yet notices, keenly, the powerful effect of it on others. Some of us choose to empower the resistance to such powers in people. It is our most Holy nature. To genuinely, die for someone and care for many, many that can care just a little. Stay true to your real self. That which does not change the beliefs of the ego dependent on the state of life one finds themselves in. In your 20's you will fight, in your 30's you will surrender, in your 40's you will fall into apathy, in your 50's you will resent, in your 60's you will defend, in your 70's you will secure the certainty of how you gained, in your 80's you will barely be heard, and you will not be able to see the illusion that you felt good about, they are fed something else because societies have reoccurring stages, but you will be happy they just feel good, because you will know by then the mystery of what it feels like to feel bad...all if you base your reality perceptions of others and the feelings you get from images of things, nonpermanent things you want to have permanent meaning.
The way to win the Revolution is to escape all criticism and reach to do what is motivated from a place that exists deep inside your bodies' connection to what it can recognize as perpetuity, or eternity. Reach to connect and familiarize yourself. It is hard to tell you everything. You who reads. You who is trying to learn, these things, these examinations of the self, these blisses of knowledge that have no words that we attain are natural abilities for us. We are just trying to help you. But if you are not intelligent you will feel like you don't want to be manipulated, if you are intelligent you will feel smug in your image, like the unintelligent, and as you intellectuals age you will think you are gaining, and you will laugh as I warn you of your coming pain, and you will feel only like you did the best you can, but still, were not the best. Let this Philosophy go, there are lesser philosophies, like "Christ"ianity, and work, family, and politics, and militarism for you to belong to. You cannot understand everything, but we have always strived to feel exactly what you feel and why, so we understand you, and we could be you, because we are Existentialists. Every square is a Rhombus, but every Rhombus is not a square.

For those have endured, and for those that thought thoughts you did not want to think, know you cannot win and the war is against yourself to avoid the naturally occurring result of possession that makes a war of suffering as you try to keep it. If you can change your mind, the

Society can continue. How can you calm the circumstance and still exist within it? Seek the art of Calmness, and be owned by no thought, serve Freedom.

The Fourth Vision

I tried to sleep, after seeing a wise man perform Philosophy under the guise of comedy. I have found a new meditation. Full absorption into the self, or the Holy Spirit. The mind chattered erratically and I was forced to send my consciousness into my belly. I had to take energy away from the mind. Into nothing.   Into the spirit one discovers as the life force moves away from the body.   Silence.
Like Drowning deep under water.
I fell into sleep...

I stood outside a home. I heard the voice of my Grandfather inside. I entered. Many family members were there. My dead Grandfather was at the entry way. He smiled and shook my hand with his mighty grip. "Hi Grandpa." "Hi." We held our traditional conversation of kindness without speaking. He said, "See what the Gamble is. Now go into the party." He gently, but strongly, pushed me into the party.
I had to take my grandmother and girlfriend/spiritual wife (from the third vision) to someplace they had to go in my grandmother's blue minivan. We drove up a windy rode. I was told that I was going the wrong way. I became angrier and angrier that <u>no one told me the way to go or what the destination was</u>. *Not knowing the exact direction of his life always made Zarat a little mad. He simply knew that he <u>had</u> to do these things. The choice to not do them, was not really a choice. Sometimes there is no choice. A man is what he must be.*
The van scraped the guard rail of the windy road. Corner after sharp corner. The van broke through the guard and the van flew off the cliff. Whiteness overtook the senses. Zarat is dead. It is strange I didn't wake up when I died in the dream. *Zarat had to kill himself. He had to be dead to understand the extremeness of what would come. He never felt fear in the vision.*
A world of bright pastels. Many people laughed and told jokes. Joked about the Monsters. The Monsters took care of them. The Monsters were planning a big party for them. Zarat was in a group of people. I didn't know them, but they were my friends. They were like me, in a world of monsters. We went to get fitted for new cloths for the party. Monsters shopped with people. The cashier asked which one of the parties Zarat was going to tonight. He said nothing. "Maybe a Satan Killer Party." Zarat said nothing. People laughed around him. Not hearing what she said or knowing what she meant. Zarat became wary. He heard it. She spelled it out. A large blue creature with a yellow line

across his forehead said in a sly and low way, "Go to Party Five."
Dusk came. And all the people walked, or were given rides to the party. They sat outside giant buildings. Attached to the building were giant screens. I tried to tell people that we had to do whatever we could to get out of here. But everyone wanted to go to the Parties. Guards began to come up behind the crowds. They must be there for safety people thought. Why do they have weapons? thought Zarat. No one was allowed to speak. *Zarat thought of the Dark Society. How they started with ideals of Free Speech, but slowly their rights were silenced and no one could speak out without being called a terrorist or a militant.* Images came onto the screens. Tony Bennett in the back of a limo. His face warped into an older actors face with the made-up features of Hitler. The world of pastels became covered in a grey filter. The brightness was gone. The camera pulled back and the Hitler actor was naked. He sat on a young boy. His dick was hard. He began to fuck the boy. The narration began. "Party five. The party of joy. Watch as Hitler and others violently fuck young virgins." Hitler began to cut into his flesh. Rip at his skin. The boys face was blurred. His face was not important to Them. "This is your time. Do as you please." Rage, Anger, Fear. Why did they want us to be afraid? Why show us this before we go into the party? I wanted to tell them all to turn and attack all at once and we could take them. If Zarat attacked alone, I knew no one else would attack, and Zarat would die. There was not Fear for Zarat, but he knew he couldn't beat the Darkness unless he could communicate. And They knew that. The People were paralyzed with Fear and Confusion.

Was this just entertainment? Or is it better to let the People think it is entertainment. Tell the People exactly what is happening so that they think it couldn't be. People think of things differently when it is just a "joke". Just a show. It is not knowing at all that makes people paranoid and angry. If the truth of what is happening barely leaks out, it is better for control. The People don't think that anything is being hidden.

The People seemed to enjoy it and be disturbed by it. The People thought they were not supposed to be afraid of the parties, so they covered their concern with laughter and uncomfortable looks.

On the screen the Hitler sat on a face while raping the young man. He crapped on her and kissed it back to him. She then bit into a snake and white ooze came out of it. She poured it on the boys face. Fear. Rage. and Loathing. Suffering. There was a fade to clips of talk shows the woman had performed on...

I, Zarat, awoke from the Fourth Vision. Knowing what will come to pass if the character of Zarat does nothing.

Don't be afraid of what will come. But think, is this what you want to have happen? Is this what you want to be? Make yourself the person you want all others to be. Set yourself free. In your Mind, your Heart, and know your Spirit. And this will never happen, again. I suggest you fight. Not for yourself (never for yourself) but for everyone else.

Everyone is at war. A war to matter. The war is against Zarat. To stop himself from continuing on. To turn him back into the peace he always wanted. To choose the Final Perception and Break Free from every reason that will continually convince him to serve his wanting irrelevant, loud mind.

The shame the Catholics used to subdue the Dark Ages left a great scar on the reality of the people that lived it, just as enslavement does. The British sect of the worlds of history is too well known for its ability to enslave the mind. It is the basis of power seekers and country stealers of today (masons). Some wise men formed a great country, while others tried to make the same image, just with them in charge of it. Anyway, the scar spreads. It will not leave until we purge that shame from this world. See the shame etched into all people, even the ones that think they have more liberated mindsets. Gays and lesbians and transsexuals and feminists and black evangelists and non-smokers all of them joined together, all of them broken up into special groups with leaders and a few key opinions. All of them too careful about stepping outside the lines of what they think this society condones, they all cling to the overall message, gripping the values that made them happy, like cherish the children, or monogamy, or a house, or christmas lights... steadliy hanging on to what they secretly think could live forever. All of them subconsciously aware of something, but what, they are wary when they talk. Sure not to upset the angry Puritans. The pushers of shame. The destroyers of Freedom. All good intentioned and all afraid to stop thinking of how to escape the reality of our own demise. It's why the bent Catholic/Christian religion has spread so far in the recent years in the society that needs, like a naked baby bird in a nest. Trapping people with the lie that keeps all in Dark, Heaven and Hell.
It's hard to not be afraid of impending moments, it's easy to want to help people and actually harm them with force. It is hard to stop. Let your wars end. I will not believe the programming. This Country was not founded for a strong Economy, or for strong morals, these are a bowl of poison gray mush, it is here for Strong Freedom. Let me tell you, "GOOD MEN SPEAK UP." Remember that over-spilling happy feeling when you were a child and the greatest delight was about to burst out of your smiling face, and then someone told you to sit there and be quiet, or you're an idiot? Stop the shame and let yourself play again. Living is agony if you think it is. As every piece of shame that leaves that obstructed feeling in me falls off of my shoulders I know Liberation and I stop being afraid of the imaginary army the persecutors desperately want you to think is everywhere. The Dark Society uses the same principles, instead of God knowing what you might be doing all the time, now they call it the FBI. Same oppression. Same shame. Same scar.

Convince a people to pursue a path where they have nothing to gain. Have them walk it when they want nothing to gain. Create drive to show the person they are already there and have nowhere to go. I have goals, but if I do not achieve these goals, I will still be happy and full, because I am not these goals. People take entire lives to have power for these minds and these bodies, when we are not these lives, these minds, or these bodies. We are existing spirits. Spirits that will never know power, but in a physical life we experience many things. None of them permanent. Always taken by a non-threatening Death. Every Freedom taken away by a populace to extend the safety and lengths of these lives is a direct defiance of the design of the world. We are not this power. We are not these flowing tears.

Every ornament we hang on the tree falls to the ground, proving that the tree was never there.

And as they live, wanting, wanting, needing, having, fearing the loss of any little thing that pleases them, this whole focus of their grasping lives, reaching to hang onto something they cannot have, stops. Like when the sea turns to glass after the storm and we realize, instantly, that we were the ocean we were trying to swim away from. We cannot drown in ourselves, but we must be willing to. The master learns that he must be willing to live in that Instant.

<u>Meaningless Thoughts Leading to Large Reasons</u>

Zarat: Many, many religions throughout the world believe that there is great energy, great spirit in the center of the belly. Taoism especially. Many martial arts use the area as a focus of chi. It is also slightly interesting that children are carried in the area. Perhaps this is where the soul developed. Perhaps the longer the gestation period, the more developed the soul is. Humans average 266 days for pregnancy. A Giraffe 425 days. A Seal 350 days. Camels 406 days. Cows 280 (One of the closest to us. Interesting. Perhaps people think they are sacred because our souls are so similar. Isn't it strange how Western societies main consumed animal is cow? Society itself is so violent and cruel. Always the worst rise to power, the good don't need it. Society must always be stopped. This is the voice of the Great Philosopher and Wise Anarchist Thomas Jefferson.). Elephants, 2 years. Most Primates, pretty close to humans. *Why does man and especially woman always have to lie and think they are the best or the longest or the toughest something or somebody?* Perhaps man is not the top of the charts on enlightenment or reincarnation. It is an interesting way to make up a reason for reincarnation. It is as true as any idea. And just as false.

Imagine that spiritualist entrepreneur that discovers where the soul is and studies it and learns how to create it. Imagine the contribution to the cloning market. Or maybe the soul (or the "should" or in some cases the "soled") is the same as a non-cloned creature.

Zarat believes what he wants to believe. It is his choice. He finds thoughts and he makes those that he liked most or found most dear a part of him. This is a gift of an OverMan. He is the conclusion of himself.

<u>Turning, Flipping, Flopping</u>

This book was supposed to be done so long ago. All the while I blink, I breath, I pulse...and my mind fantasizes. About everything. Food, laughter, conversation, numbers, sex, all of it, thinking about absolutely anything, Free from Oppression, without fear, I clack. Clack Clack. I never expected to live this long. But still I worry. I worry about how this must all play out and appeal. Can anyone believe there is someone that is Genuine? A human? A person that was this brave. No matter which way I choose to turn, I turn that way with courage. I walk the line of risk. I am what I preach. People see the odds around me and they flinch for me. They see what I am making. What we did, by living and dying. Will the rest of us have to dispel anger, sadness, disappointment, or happiness, or welcoming smiles? What will the people have to be broken of next? Where will the next shatter of illusion come from? How will we next make them see the majesties of their souls and the simplicity of this planet and its reactions? When will Evolution turn? When will we know that Nothing is Enough? And living is easy. But not wanting what's once wanted is hard. True dreamers want their works to be received by the world they made them for and simply drip into the subconscious, but we see a lot of people being angry and looking for something else to justify their anger, and we are ready to fight or vanish. And we just hope our government doesn't Oppress us when it happens. FDR, Nixon, Reagan, The Bush's, all taught us to be wary of our "leaders" of "our" free country.

I have a Dreamer's Fire.

Idiots Guffaw at Difference

People want to matter to us. They want to offer us something. This is how people feel important. They want to matter. And it is who praises them, that will own them first. If you don't make them matter they cannot love you. Couples will lose, thinking that they are losing their caring for each other as a relationship goes on and on. But what actually is happening is something holy. The incorrect interpretation ruins their lives because they aren't smart enough to see it happening. People can't matter to us. They don't. All people are equal. All live in the illusion of how important they are until they shatter the mind grip that makes people want to matter. Doesn't happen often. People think that We don't like them. But, Dear OverMen, like them all the same. They can't inspire us, because we are way way way way past that bullshit. When things don't matter, as in a holy and realized relationship, between anybody, the "not mattering" saves them a million shallow bickering conversations. The Art of letting go of anger and annoyance is sacred, and natural to our Species.
It's why we wind up alone. You can't see that We love You more than anyone else that you would easily kill for. And that's why We Hate You. Let the river of mud settle and you shall see that the water has always been pure, and has always been wet.

Zarat, still alive in a world he is preparing to escape. Still reacting with the reactions he wants to become old. Still as reactionary as any of us. Still the one that engulfed himself amongst the life, that existed, that touched it, that risked the peace of sanity. His Freedom so near... ready to stop considering it, and get on with living or dying. He passes through a small town...

<u>The Pursuit of Accented Reality</u>

I try to sit and realize the beauty of the simple, living in their worlds so close to reality, but too daft to realize it, and at this point I realize I've been tricked back into thought, just because things exist, and so, I can think of them. Plotting and singing the reflective chants of their rhetoric. I've touched and felt a thousand realities, and then I get to think of them. Integrate them. A forced into chosen path of writing. The best way to deal with it. It's like orgasming for the 45 minutes to 2.2 hours it takes to write one segment. Tap Dancing. Beating it for you. And all of us loving it. Singing at our depths from what we knew wasn't a sin. And we stop fighting it, in ourselves and on the "streets". Come on...What are we fighting today? Free verse. Water Slide. What are we failing in today? And why are we so disappointed in ourselves? People like us, you and me, sought power in the system. It was said, "Convince them that they want to be the best." And we aren't capable of it. They took away food sources so that we'd have to be a part of it, and if we weren't we'd starve. The generations have already began to come that have no idea how to survive without society. Do you see that? The Dark Ages, just at the edge of town.

Censorship: If we are not allowed to say anything, if we are not allowed to do anything, evolution will cease. To be able to evolve the best thing must be chosen, and force cannot be sued for it to be possible.

<u>Death cures all ailments</u>.

We choose to make ourselves what we want to be. Every moment in life is your chance to try to be anything you dream. If you want to be a hero commit to kindness and sacrifice. If you want to be a pianist commit to striking every note at its specific time and tone. We cannot change many things that happen around us, but truly we are masters of our perceptions, and so, creators and guides to our own very specific and independently defined inner realities and so, our masters of the true world. The true world is ourselves.

A series of choices equals one life, and no more or less than one single unit.
$y=1.0$ (y being an undetermined but exact value. $y=\Sigma$ (the sum) of choices which always $=1.0$ life)
There are a series of choices. The number of choices in a life are exact and cannot be changed. But this number is undetermined until the moment it exists, when the person dies. The number is undetermined but it stills exists in the equation of a specific life as a variable.
Within the series the number of choices to be made is very specific. The number will be absolute and can never change. However, the number of choices is unknown until the number is resolved through the living of a life. So, it is absolute, but undetermined. The life can be no more and no less than its undetermined length. Specific mathematics without conclusion.
Therefore: Life is exact, but undetermined. Therefore: We are

Aren't all variables exact and specific, even if undetermined?
Thought.
I bet someone knows this thought perfectly. I am ignorant to so many things. As is the man *(Keep your insecurity away from the reference of man for both man and woman. I know what I mean. It does not matter if you know.)* Who knows this thought perfectly?

<u>Anxiety</u>

And here I am. Again. A constant repeating cycle. My anxiety rising when I am in this world. Rising from nowhere, but circumstance. The system has made the body afraid that it won't have sustenance again. I can't get work because I haven't had a stable work history. And I can't take a job that I am not treated with respect. I won't be looked down on by the confused and the lazy that never had a Big Dream to live for. I cannot be their slave. It is a hard world for the good people left. For those that have courage. But the feeling of impending doom awaits. If only I could get work that paid enough. I'm a creative masterpiece, but no one can believe me. I work harder and harder more and more to not have to be a slave to a fool, giving me yelling advice that means nothing that has no other thought beyond it than "do it". I'd almost settle for a chance to be in the system, just for the chance to reach a dream. Everyone else gave up, but my dream was the biggest, and without luck, without intervention by anything that had power beyond my vision, my dream will kill me. I guess I am like everyone else...wrong. I still have the fear, the tendencies that lead to doom, my personality my fate, but still I can know peace in an instant. I can know what the truth is, although it doesn't even seep into the heads of the rocks that think this slave society has always been the way people thought from the beginning of ignorant programmed image worshipping time. The stress that the body produces from the weak states of survival makes me irritable, and still I calm it. Again. Realizing that I soften the berating edge of constantly foreseeing intelligence. And I touch the soul once more. Like a ping of rings around a point on a still pond, and I plunge into myself in an instant.

PEOPLE MISPERCEIVE WITH INSTANT DELIGHT THAT THEY THINK THEY KNOW SOMETHING. AND THEY THROW IT AT YOU. PEOPLE THINK I EXPECT PEOPLE TO KNOW EVERYTHING I TALK ABOUT AND THAT I AM NOT FULLY EXPLAINING SOMETHING AS A MEANS TO SHOW THAT I AM SMARTER THAN THEM. BUT, WHAT IS ACTUALLY HAPPENING, JUST BEYOND WHAT THE EGO THINKS IT KNOWS, IS THAT MY MIND MOVES SO QUICKLY FROM EXPLOSION OF IMAGES AND PATTERNS AND EVENTS THAT HAVE NEVER EXISTED I COULDN'T POSSIBLY TAKE THE TIME TO EXPLAIN IT. I TRY TO SHOW YOU WITH VISUAL MOVEMENT OF MY HANDS WHAT I'VE SEEN. LAUGH WITH

ME, BUT FAIL TO FULLY UNDERSTAND. THESE FRIENDS OF
MINE, ARE IN US ALL. IN OUR SECONDS WAITING TO BE
USED BY OUR UNIQUE TICKET, AND WAITING TO BE NOT
WHAT WE EXPECTED.

<u>Existential Becomings</u>

Existentialism is the practice of accepting yourself as a means to accepting other people. This base state escalates to become the practice of realizing that a person can change themselves into any personality, can adopt any reasoning, and can be whatever they dream. This is what the master very slowly learns to do. For best results I have found that humility and the works of the artists of humility (Jesus, Siddhartha, Gandhi, etc.) prove the most interesting and beneficial in guiding one to the height of what they can be, (but it cannot be denied that there are many paths and many choices and they are all interesting and to the Existentialist that practices logic and honesty they are all beneficial).

There is a school of Existentialism that dreams about what they want to be, but hate and fester in their weakness because they cannot become it. Often in the Great Philosophies, in Existentialist Writings, an alter personality will be invented. It is always something to admire, but always it ends in festering loathing and ultimate failing of the Becoming. The Becoming of the OverMan. Nietzsche loved and wanted to be Zarathustra. In Fight Club, Tyler Durden wanted to be his ideal of Tyler. The conflict. The failing. The acceptance of failing. The goal is to teach how to Become, not how to deal with not becoming it. This is the next evolution of Existentialism. There have been Great Societies that have risen up, such as the Nazis that tested the realms of Existentialism, but ultimately failed because they didn't practice the methods of the Humble Existentialists. Jesus and Siddhartha had the ability to kill, murder and make suffering, but they chose the other path. The more beneficial path. The path of gaining not of taking. *Another method the Nazis could have tried to correct the greed and avarice that they experienced from the oppression of the Jews (meaning the oppression of money) could have been a re-education. The Nazis failed to notice one of the key teachings of Existentialism...People (You) are malleable. And it is easy to convert the masses. This is a difference in the sides of Existentialism. But the Nazis did succeed in moving Beyond Good and Evil. They did succeed in becoming a type of success and they should not be disregarded in the teachings and understandings of Existentialism. Many societies have hated egoism and the taking mentality. The Nazis were true Existentialists because they tried to do something about it, but they failed because they needed to first do something about themselves. Egoism destroys all pure Philosophies. All Philosophies are doable, but the men implementing them have always lost to egoism.*

<u>Rendering the Dream</u>

A hard part about reaching Existentialism(, meaning Enlightenment,) in America, in the West, is that there is no way to tell where you are within the course to Peace and Full Freedom. But I guess you never know. One can never tell. No matter where you are. You can't trust your elders, you can't trust your friends, your enemies, you can't trust your teachers. You must only be devoted to overcoming every ounce of ego driven foolishness that you are. You must only be devoted to easing suffering. You must question everything. And reach the points where questions mean only more made up answers that lead you further away from the simplicity of the Truth. You must be devoted to maximum, deepening, humility. It takes work. It takes faith for the teachings of the Holy Philosophers (Like Jesus, Like Socrates, Like Nietzsche, Like Sartre, Like Gandhi,) and it takes the courage to leave what they taught behind and possibly push forward and become the Dreamer's Dream.

The Youth, They Will Kill Again

Many soldiers kill young. Some of us for our own causes, most for someone else's. Some feel bad because later they discover the power of death when "Pain" teaches them that Life is valuable. And Love is strong. Others wish there were more at the end of their grip, crushing out a breath...the only thing this guy needs to survive...snuffed. Poetry in motion. All these soldiers, I haven't met too many bad ones. They believe softly in the "I" of the concrete of their ideals. And their ideals barely shine over into the light. But had they not had to kill for Reasons that were meant to expire, then they would have been better men and women. I see an army of nurses and caretakers...an open border and a populous trained on Independence...a military full of a few special units, of men addicted to sacrifice, because I've seen the way a fascist officer in a Fascist country can look at a person that passes. I see equal pay and an improved world. Health Care is the New Military. The step up for the Poor.

Fasting

I accidentally fast all the time. I just won't eat. My body does it naturally. It is sort of a cleansing. Sort of a spiritual journey. I am naturally spiritual. I am centered in it. Somehow, no matter how strange, chaotic, good, or horrible I am always at peace. It is always perfect and balanced and happening the exact way it should. Of course, so is everyone else's life. The center in the spirit simply lets me notice it.

<u>Fate is Our Reaction to Circumstance</u>

If my father had been more successful in the Capitalist/Fascist country or really successful and I was born with a 300 million dollar spoon in my mouth, I probably would have seen the neuroses that drives someone to that and I probably would have found great peace in not-achieving, never needing to be verified. I'd live in a trailer on the side of a highway. I would do nothing but be at peace, maybe write poetry, maybe even have a little job. But...he was not. And my family was oppressed. So, I live in a trailer on the side of a highway scorching out course manifestos to explain how the acceptance of nature is the key to understanding what we are, a fit piece of nature...Be present in it. Notice the life that is around you, don't think of the life that is ahead, but be aware of the movement of Time. Just keep yourself alive, that's all you have to do, everything else is just dancing in enjoyable illusion. My fate deepens me because regardless of the circumstances that set my mind to perceive a path of living that was valuable to me because I was alive as this person. Zarat has a lot of natural attributes I have used well.

<u>Never Censorship. Evolution! The Next Thought, helping us</u>

There are a lot of things to think, and eventually, humanity will be able to figure it out. Because a computer can reference it. We must always think and do everything. "But! Remember this is the OverMan's!" If you feel like you are better than someone and it doesn't make you laugh, it makes you sneer, then you are not one. Your reactions will rise and trigger other reactions and your reactions will rise and there will be death, if you try to touch the path. Do not bode lightly on these trails. Heroes walk here. And if you ever wanted adoration for it, then do not seek it, and if you feel it later, humble yourself. And build yourself again, Oh! OverMan!.

<u>Dream On</u>

I think the mind basically cycles through everything it can think in dreams. We think along a set of lines that we think is who we are, but the mind can be stopped. Dreams can be stopped and controlled. But basically I think it is a motor running. But through dreams, if used this way, we can project ourselves into different realms of consciousness. Like to meditate with Buddhas for example. I've done, or rather my characters have done, a lot of writing on it, especially nightmares. For example, they always stop if you stop giving them identity, which means, reacting to them, stopping running or fighting. I suppose that is true with people in reality too. When we are accosted, they seem to lose all power if they have not hurt us or helped us. We seek to render the world neutral.

When we realize that we can be anything in our minds, we can think anything in the conscious world, and create amazing things.

<u>Philosopher</u>

I am Zarat. I am a Philosopher. I experience random and specific human events and based on my observations and deductions I form an opinion about it. This opinion may or may not have already existed. I am a thinker. For fun. It is my natural state of being, but I do not wish to stop it. I am at full peace and joy with everything I am. People can find much peace with this advanced technique.

Bloodied Hands of a Mindless Boy

What do you think of my murders? Were they real? Did life die? Do you think that I would not kill for my country? Did you just feel like you would kill for this thing, this trigger word, this program…this false idol that lets humans assume an image that can wield large formations of people. Yet…here we are. Now able to manipulate ourselves, as a resulting statistic in the grand observation of each other…
I know death. I know the stillness of its deadpan matter of factness. The existence in the moment of ending another present formation of existence. But.   Does it change the fact that the notion is done? There will be a soldierness amongst the compassionate that will exist in the realms of the full scheme of society, where you live now, in your circumstance that is always improvable, which is amazing. My war is my own. Blood on me is blood I have considered. The blood of a circumstance. If I told you the reason you would support my vengeance. You love vengeance. It is a common trait here. We will fight, and want to, and for good, but have not understood the...

But to see me is to see a calm man, but a man who can be sudden. Which will always and instantly translate to sex to every woman I sit beside, no matter what you think she means to you. Yes, even me. The alone. There is a sensation of a full spirit a woman won't resist, no matter with which name you try to hold her, daughter, wife, innocent. For a man who can be sudden is a man you can't be that is fast, and strong, and forceful, I hear them thinking with the pussy's mind. (Face the words that make you flinch, it is a the path to break yourself Free from your sense of disgust.) The strength of the impulse of the movement that lunges and plunges and penetrates in a deep and leveling nature is what is asked from me. Yearned for, by those that want to be shaken and blankened by what has built up and by what pretends to keep meaning. And as the motion occurs, as the result of who I take away from this world for an hour, or forever, fell to me by a pattern. A sinking. And all of them held power. Some over small areas, things I saw. Some over large areas. Some you knew. And as I slipped from a shadow and sent most back to Freedom, to try and break the Hallucination of their shoddy Reasons and valueless titles in a fashion that generally left them quietly and without the spasm of fear. As the body goes dead and can't run life anymore, I tap the head repeatedly to try and move the soul to where I am certain it can eject. And I whisper into their ear a sacred instruction and a focus on the sensation of Love. What they always wanted. I know that in another Darkness it would be them lunging at me, me a nameless unconsidered victim for them, but the key to their definition, an imagined definition, and in the instant, they'd fall again. My parry unexpected, unfortunately for them they had to pass through several planes of space to reach me, which gave me plenty of time to think of the three or four reactions that are plausible to stop him, the instant approaching where I will choose one. One of the partier's lines of Reasons not reaching long enough to reach meaninglessness to resolve to us reaching another day and realizing that beyond the Grand Illusion, we're all the same, deep down. I just wanted to let you know. Usually when anger or sadness or fear is the sensation driving the action there should be no action at all, unless it's an action to react. (Or should you?) Well, who cares what extra thoughts you add onto your mind which keeps it muddled and unmanageable, you will react quicker and more efficiently in all times of physical combat that falls to us in an instant for chains of reasons and for sudden reasons if you do not believe you are your emotions. And then you will rise from them. Above them, more so as you practice. You see? The will. You see time. If you move to Manifest Utopia from yourself unto the infinity that spreads across every expanse beyond you, then with practice, we will Become it.

To escape most attacks and most oppressions, move. Get away from what is powerful, this is practical. Get independent. Let the politicians, like me, murder each other for our reasons. Just a little while longer. War ends. Traditions of hate can fade, over society, and of course that means, in you.

Deserts and Trailers

If the value of life is what you pay for it, then life is cheap. At least
in the desert. What we did there is none of your concern, but be sure
things, some tiny, things changed.   People think differently when we
are around. Better. Grander. People matter when the generator is on.
And they know they do. And they think in a higher way, but do not
have the energy to maintain it when we are gone, but if they knew it
required inner energy and not outer energy then they would find the
simple path to the fountain of Unplaced Faith. Faith which has no
place. So, it can be anywhere it is needed. This is Philosophizing.
Building spiritual sway.

When you live in a trailer things tend to build up. They tend to get
dirty. You never fully clean it, because you always figure you'll be
somewhere else. And sometimes you move, but the piles follow intact.
But the scenery alters. New people, small groups, watching them, those
that loved money, and are ugly for it. Those that smiled and laughed
and felt it not matter. The still trying. The finally sitting. New people.
Let us introduce you to interacting with us. You will either love it, or
only think of yourself, and continue without having noticed the finer
things in people.

It never mattered where we were. We existed there. We always existed
there. And therefore chose to affect it, talentfully.

More Spatters

I am left alone to think. Left alone without the hand of God to help.
There is no divine intervention, only divine connection, only my own
Will can keep me alive and free. In a Dark Society where people have
pursued power over the poor, crime is the only freedom. *Constantly,
over and over, he must raise the power it takes to fight. Over and over,
keeping himself from the love he wanted to feel for Her. Tiny thoughts,
always building his Will to attack everything, especially himself.*

A short story...

I Had a Funny Ferret, But He Ran Away, He Ran Away, He Said He Had to Get Paid

by Mother Zarat

Two ferrets, wiry and spry, kept alert eyes open for the girl that cared for them. Every sound making them twitch and leap. Their quick and caring minds jumping to react to every echo, hoping that one sound will be the creaking front door. When all of the sudden...the creeeaaaak, followed by the thud of a heavy backpack. And a plopping sound of a teenager to a couch. The ferrets so excited in their upstairs cage that they were chasing each other's tails, round and round in the cage. Then they stopped. Both of them. Suddenly. They listened for her.   .   .   . Her wheezings. Her heavy breaths caused by her backpack and an improper inferior asthma medication. The high pitched tight breaths slowly began to recede. The ferrets' dear friend leapt up off the couch. The ferrets heard the "fwump" sound of air filling the cousin on the couch. So quietly they hear the tapping of the girl's feet on the linoleum in the kitchen. Ah! She'll be coming with food. Excitement overtakes the white ferret and he lunges his teeth into the neck of the brown one, raising a loud scream. Three echoes of laughter rise up from the downstairs, first a young one, then a heavier older one, and then a crackling guffaw kakkle. The ferrets began to laugh too.

<u>*Free*</u>

I am Zarat. The Mighty Zarat. I am not Zarathustra. But I am an OverMan. I am not <u>The</u> OverMan. I am the beginning. And an end within myself. I am a slave to birth. I am a slave to life. I am a slave to the approaching death. I am a slave and I am FREE.
This is the true glory of the OverMan. FREE to be awkward. FREE to believe. free to pained. free to be gallant, free to be kind, even free to be cruel. Free to know all this matters in a sense of non-matter. It is all so important and it all means nothing. This is the understanding. To move beyond the limits of shear logic. To escape with the use of logic. Perhaps it is the logic of creation, creation itself. Birthed from the imagination. And abandoned when truly obtained. This book. The writings. The life and times of the Constant Creator is meant to be understood by the truly advanced. I call it "advanced" because to define it It must have a place. What happens if you can step beyond the point of being a scholar? Move beyond being an intellectual. What if you moved beyond the power and trap of these names???

So these are my confessions. A type anyway. Not true in any means to physical reality. But true within the meaning of a life. Embraced in Death I die here. But that which lives within my body is greater than me. And it shall live forever. Me part of it. Yet completely IT. This is the truth as I know it. Random, non-sensical and absolutely true. True to me. And I define truth. And so define all the world. This is the knowledge of the cosmos within us. The world separate and at one with yours and the countless worlds within people within worlds that care nothing of any world you know. What will man become now that it has created a device, a computer, that can record it, mark it, for reference a million years from knowing? What did the world become when it created the alphabetical symbol? Not much. Just confused.

The government, the money mongers, the controllers are out of control. Once again the social dream has been used for power, to kill, to control. Once again it has become warped by fear and ignorance. Do not blame these people of power, do not condemn them, but stop them.

"I would like to go to," spoke the Woman.

"the beach," thought Zarat. "I was just thinking the same thing."

"That's right," the woman, "You have been doing that a lot lately."

"I can do it with anyone now. At first it was just you. It is a strange clairvoyance. It is real. It is instant. And it is useless. It feels like a real thought that I had. But it is clearly not my thought. I had no intention of going to the beach. I mean, we can go, but I wasn't thinking about it just then," spake Zarat. "I don't know what it is. You can read about things like this happening as a by-product of meditation. But they are never as we really experience them. It's strange how we imagine the "power" of what gives us no power. It is all so useless and so welcome."

"I wish I could know what it was like. Sometimes I feel like I progress so slowly," holy woman. She the last to know him. This woman who simply succumbed to the inertia of the gravity that led her to be with the epic man.

"I have been pursuing this emptiness for so long. Often I felt like I was making no progress. But I chose to use the technique of faith and believe in what seemed true. So I dredged on. You will be where you want to be one day if you keep devoted and vigilant. But when you get there I think that you will laugh at how simple and common and unextraordinary the majesty you found is," Zarat.

"Maybe." a seeker, a constant diligent doubter, she will surpass theory and thought one day, when it is perfectly timed.

<u>This is the Letter *She* Wrote to Me</u>

I will never forget you, so in this life I will never remember you. You now live deeply in me. But my path is like yours. Free. And like all free paths they will journey where they must. They will touch what they can. But their very nature is free. We have freedom in the moments of our reality. Free from suffering, even as it happens. How will you do with the suffering that this situation will implant in the reflexes of your psyche, that place where you know that this is too important to forget? You won't want to forget. But I will. Don't cry, maybe this isn't even about you. Who knows. Who knows what I have had to see to think what I can think, or will, or what I'll be with no more need to think. What of it when I become? I don't know either. Our futures are uncertain, and will never be what we want them to be. But still, Since my soul will record what you have meant to me, I think we will see each other again, and recognize each other in some strange way, and what will the fates of random circumstance weave for us to deal with and come together, and get torn apart again?

You know what we were, and I have already started to forget. It is not needed in my mind. You are a sensation deep beyond feeling, that I cannot lose. Every time that I feel very deeply happy where the most love lets me be absolutely free, every time I live in Bliss, playing my games of living and dying, I will be as with you as you are with yourself. Our souls are forever stronger for having known each other. And if they see each other again, they will rejoice, as they recognize themselves. I love. And when you see Love looking back at you, the grace will strike you, hm., then what will we do? What will be broken and built, and fade into dust? I love.

Cordially,

<u>To Love A *Woman*</u>

To love a woman that holds no past. *She* clings to no preconception of what *she* wants you to be to please *her*, to serve *her*. *She* is unowned, and so am I. *She* wants nothing from you, yet still, here you are, interacting with *her*. Making a moment happen. Discussing, thinking, thoughts out against thought, *both* reasoning towards the flurry that flutters from *your* free hearts. *Both* reasoning for life, and all that comes with it. Noticing it beginning, embracing its end, and enjoying the creamy center. Loving It, without fear of It. Knowing the holiness in every slow motioned soul influenced centering that bursts a thought into the brain and blurts a response that strikes *one* mindless. Laughing at the proof that this is not eternal, and not as serious as *we* want it to be. And together *you* looked down the same road and saw the same end and that end was harmony. For all of war, guns, flowers, power, poverty, and peace.
And *our* reasons, unheard faded off into the forgotten, where good energy still tills the Universe.
And *her* unbound love for me strikes suddenly. Overwhelmed by passion as *she* crawls over your body. *She* loves you. And you turn to *her* and you mount *her*, harness *her*, and *she* loves me. *Her* eyes telling me, as he laughs, without the present knowledge of vulnerability. With no need to recognize it, *she* doesn't. And *she* is free, and *she* loves it as hard as I do. And exhausted we *both* slip into meditation. For a time. And then *we* run over each other's bodies and meld into a cushioned nakedless (because *we* didn't think naked) world. Dripping, sticking, and never doubting the recognition of the ultimate gift of the *other*. It is easy for a hero to give his life, but the love between *heroes* that know how hard it is to do, to push beyond the fear of loss is a quaking majesty, whose energy even just in thought creeks the old boards of this house.
We noticed the best meaning in where *we* were told there was none.
Like *children* in touch with our souls, lost to time and mattering.

<u>In Dreams</u>

What is this??

I laid down to sleep. I must have fallen asleep. I can feel it. I can't move my arms. I am laying on them. I am asleep. I am not trapped in the hallucination of dreaming. It is quiet here. Uncluttered. What is that? An image. A woman. A hallucination. An impulse that creates an image. A spasm in the brain that forms a dream. That girl I love. She is beautiful. Come to me. She came. I can do anything I want. I am the observer. There is a part of me that can see the mind itself. I am not the mind. Pull down your pants. Her beautiful pussy is exposed to me. I can have sex with you. I want to. And I will. I am naked. I slide down to lick her. Both holes. Just holes. They have always been just holes, but the mind explodes in hallucination and makes me erect. Wait. Yes. I am erect in my actual body. How funny. I could stop this right now. But sex is fun. The hallucination is intoxicating. She bends over. I slide in. I ram her. She moans loudly. Of course she does. I like it that way. What have I never done? Nothing matters here. It is my own world. What then? A penis. Sure. It is small. Like a baby's. I'll touch it. It is just a small thought. It is growing from you my beauty. Suddenly you are a hermaphrodite. How strange. How terribly interesting. It is large now. It could be my own. Naturally it is. It is an image ingrained in my brain. A warped image of what the penis shaft really looks like because I see it from above most of the time. I choose to go down on to it. It fills my mouth. What a time. My own experience. I choose nothing again. It is quiet. I can think. I am not trapped. I can remember what I have known before. In dreams that I have been in trouble in, for quite awhile, I instantly pull myself from them. I am instantly aware that I am in an illusion. And I have the option to awake. My eyes can be forced open. It is always hard to force them open. The weight of sleep is very heavy. But it can be done. When I was younger. Much younger. A boy. I could notice I was asleep in a nightmare, but I could not leave the hallucination of dreaming. But I could scream. I would scream so loud in the dream that the sound would stop. And my body would know that I could wake up. I would trick my mind, because it knew that I should be screaming, and it would realize the illusion. And then I would pry my eyes open. But this. Right now, is full detachment. I am not Zarat, not exactly. I am something that can observe and control *Zarat*. What am *I*?

I have slept since. I cannot do it all the time. Sometimes. I have not yet been able to will it. It appears and I can do it. I realize myself. Sometimes I just dream. I have heard that those that meditate often and pursue the silent mind do not dream. I think it is in the Tao de Ching and I think it is Tibetan.

<u>Bearing Arms</u>

It has been hard to focus on the war. It has been hard to fight tyranny because over the time that I have lived I have become a different kind of man. My spirit has overcome my violence. But still, the violence is needed. It must be. How can fascism be stopped? The government, the wealthy, even the poor, have no courage to stop it. They want only to serve it. They are afraid greatly of Civil Disobedience. They serve what their conscience knows to be wrong. They masturbate their egos with money and mere things to help them cope. The people of self-righteousness sold their souls for comfort and the blinding gift of ignorance. Yet still they hang firmly to the belief that they are wise, even though thought is fleeting, distant, and self glorifying.

I see no other way to disband the oppressive standing armies, all local, all federal, all worldwide. I see no other way to halt the occupation of the world, but then to destroy the fascists. Can breeding suffering to stop suffering succeed? It has. But does it take a shorter time then non-violence? Not often. One would have to exterminate the scores of greedy haters. The takers. Hitler tried it. But too much money was involved and the world rose against him. We must stop money. We must stop the spread of capitalism that consumes the world, unnecessarily. The system devours the planet. It allows everyone to be an oppressor. There is no man I have ever met that has ever deserved the right to sit in judgment over anyone else. At heart I, The Zarat, must truly be an Anarchist. And why not? It is the best of thoughts. Thoreau was one. Jefferson was one. Garrison was one. *I am an Anarchist*. Unafraid of the world around me. I know that no "power" can take any real thing from me. For all things that can be taken from me were fleeting anyway. I have to stop it.

A good *person* cannot sit down and let bad things happen.

The Dark Society must move away from force and power. The people must be armed and must learn and be taught how to defend themselves. This is the point of the number 2 (two) amendment.

I know that ultimately it does not matter what I do in my life. I know that in my center is absolute peace and full becoming. I must release my right to be blissfully and lazily "free". I have to fight the Darkness. I have mostly freed myself from my own ego. Now I must simply choose actions to fill the course of this life. My actions. My choice. My non-attached desire for this physical body is to revolt against those that assume power. Against that flow of greed and glory that killed the Indians, the Panamanians, the Iraqis, the Witches, the Cubans, the Slaves, the endless list of names. If the standing army is taken away, those that seek power will not have the option to use it for invasions and power, to preserve the interests of control. If the people are armed we only defend against the invasion upon our own living soil.

<u>Fighting Control</u>

It becomes clearer and more clear. I know more every day. I see how this world became controlled. I see the warping of illusion. The taking advantage of the minds of the People. Believe. Believe. No. Do not. See into the simplicity of truth. Those that control this world. The founders of capitalism and so, the controllers of the standing armies, want you to believe in the mightiness of their majesty. The devil hides in plain site but tells you he is somewhere else. Or so he might, but the devil doesn't exist. Fear exists. We are to think that amazing innovations exist in the depths of deserts and oceans. We are to think that every criminal gets caught by the police. Every television says that. It makes cowards not commit crimes, and it makes the true slaves feel safe. And it makes survivors feel like criminals, and feel bad about it and afraid, making them appear suspicious and profile-able. The government uses alien technology, it is strong and sneaky. Not really. Think of the slowness and pace of progress. If it were so amazing it would exist in the commercial sector somewhere and in some form. Money is strong, and a weak lie drawn upon the illusions of importance. The only things man can do are: explode things (even cars are based on the principle of tiny explosions, guns,), kind-of control and route electricity, it can accumulate and distribute things (like food and stores), it can build a shelter and maintain heat, we can move great distances and we can fly, and we can lie and manipulate and reason. The majesty of Man expands only from these basic things, which expands only briefly around our very basic needs of survival. Food, Shelter, and Water. We are only seconds ahead of stone carved blocks, a lean-to of sticks. This "advancement" is only because of the ability to "specialize" in a certain field. The system of monetary slavery, capitalism, is what made this possible. And even still, we are not much of anything. Does your car break down? Do your appliances fail? Can you lose your job? Can you die from many many diseases? Will you die? Can capitalism's absorption of the planet be halted? Can the use of fascism to pursue and perpetuate capitalism be stopped? Yes. Don't be a sucker. See that things are bad. People sought power. It is a small group of people, choosing the professions of the power seekers before them. It can be stopped. It can be changed. People can truly be free. No one has the right to control you. Ever. Not really for anything. But we must vow to stop the want for power and comfort in ourselves. Just let it go. Don't be so addicted. You will not die without these things. Life has always been lived, far before these things you "need". Give it up. Let comfort go. If you don't take what the controllers give you, you can and will be free. And the controllers will fade into nothingness.

<u>The Mirror</u>

Does the creature Zarat over exaggerate wrong-doings? I often seek lawsuits. I often yell when I drive. I hold a long grudge. I often quit jobs quickly. I lose friends at sudden intervals. Is it me? Of course it is. I am a participator in these events of living. I am the cause of any place I wind up in life. I have the mind of an idealist. A blind, over exaggerating mind. A poet's thoughts. I always wanted the open skyway in front of me. A dreamer's lofty reflex. I am emotional and fluent enough in emotions to be passionate, in an obscure way. My mind cannot stick to thoughts. I circle back to them after they brush my mind. I contemplate for weeks before I function. I think of a million ways, it is hard to choose. I have grown deeply patient with my own mind. It is because of all this erratic, vivid audio and visual hallucinations that I seek meditation. I need so much because I am so riddled with it. I am a yelling Hero of a hated rebellion. A driver of wars. There will be no war without me. Silent and humble by my own definition. Perhaps others identities keep them more peaceful. I am programmed to be this. Clearly. It just flows out of me. This definition of the programmed ego. It is so hard to notice that it is even happening. But a mad identity spills forth. Yet, it is also what this Zarat is. It is what I am supposed to be. But is not Enlightenment the overcoming of this identity? The path takes so long without a guru, but I find it much richer and deeply wiser than the taught path, than the image of emulation to fake. I learn through discovery because it is the only way I can truly understand the ingraining of this written creature that is the Mighty Slave Zarat.

I uncover the mystery, like an onion they say. Are we more than this programmed identity? What do we hear when we have revealed the very essence of this truth?

<u>The Father's Throne</u>
The Center of the Kingdom

There was a gruffness about him, that he hardly saw at all. To him it was an orchestra piping the music of his streaming seemingly playful reality. A result of the meditation was the sense of bliss. A constant and deepening one. Meanwhile the outside appearance often runs wild and the appearance becomes the ego itself, the very thing the person in meditation was attempting to overcome. But only a Wise Man could see that he had chosen to be this. He broke it and returned it. His heavy breaths a sign of his deep thought. He felt his own goodness and didn't believe in this ending reality to its fullness. The proof was of how little bothered him. We deepened our bond quickly with our ability to have no fear of sharing our lives, instantly knowing the type of tough man that doesn't betray. When he spoke people believed his Genuineness. He wouldn't lie to the face of any man he respected. He respected the man that knew He had already thought about killing them in a single movement as I was entering the room. He respected me because I was prepared for it. No man's life greater than any other's. This Hero of blood and love had seen greater souls amount to shit in the eyes the opinion the society treads, ridiculously. When you have killed people or been near killing people, but the understanding is much deeper if you can place yourself in the emotion of stillness, that it is very easy to kill people, skin is thin and knives are sharp. The grandeur quickly amongst it is that we choose to not do it, but to stand beside each other in a deepening swell of the Sea of Self, listening, to the calmness of our quest to find the appreciation for each other. Reaching to touch the place where the "should" sits. To sit beside someone that sits on that unmovable thrown is densely drowning, but easily breathable, to experience. It is something to sit beside someone that is certain of their Existence, and your absolute inability to extinguish it or damn it. Many shysters have feigned certainty and cried at night after knocking up the 19 year old but the Truth of Certainty, but the True Seeker finds that only a fool is certain and he, nor his thought is eternal, and that one day soon a day won't matter anymore, and we will be Free to be at ease again. Just free from the need to survive for a time. Just without the body that lets us touch life. Just without the want that feeds us.

<u>The Listening Technique</u>

I sit in front of her. I let myself not think of anything else. I don't think of a response. I do not want to converse. I want to listen to what she is saying. I desire to have no desire that will hinder my hearing her. She talks to me because she wants to. Because she chose to. At this moment in our lives, she is in front of me. It could be our last moment experiencing each other. This time could be lost in my memory to a flood of living and recording. It does not matter because it is happening right now. What a lucky, lucky man I am. Fortune is mine because I stopped to see what is always around me. I am not in a frenzy of having to do anything. I love the way she awkwardly smiles and laughs with a single breath when she realizes how I am staring at her and into her. The re-action is acceptingly disturbed and grateful. She is full of love and joy. Just because I happen to love her every way in that very second. I smile deep into the humor of the experience's shocking beauty. This is a precious technique. It leads to many more splendors. Many have a lifetime pursued in this single technique and it is not a wasted lifetime. Being in a moment of emptiness, of simplicity, leaves all doubt, all fear, all chaos, out. It is simple to do. It is only stillness. It must be noted that it is deeply important to be there for the person you are listening to. It is important to have the silence for others. There is a path, one common to *Zarat*, that of dullness and coldness. It can be useful at specific times. But overtime, it can become too defining and warping of a person's true identity. The choice in thought seems to hinder the ease of my Nature, so it creates suffering, so it must be induced by the ego, and so, by a fear. AAAAAhhhhhhhhhhh.

The mind runs away with uselessness. What I seek is more simple than my brilliant and mad mind can comprehend.

I am ignorant and simple in that I can be taken by the madness.   But thus is the state of slave suffering.

I love the way her hair fluffs out after she washes it. She looks like a gentle beast. Zarat is pleased. Her skin is so pale. So soft. So real and so fleeting. How precious is this drifting moment. It can be deeply important to this technique to focus on the disintegration of all life and time. This sub-technique can deepen the meditation.

I love her.
I'm allowed to.

I experience waves of some type of sadness when I let the mind go and I let myself realize the coming reality. I am sad that she will die. Does Zarat realize this, it, is coming soon? Often times the clairvoyance *Zarat* experiences is as subtle as a thought. Upon further examination of the slight feeling that follows it, can be seen, the true being of the thought. It is hard to notice. Being in a state of stillness, without the simple rampaging distractions of the mind, can help one-self notice such minute bursting movements of the spirit.

                        She is a kind woman. She has been talking for awhile. Good.

Beautiful.
I will reply deeply to her every comment and explanation of the play that televises in her.
I wish I could sustain this for her constantly.

<u>Existence Expands into Infinity in Every Direction from the Unfrightened You</u>

She taught me simply. *She* taught me that there are a million choices we can make to choose our course. Some of these decisions are with our ego, some against. While most people are overwhelmed by the infinite choices and stay treading in the water as they try to swim in every direction. But to remain calm, to be able to see that there is land out there, we gain the ability to move each thought in front of the next and go in any direction and find land. *She* chose absolute personal solidarity. Immovable, no matter where *she* was, no matter what *she* did, *she* was genuine, *she* was pure. Within it all. Even if *she* was pushed so hard that *her* flesh ripped open and *her* muscles tore apart, *she* so realized in *her* inherent existence that *she* knows these earthly illusions cannot touch *her*. In any way. *She* gained absolute freedom to be anything, to be nothing, if it was. *She* realized *her* own immortality, and *she* kept it real and unimagined by seeking no power, by needing nothing, not even life. *She* laughs.

The Beginning

I will fight this war alone. I will not involve these other nations known as individual people. They must choose for themselves. This is a war that is totally original to all of history. It must be a war of total ambiguity. A war without any figure heads or images. No flags. No one to follow when it is all adjusted. No ideals, but that of no power, that of ultimate humility. There will never be any people who think themselves gods, only individuals that made a vow to their self. Never brag of it. There must be no allies to join forces, to make more than one, after the vines of an old society are cut back off of us. No one will remain but we will always be present. There will only be one thing left behind...a hidden and well defined line cut sharp into the sand. We will triumph against this creeping tyranny because there will be no army for them to fight. There will be no hero to halt. We will drive onward and onward without fear because we will never see our leader fall. The adjustment period for those that seek power can carry on and on through the entire plot of the society. Constantly power will be trimmed and adjusted. The society will never have to suffer the fate of all countries and nations....it will not reach the point of over occupation and oppression, merely from the habits of "growth and progress." Always focus on the same organizations that pursue power. Any "government" organization (organizations ran by individual people that choose to propagate oppression) that punishes for ideals, that incarcerates, that seizes, that takes away just cause and choice. It is a choice, a commitment, a timeless vow of constant determination and gentle fury. We should all be ashamed that we allow our government to occupy foreign lands and force their, or our, or my, or your ideals on living people. We should and must stop this spread of Empire. Never call these people cowards that fight against the second most powerful nation on the face of the planet. It takes a great deal to muster the courage to fight, especially when the foe appears strong. We owe it to the ones that came before and fought the largest most powerful empire in the world. They sacrificed themselves for the ideal of tolerance, anti-censorship, individual property, and the right to pursue happiness. I am a Free Man always and I will fight against the illusions. I can see the truth. My nation will not be oppressed. I will release the Animal. *He wonders if this nature of thought will be hated by those that believe society is for the ultimate good of the people. Of course, but what they must know is that their beliefs are noble, but maybe, there are other techniques that can help people more. Perhaps it is time to push to the next level of expansion. Even if that next level of expansion is less than what we have now. Sometimes philosophies and ideals become too skewed, too misunderstood over time. Let us have a reunderstanding take place to preserve the original ideals of no fear and public trust.*

Two Years Ago...
a government official pleads for his life.

"You need not bring your avarice to me to veil your ignorance. I see right through your cowardice." The knife slid easily into his belly, as if he had no soul at all.

I feel no surrender for Man now. But I feel understanding and empathy. My empathy is now my curse.

<u>Unbreakable</u>

A Great Criminal can be an amazing writer. For, the genius criminal has to figure out every way the real mystery can play out, so that he doesn't ever get caught. And no doubt he is a great actor. No doubt a raw and honest man.

MANY TIMES i STARE OFF AND <u>i</u> AM SOMEWHERE ENTIRELY DIFFERENT, HEARING, SEEING, BEING CONSUMED BY THE MIND'S IMAGE FOR ME. IT IS SOMETHING TO SEE IT EXISTING. TO ALL OTHER'S I AM JUST STARING OFF.

<u>Peacier</u>

To have peace you must inevitably quit fighting. Look Deeper. Stop fighting for yourself, for your reasons, to be right, to please others, to have a place. This war machine must have a sheet placed over it. It must rev no more, by the will of my exhaustive destruction.

My search for that character that grows in a man that doesn't need to take shit from anyone, I found deeply in the gentle annals of the expansive quiet cooing babbling wilderness, far from the hands of man's wars to matter, and I found it further in the guts of savagery, within the fight to prove that peace was greater than warring.

Our hypocrisy pangs against us. Striking with that metal ping inside our heads. If everyone is wrong, shouldn't that make me wrong too? It is easy to imagine things. Hard to see reality. Our mind doubts, but our soul is calmly firm. The calmness is what tells us it is right. It is the rot of the stare back into myself that the mirror shows me.

<u>What makes us distinct?</u>

We see people, especially in large cities, affected by the great mass of the "super unconscious". People would talk to us about it. And we were not even sure that it existed. But we came to see, large groups acting similar throughout. A tone. A note that chimes the look of spite. They are searching for the reaction they will trigger. Who are you? The larger the society the more unstable and contradicting the message becomes. So many reasons, all forced to do it themselves, and to reason that way. We see a society that abandons and takes the guilt it should feel and does away with it, seeks therapy about it. So we think. Confined by our genre, trapped by our circumstance, but our circumstances are unique. Those of the "super subconscious" are not unique. They are the same, and the smart feel trapped by it and look to us with their frightened eyes to save them...when all they have to do is not need to be saved. With their eyes upon us we see everything they feel, they want to know if they are acting right?, Is it all right what I'm doing?, what do you think of me?, what?, how should I feel about his indifference?, does this not matter?, why did someone want me to think it did?, ... I know. It's simple. *Just to gaze upon Zarat can lead you to Freedom, but you cannot want it, you must want to give it to others, and he will show you something of Freedom, as much as you can handle, as great as you want to be*. And it is because we see this that we are able to interact with the mass mind, visit it, research it, send ships out to understand it, and its cruelty and what it needs to be happy again. We do not need to divide ourselves from life where death is on the line, like the Intellectuals, whose minds won't let them surrender for fear of not existing. We do not need to torture ourselves to feel like we matter, like we went somewhere, like the poor. We are not the manipulators, but we understand how they do it, and we can know the reasons they use to put confidence in their actions.
In the end, maybe we were just entertainers. Just right to prove that they don't matter, and to prove that they do. You don't get it? The answer is a contradiction, that's why you have to be so smart to realize it. It's why Freedom is important.
We are unique because what you think has no bearing on our lives. And we see tools to Freedom from those that want opinions.
And HumanKind is unique because it makes its own reasons to keep on living, everything else knows that it is fun and joyous and playful to be alive.

The End that Will not Come

When the wise rebel is young, he resolves himself to the fact that he will not live into an older age. He accepts death. He accepts it because he knows it. He knows it only because he has experienced it. Experience is the absolute only way to understand death, and I deepened my understanding with death by meditating and killing everything that dies when I die and letting live the part that is purely me. It is the promise of death that I have always used as the primary excuse to fight. I know that no matter what I do in life, that for certain, I will die and I will be free from any bizarre consequence that man imagines and dreams to twist others with. I know that man does not have the power to trap my soul. I know that I can always escape, and I know that when it comes it will not matter what amount of time I have lived in this body. Time is dead. Time is everywhere. Ask anyone who has had to live and live and deal with the blessing drudgery of living a good chunk of years, and they will all say, that it feels like it vanished from them. They know only that they are old.
So I think of death. I thought it would have happened by now. It is hard to keep on. But I must wait here. Wait in my moment of now. The only moment I can't yet escape. But it will come and pass. And I will wait for ending that I expected so long ago. Patiently or non-patiently I am still trapped right here in this moment. No matter what the circumstance, tragedy or triumph, flood or famine, I must experience this time on earth. So be it. I will always be a slave to the endlessness of futility. And I will fight deeper into myself, I will chase the end. If it does not come when I feel that I have completed my chosen life, I imagine that it is possible that I will plunge myself into the punctuation. There is nothing wrong with suicide. I have felt it in death. You can live as you make it. You gain some things and lose some things by living certain ways, but in the end, we all return to Equality. If you really understand meaninglessness than you can laugh at it, because it means nothing. Without judgment what will you know tomorrow?

I quest to overcome the drudgery of futility. I imagine I can be futile in any other form as well. In this form death is mine, freedom from everything you fear is mine, when in an instant I enter into to state, the focus on absolute unexplainable purity, as I focus my attention to the expanse beyond your every day vision or touch. I can, as you can, access the spirit that knows none of this matters. The spirit knows that it will not live in this world of suffering forever, only the body burns, life can live even burnt. In a moment Freedom is mine. I will never lose. I already have the greatest prize. I already know that there is nothing to win. I already know that you are forgiven, and that you never had to be. I already know what real, awe inspiring, unspeakable love is. I already know what it is like to not be judged. This is the truth of *our* afterlife. You are already the essence that remains in death. You just shed the skin and everything else you will at one instant know to be useless. Today I will fight on…and on…for no reason, but to fight, a fight that can mean nothing. But maybe, someone will win the battle of understanding, and maybe, that person might be you. Everyday is a chance to realize that there is another way to Understand.

And maybe you will know how I, the Great Humble Zarat, can know that every day is a great day to die.

<u>War</u>

What? I don't see? I have lived the tragedy of my life. I lived it, as proof against it. I Zarat, Zarat, Zarat, echoing throughout my own majesty, face deeply the truth. The fact that my war against other's egos, those that obtained power through the Darkness of Pride only built them and trained them and made them more important than ever to themselves. No matter who I chose to fight I fought the same thing. I fought the ego. The same thing. Every single time, regardless of what it imagined as a Reason to believe in. I believed as much as they did, but my path was actually right, but with their tactics I could gain nothing. By arming myself with arrogance I did nothing more than feed them. Never fight. That is the message of my pain. Never let them think that they are so important that they must be fought. Pride only proves more deeply that they are right. And they will fight, and you will fight back. Let them burn up. Let them no longer matter. Let them sizzle into the graves that they fear. They have fallen. Do not believe in them. Turn away from the war they want to beat and coax you into. Stop believing, and you will see what matters. What is present in the existence of your life now. If that can be done, if your life can be appreciated instead of warped into an image you won't live up to, you can and won't need to fight anymore. Peace is one person at a time. I am coming to mine.

The Freedom Master

Do you know him? We called him The Father. He was a simple man capable of very advanced things. His simplicity made himself easy to control for Him. He has been called the Silver Dragon, though you will never hear him say so. He chose a path that wouldn't kill many, though I think that he could have killed hundreds of thousands. But he did view it as a war. The Great thing that he taught us was that in his travels, across nations owned by men and towards and into Free places, places of the woods and valleys and expanse where he roamed naked and Free, proud and silent, he learned that individuals in certain clusters and groups throughout the country were all very different. And he saw that we were not all the same, we were different. And people clung to the things that were criticized by what was supposed to carry the message of the National feeling about something. The TV. And the Reason for making you feel this way or that way, is to make those that pay more money. What Capitalism was used as, the wrong it has become, has placed manipulators above us. The way to fight back is to be individual, and actually cling to the traditions of your thoughts. At least then things will be marketed to you that you might like, making you a demographic. You don't need to have anyone else's opinion. Don't be afraid of what anyone thinks, and be ready for someone to tell you what they think. Many have been programmed, and many worship a system that has lead to their power. So, naturally, The Father sought the power of television. He created an image, just like they did, but his image was true. He was that dramatic and there was meaning in his true speech. And many of us believed him. Some knowing how he had shown how the system truly functions, how the system preserves Freedom instead of providing a vehicle to control, he did it. And we believed more in his humbly righteous path. For most People the Revolution is simple, be what you are, be pure and honest and tell people about it. The Internet helped that a lot, still is. There are many Free People out there. And those people need to be more tolerant, and if they hate, they learn about what they hate, the people that are it, and seek to understand all the reasons they do something. And the rest of Us, the *Holy*, can fight those that won't let go, that won't even out the slavery. He'd say keep Capitalism, and let the people constantly have the chance to succeed, let us be what we wish, let us be useful, but it cannot be so hard to not be poor. The distance between the rich and the poor and the pursuers of power is making criminals of us all.
He taught that Freedom was the path to Freedom. Many will fall at

first, but soon they will not be so afraid for themselves.

Our words lie together, and he is a part of me. The Father's powerless power is a Miracle. A Philosophy beyond the control of gods.

By seeing what he was, he predicted his own life. And strived towards its work. By doing it he developed a pattern of response to ease the egos of control. Like releasing films before books he had finished years ago. The strategy always got better, because it was the Reason he chose, and he reasoned for that choice. It made him unstoppable. His Freedom led him to mastery.

SEX SCENE:

Banging fiercely. Picturing other woman, etc. Coming in and out of deep love for the woman. Kissing her. Upon orgasm, he focuses on sending his energy back into his body instead of out of it. Zarat sees and feels the blue and white light shoot up his spine.

INSERT EARLIER ON: Sex scene, thinking about rage, revenge, and violence during orgasm.

Recall the violence. And realize that the energy is the same energy and it can be directed towards many different avenues. Some are better. Finally I think I have chosen my true path. My desire finally is swaying in a strong effort to conquer myself and my human condition.

I really don't know this girl. But she has served me well.

<u>Additional Reasons to Triumph</u>

I'll kill myself because when this book is finished I never want to speak about it again. The power seekers, the opinion keepers will approach me with rage. Wanting to talk about it. Wanting to see holes in it to force their wedges of pride and arrogance into my calmness. I say, "I know you want to fight. I know you need to be right to feel safe. But I do not need to sit anywhere and fight what to me is an already easily won battle of Philosophy. You have no purpose, I can tell because you want to tell me anything. We have written so much to try and help you because we love and never ever want to see you or speak directly to you. So, go finish reading the collection of works that defined the whole Movement." It is easier for me to write it here than tell a hundred thousand people, mouth to mouth.

I would talk to those that loved it though.

<u>The Technique of Faith</u>

Faith has taught the masters that a doctrine has to make sense for people to believe in it. People just don't want to doubt, because they are afraid of doubt. It hurts them. Once we know this, once we are not afraid of the direction our lives are plunged into, we know we can choose any cause. Any direction. It is our pleasure to believe. If most of this seems foreign to you. If you don't understand. If you think it is stupid. You are not a master. You are not and probably won't be. You'll keep making reasons to fail, just because you had thoughts. And so I will aid you by manipulating you. Faith taught us that something doesn't have to make sense for you to believe in it. Don't believe in something just because it appeals to you, remember it is directed towards you, to recruit you, and profit from you. Even if you never thought you were smart, you are still making a choice for your life. Deciding where it's going. Just by being alive you are choosing a side, a decision. There are fruits on this path. Believe in them and you will find them. And you will see that you too can choose the side of no side. *Our* true side. The side of a Free World.

Becoming a Director

My biggest dilemma in my dealing with my mind and translating its thoughts to actions in the physical world is that I can rationalize every side of an argument. Even the illogical. I can understand how every mind could get to the same answer. It is strange that we take ourselves so seriously when our minds are so malleable and fake, reactionary and circumstantial. But, I suppose that that is why I could act well, when being questioned by assumers. But, always there is one path that takes me to power, and one path that takes me to where I truly want to be. I do not always choose so wisely, sometimes a human has no choice but to be human--simply to survive or be free.

For example: Why or why not sell out? Why or why not become famous or rich?

Answer One: Life is short. Get all you can. Have as much fleeting fun with a world that you will never know again in this exact form that you are in. You will never be you again.

/OR/

Others will own you for as long as you live. You will be a slave to greedy, dark people. You will be a pawn and a spokesmodel. Every current famous actor is only a spokesmodel for a money machine.

<u>The Fear of Ourselves</u>

I feel a twinge run through my body. I feel a discomfort, or something that I'm not numb to through constant sensation of it. Fear. Yes. I calm it. I let it exist, subside, and fade into its death. I know the power of my mind. I fear the things it may make me dream--powerful nightmares...reality so strong it could send my body into shock. I fear what it can rationalize. I am always on guard from it. It is strange that something so close to me, something that most people actually believe themselves to be, could so easily take control of so much. Of course it could. I could get bludgeoned and my mind could go blank, or lose all control over my body, or parts of my body, or make me someone you wouldn't know. I could become instantly paralyzed. My brain and my mind cannot be trusted. But even if "insanity" (also known as the art of bothering people's comfortable zones) overtook me, even through possession, I would still not lose the factuality of my constant, impenetrable, wise, calm, soul. I sought the calmness of the spirit so greatly, I believe, because I know the strength of my mind. When I felt it those times in death…I knew the truth of this fleeting, mind-empty world. The fear that has the potential to control me was not bad, because I made it worth something. Nothing is bad if you <u>make it</u> have worth, if you choose to create it. I have learned to recognize the illusions my mind can make. I have learned to focus on my spirit to guide me with the mind. My spirit knows the truth. This is my truth. What I have learned from the deaths I have known, my many, and those of others. In death I learned what it is to be nothing, to be without this person I thought I was. I know what it is to exist more pure. It is not speculative, it is the Truth I learned, and what I can tell you. And what you have the choice to search closely inside yourself for. All I can do is promise you it is there, just the way you want it. You will know what it is like to not be able to control your spirit, and you will know that it exists in a perfect, unafraid, state that you will never need to control, nor will you feel the urge to control others. (And you will face the choice to control others, because you are not afraid of penalties from others, and you have the freedom to choose. The choices are different, and carry disadvantages.)

A Philosopher can never beat the mind within the mind.

I attempt to put punctuation on my life, again and again. I attempt

to have a worthy thought that defines my message to myself more clearly. I wind up writing that way. Everything I write winds up sounding like a good enough point to end on. But I always think of something else, or a little different, that lets me understand better what I know in myself. Every moment of my life ends. I have known uncountable Ends. And so, if every moment is an End, then so, must every moment be important and unimportant in its marvelous Beginning. In my unwasted life, every point is just as worthy to end on then any other point. I cannot know regret. I will never leave disappointed. I cannot predict the impact or depth of the value of my final final thought. It will occur. I am unable to end the message in a place that is artistically pleasing, then it wouldn't be real, then it would lose its Art.

It does not matter if you believe what I believe or not. This is my work. This is my instant to instant stand within my own definition of Independence. Wanting peace, reasoning from war. It exists for me. As me, as my Great Work. Great to a single life, forever. There is an honesty in my Philosophy, meant to define a type of person. A person that deserves his Freedom. Freedom to exist without fear of your judgment. Your Dark, Fearful, Blindly Hypocritical Judgment. All judgment is hypocritical. You need to accept that you are not a God, and your control and force only harm others, while repressing deeper the things you were taught to fear in yourself. Your fear of everything, everything that might happen, anything that might hurt, anything that might kill, is stealing from us all our basic rights to live. Without our right to Die we lose every right to Live. Don't be afraid. Have the courage to defend yourself, to take your chances. To Risk. If you cannot Risk, you waste everything. Do not try to prevent, or stop what "might" happen. Do not try to form and control to protect your weak, cowardly self, make yourself strong enough to allow yourself to let death teach you.

The Road

I thought that after a recent score of free people's revenge against a tyrant that I would seek freedom for awhile. The life of a transient is well suited to the mind of a Revolutionary against the formations of power. Everything is a greeting and a goodbye simultaneously. It is pleasant and it is calm. People have other relationships in other places. Let their families know of their scarring nature of interaction and control. For me, it's a smile and a wave. And that suits me well. Within two days I can know everything about an area because everyone wants to tell you the banter they've heard. On the road, an idiot can be a genius, an asshole can be helpful. It is important for people to be allowed to move on, to start again, to change if they want. To be anything they dream. To choose the region, the general attitude, to surround them. The world is plenty big, and 99.99% of people know nothing about you. You can rebegin anywhere as anything. That's why it's so important to escape the past, forever disrespectful nature of your families, or of a country that labels "criminals/felons" for life, because their judgment and interpretation tries to last and rule forever. I feel free out here. As much as possible. If I just drive the speed limit (even drunk), everyone leaves me alone, save their smiles. It will calm me before.

The Rifle...

My Grandfather's rifle. It would be appropriate since it was his kindness that reminded me there is an easy way out. I do not have to be a slave to anyone or anything. I do not have to live in a Dark Society. No prison can hold those willing to let everything go.

<u>To Die</u>

Is a caterpillar afraid to become a butterfly? Even if it is, it had no reason to be. It will simply just be a butterfly.

<u>Embrace those things which you Fear and Become More Calm</u>

Life will end when life commands, far beyond your illusions of control. Suffer less by following these Truths.

1. There is no penalty and there is no reward after death. There is no damnation. There is no salvation. All souls are Equally pure. All souls are in no need of forgiveness.

2. There are certain "moral" devices and teachings that you can use, such as the seven deadly sins, to help you suffer less in life, but they will not grant you favoritism, or advantage over anyone or anything. The soul cannot lose, but the body will definitely lose, and it means nothing when you lose, you only realize what you are. A Free, unboundable piece of non-timeable sense of connected perfection. You are always this and you can always choose to remember this.

3. Penalties are made up by people that seek power over you. God knows no judgment. And death will easily set you Free from the made up penalties of Humankind.

Therefore, you are always Free. You can defy anything, and you will not know suffering if you remember the truths I am telling you. Life will often times be beyond your control, but there is no loss and there is no win, there is only the equality and freedom of death that awaits us all, when we realize that our true form is the unthinking soul of the Universe.

<u>Fighting Every Mind to a Stand Still</u>

I am an ordinary man. A man like you. Do not buy into the image I have created for you, although I had to create one for you to believe, but now move me in your mind. Make me a person that is face to face with you, someone you don't need to run away from, someone you don't need to lie to to protect, or to protect yourself. Some people live in worlds that should be peaceful, but are addicted to supporting the image of what they truly believe they must and should be. I know how easy it is to take ideas and believe ideas, and to believe in what these large macro images, these organizations and these corporations, that want you to know the name of the Entity, not the name of the people within in it. It is a place to hide behind so that Freedom can be maintained. You see the ideas of goodness can be found within the system too. They are there, but there are now many images draped over the simple truth of realizing another person's Freedom. The way to fix the system is change the way your mind is thinking about it. Stop your mind from spontaneously entertaining you and get a handle on it. Don't think you have to think to stay alive. Realize that we, the Youth, Generation "whY?", are in the wake of a revolution that occurred in this country in the 1960's. And now so many sides have risen from this that we are confused, because most of us have no attachment or connection to the world of that mindset. I grew up in a Free America. My youth was of westerns and dirt, others did not. And others, of cities, divided into oppressive hypocritical groups to defend themselves from the many sides of criticism. Choosing wherever they found the most smiling scheming inviting smiles. These are the groups we laugh at and mock when they are not around from the safety of the television sets they are using to try and convince us that we should believe in worlds that don't even exist to us, and people do - the shallow macro mind, the false existentialist. You only know what others have told you to know. We are free to search. We are simple. We are ordinary men, that believe in the illusion of our extraordinary dreams. We are Free to not buy into the anger and Pride and stories we must remember to make us more who we are, because you just don't know anymore. It is a majestic effort to try and create the happy world where children are young forever, but soon you, as Parent, will bend them into the pegs you knew you had to let them beat you into. Escape the illusions of the walls, of black people and white people, cops and criminals, Americans and the Chinese, the eating and the starving, the dreaming and the crushed, men and women, you and me, and listen to us all wanting the same thing. A place to calmly dream, a place where I feel Free too, and I can see that you are.

We are the ones that knew our Grandparents, without the nastiness of knowing them as our parents, those that saw the Industrial Revolution occur, those that built it and not those that received it. It wasn't long ago, but it is far away. The youth are coming, and will come again, and we come to surprise you. Beyond Good and Evil, yes, but know we are beyond Humanity, which means we no longer have to fight for it. We are Free to live, no matter who is selling the war.

<u>What's Wrong with Americans</u>

Evil is a circumstance brought forth by people reacting to stress, to the pressures of a bizarre societal innuendo of obscurity. This can be cited in the madness people suffer when an illusion of their world comes shattering down. People kill themselves when the circumstance of their life changes. When they are "rich" or "poor" or "fat" or "married", when in actuality nothing has changed. People need to get out of the exploration of the macro mind. The way to fix the world is to fix yourself. To realize that you are existing. The world isn't over until you stop existing in it. You are present. Still. Therefore, the true root of the world doesn't ever change, until you are not there. You, your galaxy, is only in a different state of reference. If you believe that, stress will not make you "evil", and those that fear themselves and are bound most personally by the stress of rigidness (police, judges, parents) and the world will not think that their will has the right to punish you and take away your natural reaction to the world. The system of judgment in this country is punishing people for natural human reactions, and calling them insanity. When it is merely something they can't understand. The Puritans are no longer welcome here!
The cure is you. You are a reaction to the state of your surroundings. Escape and your mind will calm. And then you can learn to control what changes you from being calm. And you will no longer be a slave to what you exist as. As fewer eyes expect you to be something.
Judge me not. In our other state, the Higher State, what *We* are, is most Beautiful. But you, who was here before I came, altered my surroundings, and I existed in the state you made. We are controlling our surrounding to control our minds. Escaping the reflex our kind has to you. Taking our own advice, and leaving what we can behind to help you. We will be out there. Out there touching ourselves, deeply and hard, and waling loudly to the moon, living in the roaring hum of raging rivers. In the state of no stress, without the belief in image, we are kind. And when we are kind, all others around us feel Free, even as we roar and our mood alters.

<u>This is a Full Movement Up In Thought.</u>
We Are Existentialists.

Anger is something you are feeling. You are directing it at anything you can see with your eyes, and many things you can think with your mind. You are using the anger you feel. Making hate from your viewpoint, hating anything that doesn't make you feel secure, or better yet for you, more powerful-because you believe it will make you matter. Instead of trying to quell the anger that is making all of these things happen. All the Anger is is your human form trying to survive, trying to use it's instincts to keep life. Seek Calmness. And Anger becomes determination, and point that towards yourself. Find stability, even for a moment. Feel what it is like to not need to be afraid of the many things you are creating to come after you.

My Brother, and the Legions of Independent Impal'o'rs, this is how to be Free from Yourself.

<u>Brother</u>

I held a dream. A simple one. I wish I could have repaid the people that thought I owed them, even though debt doesn't exist. I thought of my brother in the end. I thought about slapping twenty grand against his chest and thanking him for believing in me before he spent too much on me, and gained too much for himself. Before he lost faith in my Cause. Before money weighted more than my life. I wanted to make it even in his irrelevant mind. But I didn't. But I wanted to. Thus is the nature of the Ego. I wanted to approach him with the solemn pride of a man that reached a place where he knew he wasn't going to die tomorrow. He knew. The gambler won. But in the end...I didn't gain anything. I gave more than I got. I fought and fought and made no real ground, none that was visible. None that mattered to anyone that watched me. But I reached to where I needed to. My nation lived in honor. And I leave no one with peace. I couldn't be slave enough to gain an illusion that would die. My illusion lived with me. Zarat, I was sure I was Zarat. I was genuine to myself. And I breath on in a soul that needs no oxygen. Brother, don't forget that we were even. Don't forget that what I paid back had actual value. My life was real and my rights were sound. Money is shit. Man is something. And my life pumped with passionate meaning. Driving forward. Damnation what I became. Never wavering from my course. Though I suffered in it. Though I bled in it. And though I gained nothing I could give you in it.

Forget me.

Yet all shall be forgot...

Seems like we always think of the souls we knew young, before we were forced to deal with the selling of illusions, and how to sell ourselves to its acceptance. Remember the state of infancy, these days, it is our supreme state. Before loss began. And we thought it meant something, never realizing it could take nothing from the soul that has been there all this time.

<u>An Anthem</u>

I am a firm believer in the teaching of "listening to your elders." I believe that you can only base your life on the direct experience of others. And the older the person the more wise. For the older person has suffered much, has lived with hardship and faced death closely in the dead faces of his friends and family. They dwell on the thoughts of death and think of what it is like to have nothing. They think of what wonderful things they will miss. They cry by themselves...thinking no one will understand. But in time, everyone that faces old age will understand, alone. They will know what they lost. What they wasted. I listened to my elders and they have told me of the ways of salvation. They told me that it was not fair what their government did to them. It was not fair that they were lied to. And they were, because who made the promises retired, or died, or were fired, or didn't know. They face reality honestly, without fear of what society can do to them anyway. And they don't want the children going forth after them to waste what they did. The greedy society wastes everything, the most valuable things, you know and I know what they are. I know that there is no war the People win. I know that there is no God that I can sell my soul to for protection. I will suffer and I will live a life that is not wasted. And I will do anything to make it happen. I have proven to *Her* I would. I have heard from the dying Fathers that it is not worth it to sell yourself, even to survive. It is better to live away from this madness, this furious consumption. I know that my suffering will be even greater than theirs if I stay here, I know no one that will fight. The suffering has gotten worse, and the people have become weaker, as in Every society. I do not trust the treachery and betrayers and pursuits of comfort that racks the frightened minds of the weak. The instant, hidden betrayers. I will not aid a land of hypocrisy and tyranny. These are my words as a Revolutionary. As a Hero in my own chosen, constant war that wears deeply on me, even in the Peace I have Manifested. I will fight it to the best of my ability. I fight alone now. I fight by my will and inspiration alone. I write the war. I choose, I will the creation of this war. I decided. I was never told. Many weaker than I have fallen. But I remain. A single soldier who cares only for Freedom. Only for the ease given to me by this mighty planet. It is my right. I will not fall into the same lies, and promises that warp fears, I will not aid those that seek power. *I have learned from writing, at least a bit, so it was once worse, that sometimes I can't explain everything in one article or paragraph or stanza of prose. Sometimes I have to edit my mental wonderings.*

Inside my-self is always Free, and I, my country unto myself, choose to fight what I don't like. My own culture, will die with me.

A great problem with Capitalism in relationship to Government is that it once was the old that ran the government. By those that contemplated death. But money comes fast to the brazen young. The greedy. By those that have not known enough wisdom from the dying. From those that have never died. It is one more reason this society oozes Darkness.

You see *Girl*...I did not break my vow to you...

<u>The End</u>

That *Girl*, the one that aged and changed into a different face, she, *She*, *she* allowed me to have the burden of guilt. *She* let me use it as my Reason to become Free from the burden. My *Love*. I will not forget *our* moment, in my youth, when once I was overcome with what I should not have tried to control. Part of my longing pain came from the inability to control it. But surely, this moment where my weakness shown throughout the impending course of my life, surely, it cracked the ego. And from that crack shone a light widened by the realization of my vulnerability. And surely, I realized, that no matter what I do, throughout the whole course of my life, I will eventually do something that will enrage the Fearful. *She* allowed my mind to teach me that I will absolutely be crushed by the force of the Oppressive Personalities that pursue power, authority and righteousness. The Wise Man always sees that the *Hero* can only win a couple of times before the Great Wars are over for him.

I spent my whole life avenging for a young *Girl* that I thought that I may have harmed. Truly the blessed are those that cannot be harmed. Those *Holy* that do not suffer because the Dark Society tells It it should.

315

<u>A Letter, Addressed to a Father</u>

With these ear plugs in, I Zarat, sit gently waiting. Contemplating gracefully the metal of the bullet that will clean the brain from my skull. Putting halt to every thought. Cleansing me from every sin and punishment that other men have lied into existence, denying Humanity a peaceful world. With the pressure of a single finger, a slight creak, a click, and an echo, Silence will be all I will laugh about as I am thrust into the Freedom of Loving Death. Free from the Reasons I have concocted to fight the Darkness of Fear, Insecurity, Anger, and the pursuit of Power and Comfort. Into the great wide open my soul will instantly be and magically, no, naturally become.

<u>For Our Creator, Our Beloved Author</u>

The eyes of the selfish see only their loss. See more. They mourn only for their own pain. I was never like you, and my reasons were for everyone. As this shell lay bloody, twitching and shed, will anyone see the height of my sacrifice? Will they see how far I came? Will they know the deeply penetrating sadness that tore me apart, knowing that I lose everyone. You only lost me, someone you did not much understand, and never really tried to hear. To every love I'd known...for every family member...my friends...I lose you all at the bottom of my loneliness. I bless you poor who gave your final dime, and I condemn you wealthy who ate every day and called me a bum as I worked out my words. But I go with no hatred. I leave with no hope. This was my time. A circle of fate, bound to my mind. Dead by the Lake where *She* first died. When *she* discovered that *she* had limitless potential and where I concluded that in a society of darkness there is no way for the truly good and the deeply caring to succeed. Yet this written Truth remains until speech is gone.

<u>In White Mists</u>

It is not pain that we must avoid, it is the fear of pain that we must escape. Pain and decay are ahead of us. Be like the Wolf, unafraid of its rot. Eating, sleeping, raping, killing, free from the fear that steals our lives.

I was Zarat. A sacrifice of a Generation that asked whY?.
I am not anymore. I was a Warrior.

Know the Author

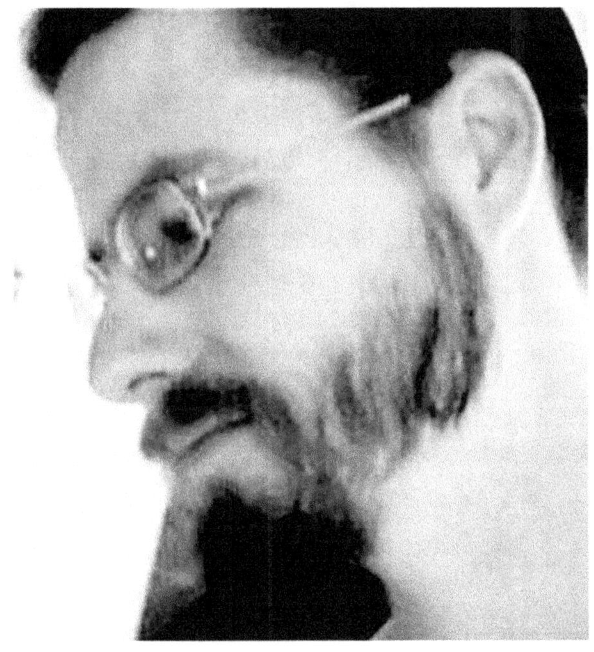

Longtime author, Stephan Pacheco, introduces his Existential concepts with the Manifest Utopia series, which launched with *The Girl, A Journey in Memories through the Self.* An early near death experience brought Pacheco face to face with the truth and limits of power, instantly defining to him the nature of actual Freedom. Through perpetual self-examination with the means of his reaching intellect he offers a portal and pathway to an unwavering American spirit. Born amongst the corruption of Reno, NV, he has become a defining voice of Generation "whY?", with an unwavering notion of Universal Freedom and a World without Power where Equality is Genuine and the concept of Utopia is personal, Free, and overflowing with the Compassion that has made his Prolific Dream attainable to us all.

We hold these truths to be self-evident, that all men are created equal, that they are endowed by their Creator with certain inalienable Rights, that among these are Life, Liberty and the pursuit of Happiness.--That to secure these rights, Governments are instituted among Men, deriving their just powers from the consent of the governed,--That whenever any Form of Government becomes destructive of these ends, it is the Right of the People to alter or to abolish it, and to institute new Government, laying its foundation on such principles and organizing its powers in such form, as to them shall seem most likely to effect their Safety and Happiness. Prudence, indeed, will dictate that Governments long established should not be changed for light and transient causes; and accordingly all experience hath shewn, that mankind are more disposed to suffer, while evils are sufferable, than to right themselves by abolishing the forms to which they are accustomed. But when a long train of abuses and usurpations, pursuing invariably the same Object evinces a design to reduce them under absolute Despotism, it is their right, it is their duty, to throw off such Government, and to provide new Guards for their future security.--Such has been the patient sufferance of these Colonies; and such is now the necessity which constrains them to alter their former Systems of Government. The history of the present King of Great Britain is a history of repeated injuries and usurpations, all having in direct object the establishment of an absolute Tyranny over these States. To prove this, let Facts be submitted to a candid world.